THE MOSCOW CODE

Other Foreign Affairs Mysteries
Escape to Havana

THE MOSCOW CODE

A Foreign Affairs Mystery

NICK WILKSHIRE

DUNDURN
TORONTO

Sipping the rich coffee, he watched as a svelte amazon in stilettos glided by, marvelling at her ability to navigate the cobblestones on four-inch heels as though padding barefoot over the softest berber. He turned at the sound of laughter from a nearby table, where two women sat smoking over empty cups — no one around him seemed to be eating much of anything, which explained why everyone seemed so tall and thin. The women could both be fashion models, but so could half the people out on the Arbat. If there was one thing Charlie had realized after a few weeks in Moscow, it was that beautiful women were as ubiquitous here as their cellphones and cigarettes.

As he breathed in the potent mixture of Marlboros, perfume, and coffee, all tinged with the hint of gasoline that permeated everything in central Moscow, Charlie fought the instinct to reach into his pocket for a Cohiba, a holdover from the past two years, which he had spent in Havana. He had a sudden longing for the smell of the ocean, too — warm, pungent, and ever-present as it had been on that quirky little island. But that was the past. Moscow was home now.

His transition to his new posting had been pretty smooth. Since arriving in mid-August, he had quickly settled into his apartment near the Moscow River and found a shortcut that reduced his walking commute to the Canadian Embassy on Starokonyushenny from twenty to fifteen minutes. It was just as well that he had sold his car to a colleague before coming to Moscow, from what he had seen of the traffic here. As for the subway, he had taken it in the evening a few times, but the constant streams emerging from every Metro station along his daily route were enough to convince him to avoid it during rush hour; he had heard that eight million Muscovites rode it every day, and he could believe it. The embassy itself was located in a quiet street in the diplomatic quarter, and though the staff seemed to like the location, the former aristocratic residence was not well suited to a modern office layout, nor big enough to accommodate the ever-increasing complement of Canada-based personnel coming to Moscow each year.

Still, though his office was cramped and musty, and the wall plaster was a web of fissures, there was a certain character to the old building that Charlie found endearing. Unfortunately he seemed to be alone in that opinion, if the number of complaints on file was any indication, and it wasn't even winter yet. He supposed that was when the reality of his first Russian winter would sink in to remind him that Moscow was a hardship posting, though for different reasons. For now, as he sat sipping his espresso and watching the endless parade of statuesque blondes on the *défilé* of the Arbat in the bright fall sunshine, Charlie wasn't feeling too hard done by.

Glancing at his watch, he directed his thoughts to the night ahead. It had been a few days since he'd received the email from an old high school buddy who was in town on business and suggesting a get-together. It had sounded like a good idea at first, but Charlie found himself questioning the wisdom of agreeing to the outing now that it was imminent. It had been more than twenty years since he had last seen Shawn Mercer, and it wasn't as though they had been best friends, even back then. On the other hand, he had no other plans. And how often was he going to bump into a fellow Newfoundlander in Moscow?

From the brief email exchange, it sounded like Mercer was an executive of some sort with a Calgary-based oil company, married with kids. It seemed at odds with Charlie's recollection of Mercer the party animal, but he supposed that people change. It occurred to him that he would have to gloss over, if not completely avoid, the topic of his own failed experiment in marriage, a thought that brought a frown to his face. But just as a gloom had begun to descend on him, it was dispersed by a cloud of Chanel that preceded a stunning brunette in a canary-yellow minidress and matching platform sandals. As she sauntered by Charlie's table, she cast a fleeting smile that he could have sworn was directed at him. Hope springs eternal.

Picking up his newspaper, Charlie glanced at the image of a familiar face under the caption "The Duma's Mr. Clean." Even as a newcomer to Moscow, Charlie had heard plenty about Pavel Zhukov, the popular former Federal Security Service agent–turned-politician, and his highly public campaign to clean up politics in the Russian legislature. One look at the crooked grin, though, and Charlie had to wonder if the guy was legit. But that was the Russian contradiction, and not just in politics — the shadier you were, the more you were revered, at least from what Charlie had seen so far. His last-minute cross-posting, direct from Havana to Moscow — do not pass go, do not stop in Ottawa — meant that the usual pre-posting briefings and cultural and language training hadn't begun until his arrival, and he was only now starting to get a sense of the city and how things worked here. Fortunately it had been a quiet summer at the embassy, and the new ambassador wouldn't arrive until Monday. Charlie didn't know much about her, other than the fact that she had been in communications and was a close friend of the Foreign Affairs deputy minister, which he figured could be good or bad. He would try his best to make a good first impression and hope that what he had learned on his last posting would take care of the rest.

Considering that he had been destined for a boring headquarters position in consular policy, Charlie felt lucky to be

posted anywhere at all. There was a general shortage of quali-
fied consular personnel, but the sudden illness of the previous
candidate for the Moscow job had been a lucky break. Being
a much bigger operation, here there would be half a dozen
people doing the work that Charlie and his Havana colleague,
Drew Landon, had shared in Cuba. He wasn't entirely sure
what area he would be asked to focus on, but Charlie was
hoping for less administrative work and more consular. For
now, he was content to try to fill in the considerable gaps
in his knowledge of the mysterious and sprawling old city
he would call home for the next two years or more. As for
his former home, though there was little in Ottawa for him
anymore, he had been buoyed to discover just a week ago
that he would be returning in mid-October for a conference.
Fall was his favourite time of year, and he hoped he wouldn't
be too late for the colours of Gatineau Park.

Abandoning his half-hearted perusal of the newspaper,
Charlie stretched and stifled a yawn, drained after the long
walk around the Kremlin. Looking at his watch, he decided
he had plenty of time to head back to his apartment for a
quick nap before meeting Mercer at seven. He felt a creeping
unease as he weaved his way back toward the river, but wrote
it off as fatigue and the gathering of clouds in the near distance. By the time he reached the now-familiar Obydensky
Lane, the sun was gone, swallowed whole by an immense
cloud dark enough to portend turbulent weather ahead.

CHAPTER 2

Charlie walked into the extravagant lobby of the Marriott Royal Aurora and took a seat on one of the plush couches, opposite a trio of sharks in bold pinstripes huddled around a laptop. Just around the corner from the Bolshoi and the exclusive shops of Tverskaya Street, the hotel attracted upscale business travellers, both Western and Russian. He unzipped his jacket and leaned back, taking in the multicoloured stained glass of the atrium ceiling, which was centred by a clear, circular skylight. A peal of laughter brought him back down to ground level, to a group gathered by the entrance to the restaurant across the lobby. He was focused on a platinum blonde in a white fur coat and patent-leather boots when he heard his name from the other direction.

"Charlie Hillier. How the hell are ya?"

Charlie stood as the other man approached. The face looked familiar, but it seemed surrounded by much more flesh than he remembered. As Shawn Mercer stuck out his hand, Charlie had one overwhelming impression — someone had shoved an air hose up his high school friend's ass and left it running.

"Shawn?"

"Who the fuck d'you think it is?" Mercer gave him a playful shot in the arm.

"How are you doing?" Charlie said as they shook hands. "I was trying to do the math, and I figure it's gotta be ..."

"Twenty-four years," Mercer said. "Hard to believe, isn't it? When I heard you were living here, I couldn't resist looking you up."

"How did you know I was in Moscow, anyway?"

"I was on the plane from Frankfurt with one of your colleagues. Susan ..." Mercer fished out a business card.

"Filmon," Charlie said, nodding. "I worked with her back in Ottawa a few years ago. She was here for the week."

"Lucky you," Mercer said. "A real piece of ass."

Charlie couldn't deny having had a similar thought upon first meeting Filmon, though he would never have voiced it, much less in terms that suggested his colleague was a slab of beef. His recollection of Mercer, the thinner version, was filling in, and it seemed his job and family hadn't changed him much after all.

"You wanna grab a drink?" Mercer jerked a thumb toward the lobby bar. "We can figure out where we're going from there."

"Sure." Charlie followed him into the crowded bar to a table in a quiet corner. They were just settling in their seats when a server arrived.

"What's your poison, Charlie?" Mercer asked, smiling at the woman, his eyes lingering around her chest.

"I'll have a beer — a Russian one."

"CC and ginger for me," Mercer said, waiting for the woman's awkward smile before adding, "That's Canadian Club and ginger ale, and make it a double." He watched as she walked off toward the bar. "You see the rack on that?" He shook his head, then turned to face Charlie. "So, you're a diplomat now, are ya?"

"I guess so." Charlie smiled. It had taken him a while to get comfortable with the description and to stop launching into an explanation of how his job really wasn't what most people had in mind when they thought of diplomacy. He enjoyed his consular work, and he was good at it. So what if he was forced to spend half of his time responding to complaints about clogged toilets in staff quarters or refereeing disputes between the embassy drivers? He was still an accredited diplomat. "How about you? I saw from your email that you're with Petroline."

"Yeah, I started my own exploration business out in Calgary ten years ago and got bought up last year. You could say it was an offer I couldn't refuse."

"So you're here to tap into the Russian market?"

Mercer grinned. "Petroline's been in the Russian market since the Iron Curtain came down. I'm here to expand our interests." He paused to leer at two women in evening gowns passing the table and leaving an intense trail of perfume in their wake. "They told me Moscow was full of hotties, but I had no idea.... Good thing I didn't bring the wife along. You married, Charlie?"

"No," he replied. He was relieved for the distraction caused by the arrival of their drinks.

"Then you're in the right place." Mercer tapped his glass off Charlie's. "Say, how's Brian doing?" Mercer asked, taking a slurp of his drink.

"Good." Charlie was trying to remember the last time he had been in touch with his brother and what the news was.

"He's still in St. John's and still with Karen?"

"Yeah, they've got a couple of kids." He felt a pang of guilt at how little he knew about his only nephews.

"Lumber business still treatin' him right?"

Charlie nodded and reached for his glass. One piece of information his brother was always keen to share was his annual sales figures, which made Charlie's AS-7 salary pale in comparison and explained the McMansion that Brian and Karen had custom-built on an oversized lot on Pine Bud Avenue in St. John's.

"Have you got kids, Shawn?" he asked, eager to switch topics.

"Yeah. Couple of 'em." Mercer pulled out his wallet and opened it to a pair of school photos.

"They're cute."

"Don't be fooled." Mercer flipped the wallet shut with a snort. "Hellions, both of them. But they're worth it." He grinned and picked up his glass. "Who'da thunk it back in high school, Charlie, that twenty years on, we'd both be sitting in a bar in Moscow, of all places."

"It's a small world, isn't it?"

"I'll drink to that."

Charlie sat at the bar in Night Sky, squinting to make out his watch face in the red glow of the smoky club. It couldn't be 3:00 a.m., surely? The place was still packed, mostly with gorgeous women, which was presumably why Mercer had insisted on coming to the Tverskaya landmark after dinner. Charlie glanced toward the washroom, where Mercer had disappeared some time ago, and was debating going after him when he heard his name being yelled over the din. He looked up and saw Mercer waving from the lounge area upstairs, like a stranded hunter signalling a search plane. He waved back, collected his drink off the bar, and made his way up the circular staircase. At the top, he looked around and spotted Mercer at a corner booth with two women.

"Over here, Charlie!"

"I was starting to wonder where you'd gotten to," Charlie said when he reached the booth.

"Meet Elena and Svetlana," Mercer said, introducing the two blondes as Charlie sat down.

"Hi, I'm Charlie," he said, as Svetlana leaned forward to offer him her hand, and the plunging neckline of her dress fell away to reveal most of her surgical enhancements.

"Svetlana, and this is my cousin Elena," she said as Charlie shook the hand of the woman next to him. She was younger and prettier than her cousin and had obviously not resorted to cosmetic surgery yet. "Shawn has told us all about you, Charlie," Svetlana went on, cozying up to a glassy-eyed Mercer. Charlie had lost count of the number of beers he himself had consumed at the club, but he had fallen well behind his old classmate, whose last drink had been a Grey Goose and Red Bull. He also noticed with some alarm a smattering of white powder on Mercer's lapel and the front of Svetlana's dress.

"You are a diplomat, yes?" Elena placed her slender hand on Charlie's arm and moved closer on the bench, so that he could feel the warmth of her hip against his.

"Are you girls from Moscow?" he asked, deflecting the question and wishing Mercer wasn't so hammered. There was something about these girls that made him wary, and the last thing he wanted to get into was his official capacity at the embassy.

"St. Petersburg," Svetlana said, as the house music thumping around them morphed into a familiar refrain. "Oh, I love this song! Come on, Shawn, we must dance." She stood and helped extricate a wobbly Mercer from the booth.

"Will you dance with me, Charlie?"

He looked into Elena's blue eyes and knew he couldn't refuse. "Sure."

They made their way onto the crowded dance floor, and Charlie's initial discomfort soon faded, aided by Elena's sultry dancing style, which emphasized her long, graceful curves and made her all the more alluring. He also found it difficult not to be aroused by her habit of swaying in close and crushing into his waist as she ran a soft hand down his arm. It was so enjoyable that Charlie had zoned out the rest of the dancers, not to mention the room and the music, when Mercer staggered into him and broke the spell. He watched as Svetlana pulled Elena by the arm toward the far end of the dance floor.

"Where are they going?" he said as Mercer continued an uncoordinated shuffle next to him, apparently oblivious to his dance partner's absence.

"What the fuck?" Realizing he was dancing with himself, Mercer squinted into the distance and spotted the women, then stumbled after them through the crush of bodies and into a narrow hallway leading to a dimly lit area with sofas. Approaching the nearest sofa, Charlie noticed a couple in the far corner, barely visible in the muted light, entwined in an intimate embrace. When he looked down again, he saw Svetlana sitting on Mercer's lap, their mouths crushed together. He felt Elena's hand pulling him down onto the opposing couch.

"Why so tense?" she whispered, her arm sliding inside his jacket and running over his chest as she pressed herself against him and placed her warm, soft lips on his. She tasted like licorice.

"Look ... I really think I should be going," he said, pulling back.

"Just relax," she purred as Charlie glanced across toward the other sofa and noticed Mercer's hand planted firmly on one of Svetlana's breasts.

"Hey Shawn," he said, leaning over a protesting Elena. "Shawn?"

"Mmmh?"

"It's almost four. I've got to go."

"Wha ...?" Mercer poked his head out from Svetlana's blond tresses. "You serious?"

"Yeah. I'm outta here. You can stay if you want." Charlie had pushed himself upright, gently forcing Elena off him as her hand slid away from his chest. She wore a resigned sulk now, and he was eager to be gone. Mercer seemed to give in to Svetlana's urgent kissing for a moment, but he broke away when he noticed that Charlie was standing.

"All right, all right. Just gimme a second...."

"Thanks for the dance," Charlie said to Elena as he waited for Mercer to extricate himself from Svetlana's grasp and clamber unsteadily to his feet, knocking over a couple of bottles on the glass table in the process.

"Wh-whash the rush anyway?" Mercer griped as they stood outside the club on the deserted street. He was swaying, as though on the deck of a tall ship rounding Cape Horn in gale-force winds.

"It's four in the morning," Charlie said, though he could tell by Mercer's expression that the time was irrelevant. "Besides, I don't know about those girls. I think they might have been pros."

"Who gives a shit ... didja see the rack on Svetlana?" Mercer protested, as Charlie started off down Tverskaya. "We're *walkin*'?"

"It's only ten minutes to your hotel. Besides, it's safer than taking a cab at this hour," Charlie added, just as a yell and the sound of breaking glass pierced the night air from somewhere across the wide street.

"I still think we shoulda s-s-stayed," Mercer muttered, his teeth chattering as he stumbled along. They had gone about thirty feet when a police car raced by, its siren wailing.

"We coulda all gone back to the hotel, or maybe to their p-p-place," he continued in his drunken stutter.

Charlie imagined them going back to Svetlana's apartment in some high-rise in the middle of nowhere, only to be robbed at gunpoint. He was shaking his head at the thought when he saw two men in uniform coming toward them on the sidewalk.

"Hey, it's the boys in b-b-blue," Mercer said as they came within earshot.

"Shut up," Charlie hissed before acknowledging the men with a nod.

The two cops seemed content to let them continue on to their hotel — until Mercer jerked up his arm in a mock salute, almost tripping over a crack in the sidewalk, and yelled, "Evenin' c-c-comrades!"

The cops made an abrupt U-turn and the older of the two approached Mercer and barked a command in Russian.

"Wha'd he say?" Mercer looked bemused.

"He wants to see our passports," Charlie said, alarmed at the darkening expression on the policeman's face and hoping passports were all he wanted. His own irritation at Mercer turned to puzzlement, then fear, as his search of his jacket pockets came up empty.

"Say, Ch-Charlie," Mercer said, as he fumbled in his own pockets and hiccupped. "You're gonna love this. My p-pashport's gone."

CHAPTER 3

Charlie was doing his best to object in Russian as the guard shoved him into the holding cell behind Mercer and slammed the metal door shut with a clang.

"This is bullshit," Mercer said for the hundredth time since the two had been bundled into the back of a van for the short ride from Tverskaya to wherever they were now. The experience of detention by the Russian police seemed to have sobered him up, at least to the point that his speech was no longer slurred.

"Do they know you're a fucking *diplomat*?" he ranted as Charlie looked around the twenty-by-forty-foot cell, suddenly aware that they were far from alone. Mercer's further protestations were abruptly halted as he came to the same realization. As a giant in a dishevelled parka growled something unintelligible at them in Russian from the corner, they backpedalled toward a bench at the opposite end of the cell.

"Seriously," Mercer whispered, "are they going to let us the fuck out of here, or what?"

"I told them I was with the embassy," Charlie said. "I'm sure we won't be here for long. Just relax."

"Hard to relax with that Siberian sasquatch over there sizing us up like we're dinner," Mercer replied in a hoarse whisper. "What about our phone call? Aren't we supposed to get a phone call?"

"This is Moscow, Shawn, not Calgary, so I wouldn't get your hopes up for a phone call." It occurred to Charlie that he was the backup emergency consular contact for the next couple of hours, but decided not to mention that to Mercer. In the unlikely event that they did get to make a call, it would go to Charlie's stolen BlackBerry if whoever was first on the call list was unavailable.

"All right, all right. You don't have to get pissy."

"I'm not getting pissy," Charlie snapped, his anger blooming. They would both be safe in their beds if Mercer hadn't opened his big yap or insisted on cozying up to a pair of grifter prostitutes in the first place. He sighed and decided to try another tack. "Look, everything will be fine. I gave them my name and told them I'm with the embassy. I'm sure they'll be back as soon as they confirm my credentials, and then we'll be out of here." He heard himself saying the words, and they sounded almost reassuring, but he was not at all convinced it was going to be that easy. Charlie didn't know the home numbers of any of the other embassy staff, other than as contacts in his BlackBerry, which Svetlana and Elena were probably using right now to text their order for all the cocaine they were going to buy when they flogged the passports.

"Jesus, it stinks in here," Mercer muttered as Charlie's mind wandered, his chest filling with dread at the thought of his rapidly approaching Monday morning. That was when he would have to report his detention, not to mention the theft of both his diplomatic passport and government-issued BlackBerry ... by a pair of hookers. If he didn't get fired, he would be the laughingstock of the entire mission. He rubbed his temples with increasing vigour, as though the friction might somehow transport him out of his current predicament.

"Charlie."

His eyes remained closed as he grasped for a plausible explanation that would leave him a shred of credibility, or at least employed.

"Uh, Charlie?"

"What?" He opened his eyes and rounded on Mercer, who had begun tugging on his sleeve as he pointed across the cell. Charlie followed his outstretched finger and noticed the parka-clad bear lumbering toward them, brushing a greasy strand of hair from his bloodshot eyes as he approached, barking something at them as spittle flew from his cracked lips.

"What the fuck's he saying?" Mercer whispered as they cowered on the bench, tensing for an attack.

"I don't know."

"Can't you tell him to go back over to his side or some —"

Mercer jumped as the ogre hurled a round of foreign expletives at them. They both turned in response to a shout from the other end of the bench and watched as a young man stood and walked over to the wild-eyed behemoth, yelling at him until he retreated and slunk back to his corner. Charlie and Mercer were rapt as the man turned to them and smiled.

"You American?"

"Uh … Canadian," Charlie said, surprised to hear unaccented English.

"No shit? Did I hear him say you're a diplomat?" He gestured to Mercer, who was making sure the sasquatch resumed his seat safely on the other side of the holding cell.

Charlie nodded. "I'm with the Canadian Embassy, but we had our passports stolen, so I guess we're stuck here for a while."

"Welcome to Moscow." The man let out a grim chuckle and took a seat on the bench next to Charlie, offering his hand. "I'm Steve Liepa, by the way. From Toronto."

"You're kidding," Charlie said as he and Mercer shook hands with their saviour. "Thanks."

"No biggie." Liepa gave a wave of his hand.

"What did you say to that nut-job, anyway?" Mercer asked.

"Ah, he's harmless. Does the same to everyone when they first come in. You just have to yell at him and he'll back off. So what do you do with the embassy, Charlie?"

"I'm, uh … I'm a consul." He glanced at the floor as he heard himself utter the words, wishing for a sinkhole large enough to swallow him whole.

"Isn't that, like, the guy you're supposed to call when you're in jail?"

"Among other things." Charlie felt himself squirming on the bench.

"This is gonna be kind of embarrassing then, eh?" Liepa grinned.

"What about you? How long have you been here?" Charlie asked in an awkward segue.

"Twenty-four hours, give or take," Liepa replied as Mercer blanched. "I told these pricks I wanted to call the embassy, but they wouldn't let me. I'm a Canadian citizen, and they're keeping me in this shithole for no reason." He sighed and the grin was back. "Lucky for me I bumped into you. Now you can help me get out of here."

Charlie looked at Liepa and guessed he was in his mid-thirties. In his cargo pants and fleece zip-up, he looked more like a backpacker than a hardened criminal. Something about Liepa's earnest expression was even harder to reconcile with their present surroundings. "What are you doing here, anyway?"

"That's a very good question," Liepa said. "They tell me I'm part of a drug ring, though that's news to me. I'm a writer by trade."

"What sort of writing?"

"Technical manuals, mostly. It's more translation than writing, really, but my real interest lies elsewhere."

"You obviously speak good Russian," Charlie commented, referring to Liepa's verbal counter-assault.

"That was Lithuanian, actually. I grew up in Toronto but I spoke it at home a bit with my parents. I read and write in Russian, but speaking it is another thing."

"And you're in here on a drug-related charge?"

Liepa snorted. "That's a joke. All I did was go to a party that got crashed by the cops. There was some weed, but that's it. I've never sold so much as a joint in my life." He stopped as the door to the holding cell swung open and the older of the two cops who had brought in Charlie and Mercer appeared. "Looks like your get-out-of-jail card's here."

Mercer was up off the bench in a flash, in response to the cop's glance in their direction. "Come on, Charlie, let's get the hell out of here."

Charlie looked to Liepa, who smiled. "Go, before he changes his mind. Just don't forget about me in here."

"Thanks for your help," Charlie said, offering his hand. "I promise to look into your case right away," he added as they shook on it. He saw the cop glare at Liepa, then mutter something in Russian. When at last they were directed through the door, Charlie turned back just as it was closing behind them and saw the smile fade from Liepa's face. It soured the relief he felt as the metallic slam echoed in his ears and he and Mercer began the short walk to freedom.

CHAPTER 4

Charlie fidgeted on the chair outside the ambassador's office, going over his version of events one last time. He had decided to keep things general — he had been out for the evening with an old drinking buddy ... No, make that just an old friend. His version didn't include the name of the club where they had ended up, the time that they had been detained, or the fact that they had spent the thirty minutes immediately prior to realizing their passports and phones had been lifted in the company of two prostitutes.

"You can go in now, Mr. Hillier."

Charlie looked up, straightened his tie, and tried without success to smile with facial muscles tense with stress. He made his way to the office and got his first look at his new boss waiting just inside the doorway.

"Good morning, Charlie."

Ambassador Brigitte Martineau was tall and elegant, with an engaging smile and grey hair complemented by the silver trim of her blue dress.

"Pleasure to meet you," Charlie began, having promised himself not to say how much her reputation as a rising star preceded her for fear of starting her off on the same line of thought. "And welcome to Moscow. I hope you had an uneventful trip."

"Thank you." She gestured for him to take a seat as she perched on an opposing chair. "Yes, it was uneventful," she said, smoothing her dress, "though I understand your weekend wasn't."

Charlie's breath caught in his chest as he tried to read her, the same smile lingering on her inscrutable face. "Well, yes.... It was really unfortunate. I —"

She held up a hand, halting his babbling. He noticed that her smile had faded, along with what remained of his hope. "I'm coming fresh off a pair of briefings from Security and Finance," she said. "Let's just say that the loss of a diplomatic passport and a BlackBerry is a bit of a double-whammy in this environment."

"I really can expla —"

Her hand was back up, but a ghost of her smile had re-appeared, too. "Are you a golfer, Charlie?"

"Uh, yeah, sure," he said, thinking that golf as a metaphor for termination an interesting choice.

You're in the rough, Hillier. The deep rough....

You're so far in the woods, you need a map to get out....

You're on the eighteenth fairway, and you're out of balls....

"Then let's just say you've had your mulligan and leave it at that, shall we?"

As the words registered, he searched her face for a sign that it was a cruel joke, but her expression was sincere. He tried to conceal his disbelief and decided he should probably say something.

"There is a silver lining," he began, his conservative inner voice screaming at him to shut up, thank her, and leave before she changed her mind. But there was a sparkle of interest in Martineau's hazel eyes, so he carried on. "I met a Canadian in the holding cell. He'd been refused consular access, from what I could gather. I've started to look into his case."

"Well, that's one way to offer consular services, Charlie, but I wouldn't recommend you make a practice of it."

"No, I suppose not." With his job no longer in imminent danger, he allowed himself a genuine grin.

Martineau leaned back in her chair. "I had an interesting lunch with Mike Stewart when I was in Ottawa."

Charlie's spine stiffened at the mention of his former boss, wondering what he might have shared with Martineau about Charlie's time in Havana. He could only hope for a high-level, positive version — *Despite some initial turbulence, Charlie was an asset to the embassy and solidified Canadian-Cuban relations in his own unique way.* The less charitable version might cast him as a loose cannon who'd concealed the discovery and destruction of narcotics, endangered the life of a visiting Department of Justice lawyer, and possibly poisoned the official dog.

"He had only good things to say about you, Charlie," she went on, allowing him to inch back from the edge of his seat. "Although he warned me your methods might be a little … unorthodox."

"Consular work can be challenging," he said, as though that explained everything.

"Indeed, but I expect you to operate within the rules of engagement here in Moscow." The smile was still there, but it had chilled a couple of degrees.

"Point taken."

"Good," she said, then moved on to her objectives for her posting and her expectations for her staff. Charlie was relieved to hear that although he would have some involvement in property matters, his primary responsibility would be consular. The administrative work, which he had come to loathe on his first posting, would continue to be handled by a full-time administrator who had been doing the job for eighteen months and would remain at post for another year at least. They discussed the consular program in Russia for a while, and he was pleased to hear that Martineau planned to expand and improve the service, though he wondered about the implications, given that no more staff were being hired. Still, he was so delighted at being relieved of administrative work that he was prepared to put in a few more hours for something he actually cared about.

"I understand you'll be attending next week's consular conference in Ottawa," Martineau said, after coming to her feet and wrapping up their meeting at precisely the end of their allotted time.

"Yes," Charlie said, pausing by the door, realizing he hadn't actually seen a sign-off on his travel request, which had been the last thing on his mind when he got in that morning.

"Assuming you can get a replacement visa in time," she added. "You know how the Russians can be when it comes to bureaucratic timelines. I'd hate to lose you for another week because they refuse to let you back in."

"I'll call the MFA right away and get the ball rolling," Charlie replied, referring to the Russian Ministry of Foreign Affairs, grateful he had something to focus on other than looking for another job.

"Very well, then," Martineau said, starting back to her desk.

"And thanks for the mulligan," Charlie added just before he left. "I promise you won't regret it."

Charlie took his coffee back to his office and began to scan the headlines from one of the online English-language Moscow media outlets. He was engrossed in the lead story as he heard a light rap at the door, looked up, and saw Rob Brooker standing there with a coffee in hand. Two years into an extended three-year posting, Brooker worked mostly on property issues and seemed to know his stuff. Charlie had been out for beer with him a couple of weekends after he first arrived, and had found Brooker to be generous with his knowledge of the workings of the embassy, and of life in Moscow generally.

"Is that the leaked tax-shelter stuff?" he said, pointing at Charlie's screen.

Charlie nodded. The leak — on a massive scale — of information about who was sheltering cash where and under which dodgy schemes, was making news around the world. In the Russian context, most of the money had been sent to Panama or Cyprus, which on its own was nothing new; the identities of many of the companies and wealthy individuals behind the money was, though. The mass disclosure was sending shock waves through Moscow's elite, which included a significant component of organized crime, not to mention some high-level bureaucrats and politicians.

"There's a lot of rich folks choking on their caviar and blini this morning," Charlie said, gesturing to the chair on the other side of his desk. "Have a seat."

"Just wondering if you're going to the reception this afternoon," Brooker said, settling his large frame in the chair.

"Who am I to turn down a free drink?" Charlie deadpanned. He had already accepted the electronic invite to attend the informal event, which he had been told would be a good opportunity to meet some of the locals providing services to the embassy.

Brooker laughed. "I just wanted to give you a heads-up that a couple of brokers are going to be there, in case you get cornered and they start asking you about the status of the relocation project."

Charlie frowned. "I didn't know there was a relocation project."

"There isn't, really. But we've been looking at various options for years." He glanced around the office and Charlie followed his gaze to the crumbling caulking at the edge of the windows, the cracks in the plaster on the walls, and the uneven floor. "Let's face it — we can't stay here forever."

"It's not so bad." Charlie shrugged.

"Wait'll you spend a winter here," Brooker said. "You're gonna want to stock up on sweaters. Anyway, one of the brokers, Oleg … I can't remember his last name for the life of me. He's a nice enough guy, but he can be a bit pushy."

"I'll consider myself warned."

"He's been pushing Petr Square on us for the past year."

"Petr Square?"

"It's a huge development up around Belorusskaya Metro station. It might actually be the largest in the city, but it's had a lot of problems with permits and whatnot."

"So I guess I tell him we're still in the feasibility stage, if he asks?"

Brooker smiled. "Couldn't have said it better myself."

"And the truth is?"

"Petr Square is on our list of possibles, but it's probably near the bottom, mostly because it's too expensive." Brooker sipped his coffee. "Plus, we just got wind of a refurbished building with a better location, and we'd be the sole occupant, which security seems to like. We're still looking into the owner, though, and I certainly wouldn't mention it to Oleg."

Charlie put a finger across his lips. "Mum's the word. Why are you looking into the owner?"

Brooker shrugged. "This is Moscow. You have to be careful who you're dealing with."

"You mean like … the mafia?"

"I don't know if I'd call it that, but there are certainly some shady operators. People we want to steer clear of. You've probably heard of Dima the Great."

"Who?"

"Vladimir Oligansky," Brooker said. "He's a big wheel in Moscow real estate and he's rumoured to have some unsavoury connections. Turns out he was part owner in a couple of buildings we looked at in the past, so we had to keep looking, if you know what I mean."

"What's with the nickname?"

"He's a former wrestler or something, and I guess that was his stage name. He goes about two-seventy-five — not someone you want to cross."

"Sounds like an interesting guy."

"Sure is." Brooker nodded. "Are you gonna be working on property much?"

"A bit, maybe," Charlie said, hedging. "But I think my main focus is going to be consular."

"Right." Brooker's eyes darted down to his coffee cup, where he proceeded to conceal his face during an extended sip.

Charlie considered ignoring the elephant in the room — he knew that there were few secrets among embassy staff, especially not ones about the new guy being tossed in the drunk tank on the weekend — but decided to try and address it.

"I take it you heard how my weekend went," he said, sensing the colour rising up his neck and into his cheeks.

Brooker gave a nervous laugh and looked back at his cup for a moment, seemingly as embarrassed as Charlie was. But when he looked back up, his expression was genuine enough. "Don't worry about it. The Russians make a sport of picking us off when they can. You're not the first and you certainly won't be the last."

"That's nice of you to say, but I can't help feeling like a moron."

Brooker gave a dismissive wave. "I hear you met a fellow Canuck in … there."

"Yeah, his name's Steve Liepa, from Toronto. He said he was in on some trumped-up drug charge." Charlie heard himself and realized that he must sound green — all consular cases, like all prisoners, were always innocent.

"So it wasn't a total waste of your Saturday night," Brooker said, as though Charlie had followed the consular handbook to its letter. "You got your first consular file."

Charlie nodded, though up until this morning's meeting with Martineau, he had been more concerned about saving his own skin. But now he saw some serendipity in being given the chance to pay Liepa back for saving his ass in the holding cell.

"I know everyone's innocent in our line of work, but he really didn't strike me as someone who should be in prison."

"You should follow your instincts." Brooker nodded. "How about your friend — the one you were with Saturday night. He okay?"

Charlie shuddered at the prospect of Shawn Mercer returning to Calgary to share his war stories at the water cooler, no doubt self-serving versions featuring Mercer rescuing Charlie from the sasquatch, or the hookers, or both. "That reminds me. I've got to check on his temporary passport. His flight leaves tomorrow morning."

"Well, I'll leave you to it." Brooker stood. "See you at the reception."

Charlie returned his attention to the online article, then entered *Oligansky* in the search box. Finding nothing of particular interest, he clicked the article shut, drained his coffee, and pulled Steve Liepa's consular file from the corner of his desk. An image sprang into Charlie's mind of Liepa's fading smile as the cell door slammed shut. He could almost smell the stench of the place as he flipped the file folder open and looked for a contact number for the prison.

CHAPTER 5

Charlie accepted a glass of white wine from a passing server and checked his watch. He had already been at the reception for almost thirty minutes, and he had no intention of staying for more than an hour. Considering he barely knew half of the embassy staff, he felt at a bit of a loss and had spent most of his time hovering on the edges of conversational clusters. He was surveying the large room, which had become crowded and stuffy since he had first arrived, when he heard his name from behind him and turned to see Rob Brooker standing there, next to a tall man with hard features.

"Charlie Hillier, I'd like you to meet Oleg Sukov."

The Russian's face opened into a broad smile as his pinstripe-clad arm shot forward, adorned by the chunkiest timepiece Charlie had ever seen.

"A pleasure to meet you, Mr. Hillier."

"Call me Charlie," he said, accepting the hand and returning the smile.

"You have just arrived in Moscow?"

"I've been here a couple of months."

"Is a nice time of year to arrive," Sukov said. "Before the cold comes. But you are from Canada, where winters are not so warm, yes?"

"That's right." Charlie watched as Sukov reached into his suit pocket and came up with an oversized business card, which Charlie accepted and scanned. It indicated Sukov as an account executive with Horizon Property Consultants.

"You're in the real-estate business?" Charlie avoided Brooker's grin.

"Yes, we offer broad services. For you, I think, brokerage is most relevant. I understand you are looking to relocate embassy?"

Charlie took a sip of wine. "Well, we've been considering a move for a long time, as you probably know. Whether it's going to happen anytime soon is another question."

"Indeed," Sukov said, looking around the room. "This building is quite charming, but not really convenient for an embassy, I think."

"That's probably a fair statement." Charlie waited for the pitch. He needn't have worried. Sukov was reaching inside his jacket pocket again, this time to pull out a folded, glossy one-pager showing an architect's rendition of a shining office tower.

"All you need is right property, at right price," Sukov said, proffering the document.

"This looks nice." Charlie took the brochure and scanned the details below the title: *Petr Square — The New Standard for Business*. The square metres meant little to him, other than to suggest a massive development. He could feel Sukov's gaze on him, like a cat eyeing a plump sparrow.

"It is largest commercial development in central Moscow," Sukov boasted as Brooker leaned in for a look. "Also, most modern."

"How far along are you?"

"About eighty percent completed." Sukov beamed.

"And where, exactly, in central Moscow is this?" he asked, as though Brooker hadn't already pointed it out to him on a map. Sukov leaned in and pointed to the flip side of the brochure, where a red star marked the development's location. It was within the Garden Ring, but at the northern extremity of the central core.

"It's perfect location," Sukov rolled on, launching into a detailed explanation of the main intersections and amenities nearby and the adjacent Metro stop, which connected to two main lines.

Charlie did his best to look impressed. "And how long to finish the last twenty percent?" he asked, curious as to whether the eighty percent figure was anywhere close to reality. From what Brooker had said about the permit problems, he was guessing they had barely progressed beyond digging the hole. Sukov made it sound like they could move in next week.

"It's perfect time for tenants to get space custom-tailored — like a good suit, hey, Charlie?"

Charlie took in Sokov's slim-cut, two-button charcoal number, accessorized with flashy cufflinks and matching silk tie and pocket square, and felt suddenly self-conscious in his off-the-rack blazer and grey cotton-polyester pants. There had been little need for suits in Havana, but people seemed to dress more formally here.

"I heard there were some problems with the building permit." Brooker jumped in, as Charlie became absorbed in an internal sartorial debate over whether his ensemble made him look more like a department store security guard or a high-schooler on his first job interview.

Sukov's disdain at the mention of permits was evident in the theatrical wave of his hand. "Is overblown bureaucracy," he railed. "You are new here, Charlie, but you will soon see how process can be frustrating." He waved his hand again. "But that's in past."

"You've got all the permits?"

"I tell you, the permit is … imminent," Sukov proclaimed with pride, whether over the status of the project or the latest addition to his vocabulary.

"That's great news," Charlie said, looking at Brooker. "So I guess that makes it easier to rent the space now." Brooker had mentioned that one of the reasons they had never seriously considered the Petr Square development was that no other tenants had committed to the space. As if reading their minds, Sukov leaned in and grinned again.

"Indeed, Charlie. We have just signed anchor tenant."

"Who's that?" Brooker asked, his interest evident despite the casual tone of the question.

Sukov cast a conspiratorial glance around the room before he spoke. "I really can't say. Is still with lawyers, but it is *big* multinational."

Charlie nodded and noticed Brooker scrutinizing Sukov, no doubt testing out his bullshit metre, but the broker seemed to revel in their curiosity.

"So you see, gentlemen, what I have been saying for many months now is true. Petr Square is well on way to full occupancy."

"How many floors did they take?" Brooker asked.

"Most of large tower," Sukov said. "We come to terms for rest soon. As for other tower, the choice is still yours, but space will go fast. I have already a lot of interest, but you can get very good rent, being such prestige tenant as Embassy of Canada," he added with an unctuous smile.

"We're still in the feasibility stage." Charlie shrugged.

Sukov's smile flattened. "Of course, I try to hold best floors for you, but I cannot promise."

"Well, thanks for the update," Charlie said, tapping the business card and handing the brochure to Sukov, who pushed it back.

"Is yours. It was pleasure to meet you, Charlie. You give me call when you are ready to discuss terms," he said, patting him on the shoulder. "But don't wait too long," he added with a wink before heading off toward the other end of the room.

"That's big news," Brooker whispered as soon as Sukov was out of earshot, "if it's true, of course."

Charlie nodded. "Maybe whoever it is knows something about the permit no one else does, if they're willing to commit."

"As full of shit as he is, Oleg's right about one thing." Brooker swallowed the last of his wine. "The rest of the space will go fast if he really has signed up a major anchor tenant. I'd better get on the horn to Ottawa and see if there's any interest in exploring terms." He checked his watch, then held out his hand for the brochure. "If you don't mind, I'll scan that thing right away and ship it off to HQ. I've got a regular call with the property bureau tomorrow and I'd like to have this on the — Oh, hi, Ekaterina."

Charlie turned to see who Brooker was talking to and found himself at eye level with a woman in a business suit.

"Charlie, meet Ekaterina Dontseva. She's with Black & Berger."

Charlie put on his best smile and accepted the woman's slender hand. "Charlie Hillier."

"Ekaterina. A pleasure." She had the prominent cheekbones so common among Russians, but her bright, friendly eyes softened her face and made for a less intimidating effect.

"Ekaterina does a lot of legal work for the mission," Brooker said. "Mostly HR-related, but she's helped me out a couple of times on property files."

"I don't suppose you deal with consular files," Charlie said hopefully.

"Charlie's just joined us as consul," Brooker said, glancing at his watch. "I'm going to have to run if I want to connect with Ottawa. That's the problem with being nine hours ahead. Excuse me."

"So, what kind of law do you practise?" Charlie asked after Brooker had left.

"I've been doing a lot of work for international companies — mostly British or American — setting up here in Moscow," Dontseva said. "Real estate, mergers, and acquisitions. Whatever they need, really. That led to some work for Western embassies, including yours."

"You don't practise criminal law, though?"

She shook her head. "Not for quite a while. You're thinking about your consular case?"

"Sorry, I'm not trying to get free advice —"

She put up a hand. "Please. I'd be happy to help you as much as I can. What sort of case is it?"

"Well, he's a Canadian, obviously," Charlie began. "He's probably early thirties, a technical writer who's been in Moscow for less than six months. He says he went to a party where there was some marijuana, and then the cops showed up and grabbed everyone and questioned them. They let them all go, except for Steve. He says he's never sold so much as a joint in his life."

"Do you believe him?"

Charlie considered the question for a moment. "Actually, I do."

"Drug cases are taken very seriously here, I'm afraid," Dontseva said, a delicate frown clouding her expression.

"I've heard that." Charlie watched as she sipped her wine with full, coral-painted lips. "I also understand there's a whole different set of rules when it comes to drug cases."

She nodded. "It can certainly seem that way, depending on the nature of the offence — or *alleged* offence in this case," she added with a flash of white teeth. "Have you been given access yet?"

"Not really," he said quickly, keen to avoid how he first came into contact with Steve Liepa. "I have a visit scheduled for tomorrow."

"Does he have a lawyer?"

Charlie shrugged. "I don't know."

"I could refer to you to some colleagues who specialize in criminal law, if you'd like."

"I'll be sure to find out if he's represented, and I may take you up on that."

"Insist on seeing his file before you leave," she added. "They will tell you it's not available, but you must be firm, otherwise they will delay and delay."

"I'll do that," Charlie said. "Thanks for the tip."

"And be careful, Charlie. The Russian system is not like in the West — they are especially hard on foreigners. I'd hate to see your client get hurt," she added.

"What do you mean?"

"Just that the prison system has its own rules, and sometimes pushing too hard on behalf of someone in detention can have … a negative effect." She paused and took a sip of wine as he tried to interpret the vague warning. "But you probably know this already."

Charlie smiled, his own glass empty and his stomach starting to growl. "Well, I appreciate the input, but I'm monopolizing your time. It was a pleasure to meet you, Ekaterina."

"You must call me Katya," she said, retrieving something from her pocket and handing it to him. "My business card. Let me know how it goes tomorrow and if you'd like a referral."

He glanced at the elegant card showing Katya as a named partner. "Thanks. I'll do that."

Leaving the reception, Charlie stopped by his office for his coat and then ventured out into the cold night air, debating whether to stop off at a grocery store on the way home or the pizza place a few blocks from his apartment. As he made his way south, his mind wandered to Katya's cryptic warning about the Russian prison system and what it might mean. His pulled the collar of his coat up around his neck in response to a blast of wind that hit him as he turned a corner.

CHAPTER 6

Charlie sat in the grim, dank interview room at Butyrka Prison waiting for Steve Liepa, recalling his own incarceration just over thirty-six hours prior and wondering how he would have coped if it had been extended indefinitely, as Liepa's seemed to have been. Despite Charlie's best efforts, the Russian police had been willing to share very little of the details of Liepa's case, other than the fact that he was to be detained pending formal charges. Following Dontseva's advice, Charlie had insisted on disclosure of the full file when he had arrived at the prison. Undeterred by the initial refusals, he had managed to secure a promise that the file would be ready for him at the end of the interview, but he had a feeling he shouldn't hold his breath. He had spent the morning doing research on the procedural aspects of the Russian legal system, and the bottom line was that things didn't look good for Liepa. As Katya had implied, it wasn't that there weren't rules covering things like how long you could be held without charge; rather, they seemed to be applied arbitrarily, at best. And Liepa's mention that he had been picked up as part of a narcotics sting was more bad news, from what Charlie could tell. In fact, the more he learned about the Russian legal system and Liepa's particular interaction with it, the less likely it seemed that the young Canadian would see the light of day anytime soon.

Charlie flinched at the sound of the metal latch giving way, and then the heavy steel door swung open to reveal a tired-looking Liepa, his hands and feet cuffed and chained as a surly guard prodded him forward. The guard grunted something in Russian and Liepa sat heavily opposite Charlie.

"Good to see you, Steve."

"You look better than last time," Liepa remarked with a thin smile, then gestured to the guard with his cuffed hands, earning only a scowl before the door slammed shut again and they was alone in the close air of the unventilated room.

"How are you holding up?" Charlie noticed that the mischievous glimmer he had seen in Liepa's eyes on the night they had first met was gone, along with a couple of pounds of body weight. Together with the several days' growth on his chin and the sallow tone of his skin, it was as though Charlie was looking at a different person.

"I've been better," Liepa replied, turning his face to reveal a dark bruise by his left cheekbone.

"What happened to your face?"

"Banged into a door," he said, his tone flat as he looked away.

"If you're being mistreated in any way ..."

"It wasn't the guards. There are plenty of people in here ready to kick the shit out of me without the guards having to lift a finger. Anyway," he said with a shrug, "I'll survive. What did you find out about my case?"

"I'm working on it, but it takes time," Charlie said, preferring to keep things general, rather than confirm that his inquiries had resulted in virtually nothing useful. "They told me you have a lawyer assigned to your case."

"Don't waste your time. He's useless."

Charlie saw the dejection in Liepa's features. He also noticed a pronounced facial twitch that he didn't recall from their first meeting. "I can get you a list of lawyers that we've referred people to in the past, if you're not happy with yours. I met one at a function yesterday and discussed your case informally."

"Yeah, what odds did he give me for getting out of here?"

Charlie couldn't help avoiding Liepa's eyes by busying himself with pulling out his notepad, but the dispirited gaze that he saw when he looked back at Liepa told him that the young man had all but given up hope.

"It's a complicated process here," Charlie said, beginning to scratch the date and time onto the top of the page. "Which is why it's important to get a local lawyer involved as soon as possible."

Liepa shrugged again. "I'll take one of your referrals, then. I have some money."

Charlie nodded. "I'll ask him or her to make an appointment to come see you as soon as possible."

"Whatever."

"Why don't you tell me your side of the story, starting with how you came to be in Moscow?" Charlie was determined to sound upbeat.

"I was in Berlin doing some freelance work," Liepa began in the same monotone, "when I saw an ad for a six-month gig in Moscow."

"You mentioned you write technical manuals?"

"Yeah, it's not the most exciting work, but the pay's not bad. Anyway, I was just doing odd jobs in Berlin. So this was the chance to do something full-time, you know?"

"Sure." Charlie began to take notes. "What's the name of the company?"

"Technion. They helped out getting me a work visa and everything else I needed." Liepa brightened for a moment. "They got me this great apartment near the Arbat for a good price, and I was set. I started work about four months ago."

"And things went well, on the work front, I mean?"

"Yeah, sure. It wasn't like the work was really hard or anything. I guess there's a shortage of people with experience writing and translating instructions on how to put a bookcase together or whatever. Strange as it sounds, it does take a certain expertise. Technion does some more complicated stuff, too, like manuals for building systems."

"So you're in Moscow for a few months, you're working at Technion, and …"

"And boom — I'm in here," Liepa said grimly.

Charlie put down his pen. "What happened on the night you were arrested?"

"I went to a friend's house for dinner, and he was going on about this party where a bunch of Ukrainian girls from his office were going. Do I have to say more?"

Charlie smiled. He had heard enough about Ukrainian women that he was looking forward to his first visit to Kiev, slated for early in the New Year. His smile faded, conscious of Liepa's slumped posture across the table — a shell of the confident and outgoing person he had met in the holding cell a couple of nights ago. He picked up his pen and started scribbling. "What's your friend's name?"

"I don't want to drag him into this." Liepa was shaking his head.

"But he wasn't arrested with you?"

"Nobody was. Just me."

"Okay." Charlie looked up from his notes. "Go on."

"There were a couple of joints going around at the party, maybe some hash. Nothing serious. Next thing we know, the place is swarming with cops. They threw a dozen of us into the back of a paddy wagon, but then they let most of us go before we even left. They let the rest go when we got here."

"Except you."

"I was the only foreigner."

"So you think they arrested you because you weren't Russian?"

"Yeah," Liepa replied, fixing Charlie with a stare as he gave a barely perceptible shake of his head. Silence reigned as an unspoken communication was made. When Charlie spoke, it was in little more than a whisper.

"You think there was another reason?"

"The walls have ears," was all Liepa said in reply, and Charlie noticed his leg was jerking under the table, and the twitch on the left side of his face had returned.

"Are you sure you're okay, Steve?"

"I'll be all right, as long as I can get the hell out of here."

"It would be helpful if you could give me your friend's name. I promise not to get him into any trouble."

Liepa sighed. "It's Sergei. Sergei Yermolov. He's a sales rep with United Pharma…. Shit! They took my phone and I can't remember his number. Wait, I think I remember his email." Liepa closed his eyes for a moment, then smiled slightly and gave the email address to Charlie.

Charlie wrote it down, then looked up from his notepad. "Is that UPI, the American pharmaceutical company?"

"Yeah, he's in sales, some kind of junior executive. Makes a lot of coin, but he's a nice guy."

"I'll find him," Charlie said.

"So you'll talk to him and then what?"

"I've got to find out more about what they intend to charge you with. I've told them I'm not leaving here without a copy of your file. Then I have to talk to your new lawyer," he added, knowing that neither activity would likely result in an early release. He looked at Liepa, his eyes lingering on the bruising on his face.

"I'm fine, really," Liepa said with apparent sincerity.

"I'll make some inquiries as soon as I leave here, but unfortunately I'm going to be out of town for a few days after tomorrow."

"Where you off to?"

"Back to Ottawa for some training."

Liepa perked up at the mention of Ottawa and seemed about to say something, then hesitated.

"Is there something I can bring you back?"

"There is someone you could contact for me. She's in Toronto. Her name's Sophie Durant. I'd prefer you spoke to her instead of sending her an email."

Charlie scribbled the name on his pad. "Sure. Your girl-friend?"

Liepa shook his head. "My older sister. I'd really appreciate it if you could let her know I'm in here. I don't want to worry her, but I might be here for a while and she'd be really pissed if I didn't get a message to her. Can you try and break it to her gently, though? She's a little … high-strung, I guess you'd say. A surgeon — need I say more?"

"Any other family I can get in touch with for you? Or anyone else you'd like me to contact?"

"She's all I have." Liepa stared off to the side. Charlie took down the sister's phone number and email address, asked a few more routine questions, and then they talked until their time was up. As he tucked away his notepad, Charlie looked across the table, struck again by the contrast in Liepa's overall appearance and demeanour since the night they had first met.

"Is there anything else I can do, Steve? I mean it — anything."

Liepa leaned slightly forward and paused, as though considering his answer before he spoke. "Just get me out of here."

As he left the prison and stepped out into a cool, grey Moscow day, Charlie had the same sensation as when he had first left Liepa behind. This time, even the fleeting relief of being clear of the place was absent, leaving just a growing unease.

CHAPTER 7

Charlie yawned and stretched his arms overhead as the cabin crew moved down the aisles picking up newspapers and coffee cups and the pilot announced the start of their final approach into Ottawa. He had slept for a record three hours on the flight from Frankfurt, and he actually felt pretty rested. Looking out the window as the plane pierced the cloud cover, he couldn't help smiling at the canvas of red and gold that appeared below. He had always loved fall in Ottawa, and his planned trip across the river to take in the colours of Gatineau Park would be well worth it. He followed the progress of a couple of dinky-size cars along a rural road southeast of the city, then checked his watch. By the time he cleared security and checked into his hotel downtown, it would almost be time for dinner, probably somewhere in the Byward Market. It would be better if he just grabbed something quick, on his own, in case jet lag set in later. It had nothing to do, he told himself, with the fact that he hadn't bothered to contact anyone in advance of his return to Ottawa for the first time in almost two years.

Charlie glanced around the plane again, just to make sure he hadn't missed a familiar face. When he showed up at the gate in Frankfurt for the direct flight to Ottawa, he had been expecting to encounter a former colleague or acquaintance of his — or, worse, his ex-wife. The fact was, with very few exceptions, his friends had really been hers, and he planned to avoid dredging up unpleasant memories as much as possible on his brief visit. He had every reason to be glad for the chance to go home after a considerable time away, but an unmistakable dread had hung over him since learning of the trip. There was a reason he had left, after all. He had never really considered Ottawa home, but it seemed that in the last couple of years, he was officially homeless.

His thoughts turned to the more pressing issue of his survival as the plane lurched through an air pocket, and his heart jumped like a startled mouse as his grasp on the armrest tightened. Charlie disliked landings even more than takeoffs. As had become his coping strategy, he reminded himself of the favourable odds of surviving most flights as the jet's powerful engines accelerated to bring it back on course and the barbed wire of the airfield perimeter came into view, followed shortly by the tarmac of the runway. He looked out the window as the sound of the engines faded, and the plane rolled slightly from side to side as the pilot levelled it off, then deposited it onto the runway with a gentle bump.

Safe again, Charlie could turn his thoughts to the upcoming conference — two days of consular training during which he would do his best to keep his head down and hopefully learn something in the process. At least it was being held at a hotel across the river in Aylmer, as opposed to the headquarters building, where a multitude of awkward encounters were a certainty. He planned to arrange for a lunch with a couple of former colleagues, including his old friend Winston Gardiner, whose directorship in HR had led to Charlie's first posting in Havana. Other than that, though, he planned to stay the hell away from anywhere and anyone that might bring him into contact with his former spouse.

As the plane pulled up to the gate and the seat belt signs went off, Charlie stayed in his seat, refusing to join in the pointless frenzy to reach the overhead bins — he had never understood it, since no one was going anywhere for a few minutes, at least. He pulled out his brand-new BlackBerry and switched it on as an overweight man in a suit elbowed an old lady out of the way to get to his carry-on. As the email folder updated, he watched the numbers climb until it hit twenty new messages, then clicked on the only one of interest — from Winston Gardiner, suggesting dinner tonight. Charlie rubbed his eyes and checked his watch. If he made good time downtown, he would have time to shower and relax a bit first. He sent the reply suggesting they meet at his hotel at seven. It looked nice outside, maybe even warm enough for an outdoor patio. It would be fun.

"So, how's Moscow?" Gardiner asked after they were seated on the balcony overlooking Dalhousie Street. For a Monday night, the Byward Market was booming, perhaps because everyone knew the nights of eating outside were coming to an end, much as they were in Moscow. Gardiner had gained a bit of weight and lost a little hair since Charlie had last seen him, but he seemed in good spirits. In part, no doubt, to his continued ascension up the management ranks, despite the rumblings about cutbacks and general austerity.

"Can't complain," Charlie said. He decided not to mention his recent incarceration to the man who had gone out on a limb for him a couple of years back — placing him in a consular stream for which he was probably unqualified. To say that Charlie's first posting had been a rocky start was to describe a hurricane as a stiff breeze, and the fallout must

have caused Gardiner some initial grief before the dust settled. But things had turned out all right in the end ... sort of.
In any event, Charlie was keen on proving that Gardiner's
faith in him was warranted. He knew that word of his arrest
might make it back to Ottawa eventually, but he certainly
wasn't going to facilitate the process.

"The new HOM in yet?" Gardiner asked, using the departmental slang for head of mission.

"Arrived this week. She seems very nice."

Gardiner nodded. "I worked with her when I first joined
the Department, in the Americas branch. She's had a couple
of postings since then and done very well for herself. I think
she's a rising star."

"You're not doing so bad yourself," Charlie said with a
smile as a server arrived to take their drinks order. "I noticed
your title's changed again."

"It's only an *Acting*, for now."

"Still, Acting Director General sounds pretty good."

Gardiner shrugged. "More headaches, not much more
pay, but I'm not complaining. They're axing people left, right,
and centre in other departments."

They ordered a couple of beers and spent a few minutes on the rumoured changes at HQ that seemed to be on
everyone's mind lately, and concluded that their respective
jobs were intact, for the foreseeable future at least.

"By the way," Gardiner said, "I bumped into Michael
Stewart last week. "He had nothing but good things to say
about you. Apparently the new embassy project's well under-
way in Havana."

Charlie nodded. "Yeah, it's still about eighteen months
out, but it will be nice when it's done."

"He tried to get you extended, you know," Gardiner
said. "He got overruled by the Assistant Deputy Minister

in the end, but he pushed hard, so he obviously thought highly of you."

"That's nice to know," Charlie said. He wasn't surprised as much as grateful, as it was looking more and more like Stewart's chat with his new boss was the only thing that had saved Charlie's ass with Martineau on Monday. "It seems I owe several favours now," he said as their drinks arrived and they raised their glasses in a toast.

"To a brave new world," Gardiner said.

"Seriously, though," Charlie said, after they had each taken a sip. "I can't thank you enough for what you did for me. I don't know what I would have done if —"

"You don't give yourself enough credit, Charlie. All I did was give you a push in the right direction." Gardiner turned his glass on the coaster for a moment. "So, no regrets, then?"

Charlie laughed. "About leaving Ottawa? God, no. And it's not just the change of scenery, either. If the new HOM's telling the truth, I'll get a chance to do a lot more consular work in Moscow."

"You like consular, then?"

"Yeah. I like helping people. Trying to, anyway." He thought of Steve Liepa sitting in a stinking cell in Moscow. "Who knows, maybe after some work in the field, I'll come back to one of the new HQ positions they're talking about creating. It's one of the few areas that seems to be expanding."

Gardiner sipped his drink and nodded, playing with the menu.

"What?"

"Hmm? Nothing, I was just —"

"Come on, Winston. I know that face."

"Have you been in touch with Sharon lately?"

Charlie froze at the sound of his ex-wife's name. "No," he said after he had gulped some beer.

"She's rising fast in the Department and she's rumoured to be the front-runner for the new Assistant Deputy Minister position."

"Which new ADM position?" Charlie asked, though he sensed the answer before the words left his lips.

"Consular."

Fuck.

In the silence that followed, Charlie felt the presence of a black cloud looming directly over his side of the table.

"Great, so she'll be my new boss," he said. All the possible ramifications ran through his brain and triggered a reach for his glass, from which the golden liquid was quickly disappearing. He imagined putting in his request to extend his Moscow posting in a couple of years' time and getting the refusal, accompanied by notice of his immediate cross-posting to Bishkek or Conakry. As his alarm spiralled into despair, Charlie had forgotten about Gardiner, whom he now realized was looking at him like a witness to a particularly gruesome wreck.

"Sorry, did you say something?" Charlie drained his beer and looked around for the server.

"I was just saying nothing's official yet."

"Maybe I should try to reconcile," Charlie said with a feigned laugh, but Gardiner's reaction was pure pity. "I was joking, obviously."

"Look, Charlie ... I wasn't sure if you already knew, but Sharon's engaged ... to Lewis McDermott."

Charlie's mouth went dry as he fumbled for the words to respond. "M-McDermott?" he stammered. "You mean the Deputy Minister?"

"I guess they've been seeing each other for a while on the q.t.," Gardiner said. "Everyone was surprised by the news."

"I'll take another Old Flame, please, but bigger." Charlie tapped his glass as the server appeared at the table. She turned to Gardiner, who waved her off, his glass half-full.

"I'm sure it's difficult to hear, but you've got your own life now, right?" Gardiner said quietly, leaning across the table. "You can stay out at post for a few more years and not have to worry about what happens around here."

Easy for you to say, Charlie thought, as the black cloud intensified. Gardiner had the type of rock-solid marriage that anyone would envy, whether because he and his wife of twenty years always seemed so happy, or because their two perfect kids seemed destined for greatness. What did Charlie have? Fifteen years of a sham that only he had believed was a marriage, and now his ex was headed to the upper echelons of the Department, well placed to rain shit down on his futile attempts at advancement for the rest of his doomed career. In a nutshell, he was fucked.

"Are you listening to me, Charlie?"

"What?"

"You've got to forget about Sharon, move on. Make a name for yourself with Brigitte Martineau, for starters. You're already off to a good start, right?"

Charlie winced, then closed his eyes altogether for a long moment. When he opened them again, a large beer was sitting there. "Yeah," he said, picking up the frosted glass and tapping it off Gardiner's. "I'm off to a great start."

CHAPTER 8

Charlie sat at the rear of the conference room, nursing his second cup of coffee and wishing he hadn't drunk quite so much the night before. He and Gardiner had left the restaurant at around nine-thirty and if Charlie had gone back to the hotel then, he would have been fine. But they'd bumped into a mutual friend outside the restaurant and while Gardiner had been smart enough to call it a night, Charlie had accepted the offer to go the Heart and Crown for a quick pint. He had lost count of the number of "last" beers he consumed before stumbling back to the hotel at 2 a.m., but it was enough to make for a ghastly morning. He was getting too old for this, he thought, as the speaker launched into a PowerPoint presentation on the Department's four-year plan for increasing the complement of consular officers abroad. He was sipping his coffee and trying to square the ambitious plan with the rumours he had heard since returning to Canada of the deep funding cuts that were on the horizon when his phone went off. He jumped up from his seat and slipped out through the double doors at the back before answering.

"Charlie Hillier," he said, his throat still raw from his late night.

"This is Sophie Durant, returning your call. I apologize for not getting back to you yesterday."

"That's okay," Charlie replied, trying to recall how much information he had left on her voice mail. "I'm with the Canadian Embassy in Moscow."

"Is this about Steve?" Her voice had already risen an octave and he hadn't even had the chance to tell her anything yet.

"Yes. He asked me to get in touch with you on his behalf."

"Is he all right?"

"He's fine, but …"

"But what?"

Charlie sighed, remembering Liepa's request to break the news gently. It had seemed simple enough at the time. Sophie picked up on the pause, and the urgency in her voice kicked up a notch. "If there's something you need to tell me about my brother, I need you to spit it out."

"When was the last time you were in touch with Steve, Dr. Durant?"

"I got a postcard from him about a month ago, I guess. And please call me Sophie." It was clear from her tone that it was not a request.

"All right, Sophie. I hate to be the bearer of bad news, but Steve's in jail."

There was silence on the other end of the line as she digested the information. "What … what for?"

"It's not entirely clear yet. He was just detained a few days ago and formal charges have not been laid, but it appears to be drug-related."

"For Christ's sake," she said, pausing to let out a sigh. "How do I get him out? I mean, there must be bail or something."

"There's really not much that can be done until formal charges are —"

"You said you were with the embassy in Moscow, but this is an Ottawa number."

"I'm in Ottawa for a few days. I'm heading back to Moscow on Sunday."

"I want to meet with you. I can come over ..." There was static on the line for a moment and the rustle of papers before her voice returned. "I've got a surgery I can't move tomorrow morning, but I could fly over after that."

"There's really no need for you to —"

"No, I have to meet with you. Steve can't be in jail. You don't understand. I have to meet with you, please."

Charlie closed his eyes. He'd been planning to take advantage of the brilliant sunshine forecast for Saturday by spending the day in Gatineau Park, not being bossed around by a high-strung surgeon. But Liepa's forlorn figure appeared in his mind's eye, still confined to his grubby Russian jail cell, and Charlie's decision was made. "I could meet with you tomorrow afternoon, if you like."

"That's fine. Give me your email address and we'll firm up a time when I have my flight details." They traded contact information and agreed to meet the next day, and as Charlie returned to his conference, he had a feeling Sophie Durant was going to be a real pain in the ass.

Charlie watched the last of the afternoon sun fade as he waited for Sophie Durant in the lobby of the Lord Elgin Hotel. He had been up early, after a quiet night and a good sleep, to beat the rush he knew he could expect on such a brilliant fall day in Gatineau Park. He had gone at a leisurely pace on the two-kilometre trail around Pink Lake, stopping frequently to take in the sparkling blue-green waters against an endless backdrop of every shade of gold, red, and brown, a recent cold spell having sharpened the fall colours just in time for his visit. After a light lunch in a Chelsea tea house, he spent the early afternoon strolling around the Byward Market before making his way to the hotel.

"Mr. Hillier?"

Charlie looked up to see a woman looming over him, clad in jeans and a sweater, her auburn hair tied back in a neat ponytail. The casual attire did nothing to downplay her beauty, as he suspected was the intent, and as he stood to greet her he noticed they were about equal in height.

"Dr. Durant."

"Please call me Sophie," she said again, and he recognized the same terseness that he had heard on the phone.

"Sure, as long as you call me Charlie."

She gave a tired smile and he pointed toward the coffee shop on the ground floor of the hotel. "Would you like to get a coffee? We can talk there."

She nodded. "I could really use some caffeine."

They went in and ordered and took a seat at a corner table.

"Good flight?" he asked, as she sipped her latte. He didn't see any immediate similarity between Sophie and her brother, other than their both being tall and thin. Sophie had high cheekbones, full lips, and emerald-green eyes that peered back at him from behind black-rimmed glasses. Whereas Steve Liepa gave off a crunchy vibe that had him most at ease lounging in a coffee shop or crashing in a hostel, his sister looked more suited to a Chamonix après-ski, if not a Milan catwalk.

"Not bad. A lot shorter than yours," she said, before putting her cup down to indicate the end of chit-chat. "I want you to be straight with me. How much trouble is Steve in?"

Charlie considered the question and the information that was missing in order for him to provide an accurate answer. He wanted very much to be the bearer of good news, but those eyes demanded honesty.

"He's in trouble, but I honestly don't know how much. Not yet. I'll know more when they actually charge him."

"How long can they hold him without charging him?"

"Russian law is a little unpredictable that way," he began. "There's a bit of a gulf between the laws and how they're actually applied, if you know what I mean." He tried a knowing smile, which withered under Sophie's stony gaze. "I talked briefly with Steve's lawyer before I left, and I understand she's looking into a petition for his release pending charges, but it's still early days."

"But you said he's been in jail a week already."

"I know, but —"

"What's it like?" she said, her brow creasing in a worried frown. "Have you seen where they're holding him?"

Charlie nodded. "Yes, I have." He sipped his coffee, avoiding her eyes but not for the reasons she likely suspected. "It's a typical Russian jail."

"It's bad, isn't it?"

"It's not like a North American facility, but it's not that bad," he lied.

"So what's his story, anyway?" she said, her tone hardening. Whether it was because of her demeanour or her Nordic features, Charlie imagined Sophie Durant was an ice queen when she wanted to be. "Let me guess. He got tangled up with some Russian slut and he didn't know it was coke she was snorting."

"Nothing like that," Charlie said with a wave of his hand, though he decided to omit the Ukrainian girls from the story Steve Liepa had told him, at least for now.

"That's just like Steve," she continued, when Charlie had conveyed the basic chronology of events that Liepa had laid out. "And I can't believe he didn't even get a hold of me," she added, shaking her head.

"Well, he probably didn't have the opportunity."

Sophie sighed and looked out the window. "Just when he seemed to be doing so well. He had a normal job and he seemed content."

"When was the last time you saw him?"

"A couple of months before he went to Moscow. I was in Berlin for a medical conference and we had dinner."

Charlie nodded as he put together the family dynamics from her tone. She was the successful, older sibling, whereas Steve was starting to look like the family fuck-up, and also the baby. Charlie had a successful older brother himself, and he didn't have to try too hard to imagine what it was like growing up with Ms. Perfect — beautiful, confident, strong-willed, and accomplished — and that was what he knew about her after five minutes.

"He was still working freelance in Berlin," she continued. "But he was finalizing the details of the Moscow job, and he seemed really pumped."

"And you say Steve isn't big into drugs, as far as you know?" Charlie asked as he took another swallow of coffee.

"Steve smokes the odd joint, but that's all. It's part of his free-spirit lifestyle, I suppose," she added, her disdain obvious.

"What do you mean?"

"I mean he's spent the past ten years bumming around Europe, working as little as humanly possible to sustain himself, staying in hostels like some eighteen-year-old while he dreams of the great novel he's always talking about writing." She sat up straight and pushed her coffee cup away. "But he's not stupid enough to get tangled up in drugs in a big way. Especially in Moscow, of all places."

"Steve's a novelist?"

She laughed. "That's just part of his fairy tale. How else do you explain someone with a Ph.D. from the University of Toronto writing technical manuals in Russia?" She took a deep breath and stared at her hands for a moment, until the anger began to recede and her posture and facial expression relaxed. "How did he look?"

"He looked fine," Charlie said, unsure whether to mention the obvious deterioration he had noticed the second time he had seen Liepa.

"I'm not sure Steve's cut out for a long jail stint. He's had some issues in the past with anxiety," she said, pulling the cup back toward her and moving her finger around the rim.

"He did seem a little different the second time I saw him."

"Different, how?" Her head snapped back up and her intense gaze bore into him. Charlie instantly regretted the comment.

"He just seemed a bit ... agitated." He recalled the jerking leg and facial twitch and knew it was more than mere agitation, but as Sophie's hard facade morphed into an anguished plea, his decision was made — there was no question of giving her the unvarnished version of her brother's condition.

"But he's all right, isn't he?"

"He said he wasn't being mistreated. I made a point of asking several times."

She seemed to take strength from this statement, and her intensity returned. "What about this lawyer, is he any good?"

"It's a she, and I don't really know. We've only spoken on the phone. I was referred to her by someone I know."

"Well, if she's a lightweight, I want you to tell Steve to replace her. Money's not an issue. You can have the bills sent straight to me. I'm not having Steve rotting in jail so some newbie can learn the ropes."

"I'll try to set something up as soon as I get back," Charlie said. "Maybe I can visit Steve with the lawyer."

"When do you go back?"

"I'll be back in Moscow on Monday."

She nodded and began to pull something out of her purse. Charlie watched as she unzipped the rectangular case and opened what looked like a cheque book. "I'm going to give you this," she said, scribbling an amount and her signature.

"What's that for?" he protested, as she tore the cheque from the pad and handed it to him.

"Expenses. For the lawyer, or a replacement if you don't think she's got what it takes, and whatever else you need to get my brother the hell out of jail, fast. I've heard how things work in Moscow."

"Look, Ms. Dur … Sophie, I can't," he began, noticing the cheque was for ten thousand dollars, drawn on the account of Dr. S. Durant, the payee line blank. If he had ten thousand dollars in his own bank account, he wouldn't dream of handing it over to someone he had just met. This woman was either loaded or far too trusting. He looked at her plaintive expression and considered a third option. Desperate.

Charlie shook his head. "I'm an embassy official, not a private eye. I can't take this."

"Well, you have to. I can't go to Moscow, not this week — I can't even apply for a visa until Monday — and I need you to make sure Steve has a good lawyer, and the good ones are never cheap. Trust me, I know."

"You don't understand —"

"This is for a retainer. Or you cash it and give the lawyer whatever she needs, I don't care."

He looked at those expressive green eyes and knew he was powerless, but he tried to hold off as long as he could. "Look, Sophie —"

"The worst thing Steve's guilty of is being naive, believe me," she said. "And I'm sure he put on a brave face and told you he's fine, but I know my brother. He simply won't survive in a Russian jail for very long." She paused and let out a sigh, adding in a lowered voice tinged with strain, "I'm begging you."

Charlie folded the cheque and tucked it into his shirt pocket. "All right, I'll hang on to this for the lawyer."

"When do you think you might get in to see Steve again?"

"I've already got an appointment for Tuesday afternoon. I'll try to talk to the lawyer beforehand," he said, thinking his first day back at the embassy was already looking unpleasant, without having to cross-examine Katya Dontseva's colleague to see if she was up to Sophie's exacting standards. "But I can't promise anything."

"Of course," she said in the confident manner of someone used to getting her way without conceding anything of substance. Charlie had already been motivated to help Steve Liepa, but meeting his sister had taken it to a different level. For any number of reasons, giving more bad news to Sophie Durant just didn't seem like an option.

CHAPTER 9

Charlie returned to his office and set the fresh cup of coffee down on the corner of his desk blotter, his eyes drawn immediately to the flashing light on his phone. As he waited for the message to play, he rubbed his tired eyes. He had barely slept on Sunday's flight, and his connection from Frankfurt had been delayed a couple of hours so that the ride in from Domodedovo International Airport had been right in the middle of rush hour. To top it all off, he had fallen asleep at nine the previous night, only to awake with a start at 4:30 a.m. Now, still only mid-morning on Tuesday, he was already exhausted. He had left a couple of messages with the lawyer that Dontseva had referred him to, but gotten no response. He listened to the message and sighed in frustration at the news that she was at a hearing all day, but willing to meet tomorrow. He had hoped to talk to her before his afternoon visit with Steve Liepa, even bring her along, but that wasn't going to happen.

He put the handset back and stared at the phone, determined to make some progress on Liepa's case before the afternoon meeting, and not just out of an obligation — professional or otherwise — to the young technical writer. He had been haunted by Sophie Durant's plaintive expression and had returned to Moscow with a fire in his belly. He grabbed the phone and dialled Dontseva's direct line.

"It's Charlie ... Hillier, from the Canadi —"

"How are you, Charlie?"

"Good, thanks. Well, actually, I was wondering if I could ask you a favour."

"Of course."

"It's to do with that consular case. I called the lawyer you referred me to."

"Valeria? Yes, I spoke to her yesterday about the case. She had some very good ideas."

Charlie paused, his coffee cup at his lips. "Really? Like what?"

"She mentioned the possibility of a petition to seek Mr. Liepa's release, pending formal charges. This is not the usual process, you understand," Dontseva added. "But there have been a few cases recently where this type of petition to the court has been successful in drug cases."

"That sounds great."

"You shouldn't get your hopes up, Charlie — I would hate to see you disappointed — but if anyone can achieve this, I think it's Valeria."

"Understood." Charlie felt an optimistic surge despite Dontseva's warning. "I'll be sure to follow up with Valeria. But the reason I was calling," he continued, glancing out the window and noticing fat flakes of snow drifting by, "is that I have a meeting at the prison this afternoon with Steve, and unfortunately Valeria's tied up in court. I know this isn't really your field anymore, but it might be encouraging for Steve if I could bring a lawyer, if only to explain the broad stro —"

"Of course, I would like to help if I can," Dontseva said, her tone warm. "What time is the meeting?"

"It's after lunch. Two o'clock."

"In that case, I would be happy to join you. Shall I come to the embassy around one-thirty?"

"That would be great. I really appreciate this, Katya."

He hung up the phone and swivelled around to face his monitor, a faint smile teasing the corners of his mouth, which he liked to attribute to a new hope that he might actually be able to get Steve Liepa out of jail, if only until the prosecutor's office decided to lay charges. His smile faded as he caught sight of one of the locally engaged assistants at his door, a look of grave concern on her usually cheerful features.

"What's wrong?"

"I received word from Butyrka Prison. Your meeting with Mr. Liepa has been cancelled."

"Cancelled? Why?" Charlie could see the alarm in her expression, but he was still unprepared for the news.

"It's Mr. Liepa. He's dead."

"If you're not up to doing this right now, we might be able to reschedule to tomorrow," he said, though he wondered how that could be achieved, given what Dontseva had been through to arrange this afternoon's appointment — not to mention his own efforts, including begging someone in the visas section of the embassy to expedite the approvals for a group of elite Russian hockey players trying to make it to a junior camp in Toronto as a *quid pro quo* for co-operation from the prison officials.

"No." She pulled a tissue out of her purse. "Waiting until tomorrow would only be worse," she said as she composed herself and looked at him. "I know you've probably got other things to do, but would it be too much to ask for you to come with me?"

"Of course not."

She blew her nose and took a deep breath, as some of her strength seemed to return. "Thanks."

Charlie, Sophie, and Dontseva were led into a meeting room on the second floor of the prison building. The room was centred by a long table with three empty chairs on either side. The window behind the empty chairs on the opposite side overlooked a courtyard, where the sound of a jackhammer could be heard through the double-paned glass. At the far end of the room, next to a closed door, were a half dozen portraits of severe-looking men whom Charlie presumed were former directors of the prison. He was about to head down for a closer inspection when the door opened and three men entered the room. The oldest was a mountain in his fifties, his thick head topped with a white brush cut that contrasted sharply with bushy black eyebrows. He spoke in a deep baritone, prompting Dontseva to step forward and introduce Charlie and Sophie to the prison director, a legal officer, and a representative from the Russian Ministry of Foreign Affairs. The MFA man pointed to the chairs behind them and spoke in British-accented English.

"Please, have a seat."

"Thank you," Dontseva said, launching into an introductory statement in Russian, which she translated briefly into English for the benefit of her clients. The MFA man responded for the other side of the table.

"First of all, Director Orlov would like to express his deepest regret to Dr. Durant for this unfortunate occurrence."

In the pause that followed, Sophie gave a nod of acknowledgement in Orlov's direction as he sat stock-still and the lawyer at his side scratched something on his legal pad.

"And he would like to assure you of his full co-operation in answering your inquiries."

"Perhaps we might begin with a brief explanation of the circumstances of Mr. Liepa's death," Dontseva said. Though Orlov's face remained impassive as he waited for the translation, Charlie had a sense that he understood what had been said. The Russian shifted his weight on his chair and set his enormous forearms on the surface of the table as he spoke first in the direction of the MFA man, then across the table. Charlie hadn't understood much of it, but he didn't need to.

"He says that while they are pleased to co-operate fully," Dontseva began, "he is bound by strict rules of procedure in cases involving the death of a ... an inmate." She began another brief exchange in Russian, before adding, "But he is pleased to provide us with the official report of the prison."

Orlov turned and nodded at the lawyer, who pulled a thin sheaf of papers from a file and passed it across the table to Dontseva. Before she had a chance to look at it, the director began speaking again, alternating his focus between Dontseva and Sophie, and ignoring Charlie completely. Dontseva translated once he was finished.

"He says Mr. Liepa was found dead in his cell on Tuesday morning by guards, who were doing a routine check."

Sophie was ashen-faced as she gave Dontseva a nod.

"Go on."

Dontseva asked another question in Russian. The answer was succinct, and Charlie understood it before Dontseva turned to Sophie and translated it: "He hanged himself."

Charlie and Dontseva stood by the door of the examination room as Sophie approached her brother's body laid out on the gurney and covered by a green sheet. As if the meeting with the prison officials wasn't difficult enough, Sophie was now faced with the task of identifying her brother's remains. Charlie wondered how she managed to maintain her composure as she stood over the body and reached for the sheet. Charlie flinched as she pulled it back and he saw Steve Liepa's lifeless face in profile. From his vantage point by the door, Charlie thought Liepa looked at peace, and he hoped his sister had the same impression. After an initial pause, Sophie traced a finger on her brother's forehead in a gesture of intimacy that made Charlie feel like an intruder.

"It's him," she said, more to herself than to the medical attendant or anyone else who stood nearby. "That's my brother."

As the lawyer translated her words, Charlie watched Sophie roll the sheet slowly down to the top of Liepa's shoulders, then step around the head of the gurney. She seemed to morph from sister to physician at that point, leaning over to inspect the neck area more closely from different angles. Even from where he stood, Charlie could see the bruising around the neck, and the attendant said something as Sophie walked around to the other side of the gurney.

"He says no touching," Dontseva relayed.

"Tell him to go fuck himself," Sophie replied without looking up. Whether or not he understood the comment, the tone was unmistakable, and the attendant had begun to move toward the gurney before Dontseva intercepted him and began an exchange in Russian. Charlie watched as Sophie turned her back to the argument and prodded Liepa's shoulder area while the discussion between Dontseva and the attendant heated up and the latter began yelling. Sophie touched her brother's forehead again, then brushed past the attendant, whose ire was still focused on Dontseva.

"Tell him to relax. I'm done."

Sophie followed Charlie out into the hall, and as they waited for Dontseva, she began pacing the floor. Charlie considered asking her if everything was all right, but the very question seemed ludicrous in these circumstances.

"Bastards," she muttered, as Dontseva appeared in the hall and looked at her.

"You must let me do the talking, so we can get your brother's personal effects before we leave, yes?"

Sophie stared back at Dontseva as the lawyer stepped closer and touched her arm. The gesture seemed to defuse some of Sophie's anger and she took a deep breath, before nodding her silent assent.

"Come on," Charlie said, "Let's get out of here."

CHAPTER II

Charlie stood in the lobby of the Marriott Grand, watching the Friday-evening crowd milling about near the entrance to the bar. For the most part, the Russian men laughed amongst themselves and smoked cigarettes, while their dates perched on stilettos nearby, looking bored. Charlie had been trying to think of a way out of an invitation to the dinner party — he had a pretty good idea that it was a blind date set up by a well-meaning but nosy colleague in consular — when Sophie Durant called with the perfect excuse. She had been given tickets to a piano concerto at the Moscow Conservatory and was hoping he could join her.

When he had dropped her off at the hotel the night before, she had been in rough shape, her mental exhaustion from grief and anger exacerbated by jet lag. Charlie had offered to show her the sights on the weekend, if only to take her mind off things until the next scheduled meeting on Monday at the Ministry of Foreign Affairs building, but her call had still been a surprise. He scanned the lobby again to make sure she wasn't waiting on the other side, and as he glanced toward the elevators, the doors slid open and his breath caught in his throat. She wore a simple black dress, and other than small diamond studs in her ears, the only accessory was a black headband with a subtle pattern of white polka dots that complimented her reddish-brown hair, but the overall effect was stunning. Charlie could sense eyes from all over the lobby fix on her as she spotted him and made her way over.

"Thanks for coming on such short notice," she said as he stood to greet her. "I hope I didn't ruin your evening."

"I had nothing planned, anyway," he lied. Sophie's face looked much less strained than the night before, but her body language still suggested a tentativeness that seemed at odds with her assertive personality.

"Do you know where it is?" she asked, slipping her coat off her arm and putting it on. "I could ask the concierge."

"I know where it is. You okay with the Metro?"

She nodded and began to head for the door. "Come on. We don't want to be late."

They walked out into the cold evening air and Charlie led the way north up Tverskaya, wondering what to make of her uncharacteristic silence. They reached Mayakovskaya station in a matter of minutes and made their way down to the turnstiles as Charlie pulled a pair of tickets out of his pocket and handed her one.

"Thanks," she said, watching as he slid his ticket into the gate and then following the same process with hers. "I'll pick up the return trip," she added as they joined the stream of people converging at the top of the escalator.

"Don't worry about it. I've got plenty."

"You take the subway a lot?" she asked. They began their descent and she peered down the steep grade.

"I'm slowly getting used to it, and Moscow traffic's a nightmare."

"How deep does this thing go?" she said, looking down the escalator, the platform below still nowhere in sight.

"Quite something, isn't it?" he said, noticing her relief as the bottom of the escalator finally came into view. "Stalin had it built deep enough that it could do double duty as a bomb shelter." They continued their descent in silence, and Charlie tried to think of something light to say, something that wouldn't remind her of why she was in Moscow. "So where did you get the tickets, anyway?"

She seemed to consider the question for a moment, and Charlie was more intrigued than ever by her preoccupation with what he thought was a straightforward question. "I don't have tickets," she said as they reached the bottom and followed the mass toward the platform. "I was told I could get them at the door."

Charlie checked the signs for the southbound train as Sophie looked up.

"It's beautiful," she said, pointing to an intricate mosaic inside one of the circular niches that lined the ceiling of the central colonnade separating the two platforms.

"This way," he said, hurrying them toward a waiting train, the red lights above its doors beginning to flash as they entered. They took standing positions in the open space at the front of the car.

"I should have told you," she said, as the train began to move, "but I was ... afraid, I guess."

"Told me what?"

"Someone left me a note at the front desk this afternoon," she said in a voice barely above a whisper. "Telling me to meet them at the Conservatory. I'm supposed to come alone."

Charlie reached for the overhead handle as the car lurched forward, catching Sophie in his free arm as she flailed for something to hold on to.

"Who left you the note?" he asked after she had righted herself and latched on to a bar.

"He said he was a friend of Steve's — no, a colleague."

"And he didn't leave a name?"

"Look, I probably shouldn't have misled you like this. I understand if you don't want to ..."

He shook his head. "It just seems a bit odd, don't you think?"

"Maybe, but I need to find out what happened in that prison," she said, the more familiar resolve returning to her features.

"What do you mean?"

She clutched the bar as they clattered over the connecting rails beneath them and the car wobbled from side to side and an ear-splitting screech announced their impending arrival at the next station. "I mean Steve didn't commit suicide."

They made it to the Moscow Conservatory twenty minutes before the scheduled start of the recital and agreed to line up separately for tickets. Since it was general admission, they agreed Charlie would sit at the back and keep an eye on Sophie while she waited for her mystery date. As the room filled up to near capacity, Charlie took his seat and watched as she settled herself near the end of a long bench ahead of him, leaving just enough room for someone to squeeze in. As the curtain came up and the crowd began to applaud, the spot next to Sophie remained vacant. The pianist took her seat behind the piano, and as she began playing, Charlie divided his attention between the Rachmaninoff and the back of Sophie's head. As the time passed, Charlie's hope that the planned meeting wouldn't materialize grew, though he couldn't imagine why someone would bother with such a hoax. More troubling was Sophie's statement in the subway about her brother's death, and the look on her face that left no doubt as to her conviction. But what made her so sure it wasn't a suicide? After all, she had said herself that her brother had some emotional problems. Charlie couldn't imagine that these would have been helped by incarceration in a Russian jail. But there was an unmistakable look in Sophie's eyes that made him wonder what she knew that he didn't. Something she felt disinclined to share with him on a crowded Moscow subway car.

Charlie watched as she subtly glanced around the room, giving him a view of that perfect profile. To describe Sophie Durant as beautiful was to call the pyramids just okay, but he wondered what lay behind her tough exterior, whether she let it down for anyone, even her husband. He hadn't noticed a wedding ring, but the fact that she had a different last name than her brother certainly suggested that she was married. Hardly a surprise, he thought, imagining a six-foot-four cardiothoracic surgeon with a lantern jaw.

As the frenzied pace set by the pianist slowed to a few final notes, then the brief silence that preceded an ovation, Charlie realized that they had reached the intermission. He watched as the audience drifted out of their seats, and when Sophie stood and made her way to the lobby, he followed at a distance. He watched from one line as she stood in another, eventually buying a glass of wine. A few minutes later he had his own and was considering crossing to the corner where she stood when he saw a man stop and engage her in conversation. Charlie leaned on a railing in the opposite corner of the lobby, trying not to stare as Sophie acknowledged the other man's presence, not with a smile, but with body language that indicated a keen interest. The man was tall and thin, in his fifties, with wavy grey hair and an angular face, which together with his worn corduroy suit, made him look distinctly Russian. He appeared relaxed as he stood next to Sophie, speaking between sips from his glass of wine. Charlie busied himself with his program on the couple of occasions when the man took his eyes off Sophie to survey the room. Whatever he was saying, it had Sophie's full attention, and from what Charlie could see from across the room, the mystery man was doing most of the talking.

As the first bell rang to announce the second half of the performance, Charlie watched the man reach over and shake Sophie's hand. She seemed surprised by the gesture and Charlie felt a surge of alarm as the handshake lingered for a tick too long. He started toward them but the handshake was suddenly broken and the man was gone, disappearing among the crowd making its way back into the concert hall. The second bell seemed to stir Sophie into action and, depositing her wineglass on a nearby table, she made her way back to her seat. As he regained his own, Charlie saw her turn and catch his eye. But instead of giving him a sign that they should leave, she returned a blank gaze, faced front, and settled in her seat. Charlie bit back his curiosity as a full orchestra assembled on stage and the pianist returned to a roar of applause.

CHAPTER 12

At the end of the performance, Charlie followed Sophie out into the evening chill, hanging back as she regained the street and headed back in the direction of the Metro. After taking only a few steps away from the Conservatory entrance, Charlie could bear it no longer and quickly closed the gap between them.

"So?" he asked when he caught up.

"I need a drink," she said, spotting the lights of a nearby restaurant.

The place was filling up with the Conservatory crowd, but they were squeezed into a small booth at the rear of the smoking section. Sophie waved off Charlie's concern for her lungs as they ordered drinks. When the server left, he waited for her to speak.

"He was a friend of Steve's," she began. It was clear that, despite the hour spent listening to the second half of the concerto, she was still shaken by the encounter. "A journalist."

When she didn't continue, Charlie finally spoke. "Why did he want to meet with you and why all the secrecy?"

"He said Steve told him, if anything ever happened to him, to get in touch with me. As for the cloak-and-dagger stuff, he was afraid — pure and simple."

Charlie looked puzzled. "Did he say why?"

"He said he and Steve had discussed journalism in Russia, and the dangers that went with the profession here. Then Steve said he was working on something ... explosive." She paused as their drinks arrived and only resumed after she had taken a long sip of her gin and tonic. "He also said that when he heard Steve had ... died, he knew that he'd been killed."

"Did he say what this explosive thing was? An article or an exposé or something? You said he was a writer."

Sophie shook her head. "I said he *wanted* to be a writer, and apparently he wouldn't say what it was. Just that it was going to make a name for him, that he knew it might piss some people off, but he was prepared to take the risk."

"How did this guy know about Steve's death, anyway?"

"He said he used to be a crime reporter, and he still has contacts. He'd heard about Steve's arrest and was trying to find out about his case when he heard ..." She trailed off and put her face in her hands. Charlie tried to think of something to say and put his hand on her arm.

"I'm sorry, Sophie. I know this must be awful for you, but even if his intentions are good, this guy's information sounds pretty vague."

She wiped away her tears and, taking a deep breath, appeared to steel herself to continue. "It wasn't suicide. I know that much for a fact."

Charlie looked at her eyes, no less piercing despite being red-rimmed. "Is there something you're not telling me?" He had lowered his voice despite the hubbub around them. She shot a look around before leaning forward to speak.

"Steve had a puncture mark on his right trapezius," she said, and Charlie remembered he was talking to a doctor. He had never asked what her specialty was, but he knew she was a surgeon of some kind. Somehow he couldn't picture her doling out antibiotics in a family clinic.

"Is that significant?" he asked, thinking the question made him sound ignorant, but his knowledge of medicine really was nil. If his inquiry frustrated her, though, she didn't show it.

"It looked a lot like the mark a twenty-five-gauge needle would make, and the trapezius muscle's an excellent injection site."

"For what?"

"A paralytic, like succinylcholine," she said, her voice down to barely more than a whisper, "which could completely incapacitate an adult within seconds, and it would be difficult to find with a blood test, even if you knew to look for it." She paused and braced herself with a healthy swallow of her drink. "If I wanted to stage a hanging, I couldn't think of a better way to do it."

"You mean the person would be unconscious?"

"Not unconscious, just paralyzed," she said as Charlie realized the implications, "for anywhere from five to fifteen minutes, depending on the dose." They sat in silence on either side of the table. Even with no medical training, Charlie had no problem conjuring up a vivid mental image of Steve Liepa's last moments on earth, and he hoped Sophie, for her sake, wasn't doing the same.

"You would like to order now?"

Charlie looked up to see a server standing there, pad and pen at the ready, the menus unopened on the table between them. "Uh, give us a couple of minutes."

"I'm not hungry," Sophie said, pushing the menu away.

"You should try to eat something. It's hard to think straight on an empty stomach."

She looked at him and the flicker of a smile graced one side of her mouth. "I suppose you're right. What do you recommend?"

"Damned if I know. I usually stick to the Western stuff. My experimentation in local cuisine has been hit-or-miss, but you can't go wrong with a BLT."

She nodded. "How long have you been in Moscow, anyway?"

"A couple of months."

"I'll bet Steve loved it here," she said, looking around the crowded restaurant. Most of the patrons were in their twenties and thirties, and whatever segment of the Russian population was suffering from the economic slowdown, it wasn't to be found in here. These people were too busy laughing and drinking through a haze of cigarette smoke. Charlie nodded as he pictured Steve Liepa sitting at one of the tables, laughing right along.

"Where did he learn his Russian?"

"Our parents were Lithuanian, and they taught us a bit of Russian, too," Sophie said. "Whatever I learned as a kid, I've long forgotten, but Steve retained it all, and he picked up French, German, and who knows what else over the years. He always had a natural aptitude for languages." She gave a little chuckle as she added, "I barely passed my one and only undergrad English course."

"You obviously have other strengths," Charlie said, trying to prolong the levity in the conversation, but he could tell by her expression that she was struggling. "He seemed like a really decent, easygoing guy," he added, after an awkward silence.

"Everyone loved him. It used to drive me nuts when we were growing up, the way our parents fawned over him, but looking back, how could I blame them? Thank God they didn't live to see him die, especially like this."

"It was just the two of you?"

She nodded. "Our parents both passed away in the last five years." The server returned for their orders and when they were alone again, she continued. "No, Steve could do no wrong in my parents' eyes, being the baby and all."

"And no matter how hard you applied yourself, as the dutiful older sibling, it was never enough?"

She looked up at him, the vacant gaze gone now, replaced by an inquisitive sparkle.

"I have a brother back in Newfoundland," he said, and Sophie slowly nodded. "Though mine's the older one and that's probably what he would say. I guess you could say *I'm* the fuck-up in our relationship, so I think I know what you mean, but what good does it do to beat yourself up about it now? Steve didn't strike me as someone who would hold a grudge, anyway."

She laughed. "I'm sure he was oblivious. I was such a bitch to him sometimes, though."

"I'm not sure he would have seen it that way, somehow."

She smiled and finished her drink, waving as the server passed by. "You want another?"

Charlie looked at the inch of beer left in his glass. "Sure."

"Two more of the same, please." She paused for a moment, looking at him with her sad eyes. "What does your brother do?"

"He owns a chain of building supply stores," he said, thinking of the mansion his brother had just had built on a prime lot in St. John's. Charlie didn't even own a home anymore, and his government salary wasn't going to make him rich, hardship bonuses or not. "He does very well, and I'm obviously in the wrong line of work."

"I guess a little sibling rivalry is par for the course in every family," she said with a small grin.

"Last time we talked," Charlie went on, "he was running a couple of stores. Now all of a sudden, he's got a whole chain and he's expanding out of province." He paused and let out a little laugh. "Listen to me. Some brother I am. Plus, you're not supposed to be consoling me."

Her face lit up in a way he hadn't seen before with her first genuine smile. "It was the reverse for me. Steve was still backpacking around Europe by the time I finished my surgical residency, but that didn't seem to matter." She sighed. "I was all set for the perfect life — great career ahead, married to Mr. Perfect when I was still in med school. He was a surgeon, of course." The smile faded, then disappeared altogether. "The promise of grandchildren kept our parents happy for a while. They didn't even seem to mind that I'd married the world's biggest asshole, and neither did I. I was so hell-bent on beating Steve at something. Boy, did that backfire on me," she said as their drinks arrived. "It didn't work out, and while Steve was hitchhiking from hostel to hostel and living on peanuts, I was busy getting divorced. Another strike for big sister."

Charlie could see her mood darkening, and he was thinking of ways to nudge her onto another topic, but she was in full swing now. "Why couldn't I just have been happy for him? He never gave a shit about prestige or status or money, and good for him. I know he didn't like Brad — my ex," she added, swirling her drink around in the glass. "But he never showed it, always put on a friendly face. Why did I have to resent him for his happiness?"

Charlie shrugged. "People like Steve have a certain innocence that can be … well, annoying," he offered. "But it's that same innocence that makes them immune to whatever resentment you might have felt. I'm sure he never even noticed."

Sophie looked at him as though half of her wanted to believe him, while the other half thought she was being fleeced. "I hope you're right," she finally said, her voice on the verge of cracking. "I just can't get what he said out of my mind." She looked at Charlie and he saw her eyes tear up. "The man at the Conservatory."

Charlie shook his head. "What do you mean?"

"Steve told him I'd know what to do if he was ever in trouble. That I'd help him." She wiped a fat tear from her cheek. "I guess he was wrong."

CHAPTER 13

It was after midnight by the time Charlie and Sophie made it back to her hotel. Standing in the lobby, Charlie was enjoying the warmth that seeped into his thin coat; the Moscow nights were distinctly colder now that fall was morphing into winter. He watched as Sophie shifted her weight unsteadily from one foot to the other, the result of several drinks superimposed on a rather insubstantial BLT.

"Thanks for coming, Charlie," she said. "It was totally unfair for me not to level with you, but I don't know what I would have done without you."

"It's fine. Next time, though, you'll tell me what's going on, right?"

"Right."

She waved at the elevators. "I'd invite you up for a nightcap, but we've probably had enough for one night, I think."

Under normal circumstances, the idea of a nightcap with Sophie Durant would have been irresistible, but these were hardly normal circumstances.

"Yeah, I'm really beat," he lied.

She nodded. "So I'll come to the embassy first thing on Monday?"

"Yeah. We can go over to the MFA meeting together."

"Well, I'll let you go." She put her hand on his arm. "Thanks again. I really mean it."

"No problem." He watched as she began to cross the lobby, a forlorn figure on her way to a weekend alone, with nothing to do but imagine her brother's final moments.

"Hey," he called out, taking a few steps toward her. "I was just thinking, it's supposed to be a nice day tomorrow. I could show you around a bit, if you like." He couldn't tell by her body language if she was thinking of accepting his offer or of how to politely refuse it, so he just kept talking. "It'd be good for you to get out of your hotel room for a bit. Maybe take your mind off —"

"I've already monopolized your Friday night. I'm sure you've got better things to do."

"You forget I'm a newbie here — haven't developed a social life yet," he said with a grin. Her face brightened in turn.

"Well, if you're sure you don't mind ..."

"I'll drop by here around ... is noon okay? We can go for a walk around Red Square and the Kremlin, maybe grab a late lunch."

"See you tomorrow, then."

"Sleep well, Sophie."

He watched her until she was safely inside an elevator, then turned and headed back out into the night for the short walk to the Metro. He had only gone fifty feet along Tverskaya when he heard his name and turned to see Sophie running toward him.

"What's the matter?" He could see the urgency on her face.

She held out her open palm and Charlie could see a small, rectangular object, its metallic surface glittering in the beam of the streetlight overhead.

"It's a USB stick," Sophie said, her voice a note higher from her excitement and the short run. "I found it in my purse when I was rummaging for my room key. He must have dropped it in there at the Conservatory."

"Do you have a laptop?"

She nodded. "Can you come back with me and have a look?"

Charlie pulled the armchair up to the table where Sophie had set up her laptop. He watched as she plugged in the USB stick.

"I hope it's not in Russian," she said as they waited for the laptop to recognize the stick. A few seconds later a new directory appeared with two files, the first of which was entitled *AS*. Sophie clicked on it and they both sat in silence while the file opened.

"It's in English," Charlie said, scanning the full screen of text. "Who's Alexander Surin?"

"I have no idea." Sophie frowned. "But this appears to be a bio on him. Looks like he's some kind of bureaucrat. Ah, look at this — he's a former KGB officer."

"That's not uncommon for Russian bureaucrats, especially if he's an older guy."

"He's fifty-five," she noted, continuing to scan the document. When she reached the end of the page, she moved the cursor to the bottom and held it there. "It's just the one page."

Charlie took a few seconds longer to finish reading, then sat back and asked, "Did the guy at the Conservatory mention anything about this Surin?"

Sophie shook her head. "No, he just said that Steve had asked him for some background information about Russian politics. It sounded like publicly available stuff, and he certainly didn't say anything about this Surin guy."

"Let's see what's in this other file." Sophie clicked it and as they waited for it to open, Charlie turned to her. "Steve never mentioned anything to you about political research?"

She shook her head. "Steve hated politics. And all he ever told me was about his work translating technical manuals."

They both turned their attention to the screen as the second document opened. Unlike the first, this one was a spreadsheet with a series of columns with abbreviated headings across the top and numbers in the rows below. There were only two rows on the left side of the chart, with the respective headings *RU* and *OS*.

"What the hell's this?" Sophie said, staring at the screen along with Charlie.

As he looked more closely, he noticed that each descending column was divided into two, with the symbols # and % at the top of each.

"I don't know."

"There must be a legend or something." She scrolled up and down but found nothing to interpret the series of letters and numbers that might as well have been hieroglyphics, for all the sense they made.

"Did the guy give you any way to contact him?"

She took her finger off the mouse and sat back in the chair with a sigh. "I tried, but he wouldn't even tell me his name. He told me he was honouring his promise to Steve."

Charlie could understand how a Muscovite, even a seasoned journalist — perhaps especially a seasoned journalist — would be reluctant to get too involved in the death of a foreigner.

"He said it was dangerous, for both of us," she added, obviously going through the same thought process. "That's it," she added, after a final series of clicks and keystrokes had satisfied her that the rest of the USB was empty. "So what now?"

Charlie pointed at the screen. "Can I get a copy of that?"

"I can email you.... Maybe not such a great idea." She reached over for a leather courier bag and fished around in one of the inside pockets. "I've got an extra USB stick in here somewhere."

Charlie watched as she shoved the stick into one of the other ports, and he noticed the outside of the key was in the shape of a teddy bear. Sophie caught his expression and laughed. "What, you didn't figure me for the teddy bear type?"

"Honestly?"

She grinned, then popped the stick out and handed it over. "Here."

He glanced at his watch. "It's getting late and we've both had a busy night. Let's sleep on it and circle up tomorrow. Maybe we can have another crack at figuring this out. Whatever it is, it must mean something."

She followed him to the door.

"Thanks again for coming with me tonight."

"It was my pleasure, really."

As he headed toward the elevators, he was already thinking of how to decipher the information on the USB and use it to shed some light on Steve Liepa's death. The night had been far from what he had expected, but he wouldn't have traded it for anything.

CHAPTER 14

Charlie sat in the café on the top floor of the GUM building, drinking coffee and looking over the rail at the stores below. Once a spartan and poorly stocked department store where citizens queued for toilet paper and bread, the enormous building had been beautifully restored and converted into a lavish, multi-level mall where Moscow's elite converged to buy the latest brand-name clothing, luggage, and skin-care products, all at dizzying prices.

"This really is a spectacular building," Sophie said, looking up at the domed glass roof that ran the length of the massive structure. The view looking down was just as impressive from their vantage point by the railing of a bridge-like strip that spanned the atrium below.

"It's nice, as long as you don't try to buy anything," Charlie cracked.

"Not even a hat and gloves? I didn't bring any."

He nodded, remembering that he was talking to a successful surgeon who probably made more in a month than he did in a year. Maybe spending two hundred bucks on a pair of gloves wasn't unusual for her. "Sure. We can have a look on the way out, if you like."

They chatted for a while longer, and inevitably their conversation returned to the mystifying contents of the USB stick.

"I did an online search for Surin last night after you left," she said, sipping her cappuccino. "I can't see any reason why he'd be of particular interest to Steve, or to anyone else, for that matter."

"I'll see if I can find out anything at the embassy on Monday. Maybe Trade or Political will have heard of him," Charlie said. He had done some web research of his own when he got back to his apartment the night before and found nothing of interest on Surin, either. It didn't help that most of the results were in Russian. "And as for that chart, I don't know what that's all about yet, either, but we'll figure it out." He said this with more certainty than he felt. He had spent an hour on his laptop that morning going through the files, after which he was no further ahead.

"What's the plan for the meeting at the MFA?" Sophie asked.

"I know I agreed that you should come first thing Monday, but I've got meetings all morning," Charlie said. "So why don't you drop by the embassy after lunch, and we can go from there."

She frowned, which Charlie took as concern over Monday's schedule. He was about to inquire when she spoke again.

"The meeting's pretty much a waste of time, isn't it?"

"What do you mean?"

"I mean, if I was hoping to get to the bottom of Steve's death."

Charlie considered the question for a moment. He had managed to tack the meeting onto one he had arranged weeks before to discuss another consular case involving a request to extend a visa, and he doubted it was the appropriate forum to make allegations of wrongful death, if that was what Sophie had in mind.

"Have you had a chance to consider your theory any further?"

"You mean am I sure he didn't kill himself?" she said, finishing her coffee and setting the cup down before answering. "I'm sure."

"Based on the mark on his shoulder? I'm no doctor, but ..."

"Well, I am. And I know an injection site when I see one."

"I'm just saying —"

"And I know my brother. He didn't kill himself."

Charlie saw the familiar resolve in her eyes and knew she had made up her mind.

"Then we'll find a way to get to the bottom of it," he said, breaking the silence that had descended over them. "But you're probably right not to expect much from the meeting. I was wondering if I should ask Dontseva to come along."

"Sure, if you think she might be useful," She began rummaging in her purse and pulled out a handful of postcards. "I meant to show you these," she said, passing them across the table. "You asked when I'd last been in touch with Steve. This was it, after I met him in Berlin last spring."

Charlie flipped through the postcards — one from Berlin, two from Moscow, and a third with a picture of a skyline at night that he didn't recognize. "Where's this?"

"Astana, Kazakhstan."

"What was he doing there?"

"Work, I think," Sophie said. "You can read them if you want."

Charlie scanned the handwriting on the Kazakh postcard, focusing on the text that followed the standard words of greeting from a foreign city: "*Man it's cold here, for summer, but I'm warming up to something new — something I've always wanted to do. Sometimes the answers are right in front of you.*"

He noted the date — July 31 — then flipped the card back over and looked at the picture again. It was a shot of a complex of glass-clad office buildings lit up against the night sky.

"Do you know what he meant by this?"

"The stuff about something he always wanted to do?" She took the card from him. "Not really. I know he always wanted to be a writer — a novelist. It would have suited him. But Steve was always talking in riddles." She smiled. "I never knew what he meant half the time."

"That's funny," Charlie said as he looked at the backs of the other postcards. "They're all postmarked from Berlin, even the Russian and Kazakh ones."

"Really?" Sophie perked up. "I didn't notice that."

"He went back to Berlin after he had moved to Moscow for work?"

She nodded. "I know he loved Berlin. It fit with his artsy side, and he liked the beer." Again she smiled.

Charlie watched as she lingered over the words scribbled on the backs of the postcards. "Maybe we should focus on getting Steve back to Canada first," he said.

"What do you mean?"

"Russia's a very bureaucratic society. If we start making inquiries that are … unconventional, we may find ourselves up against an administrative brick wall."

She looked back down at the postcards and nodded. "Maybe you're right. I don't have a lot of faith in having an independent investigation here. I need to arrange for a proper autopsy as soon as possible. It may not give us all the answers, but I guarantee it will turn something up. Do they have private investigators here?"

"I'm sure they do. I can ask Katya." Sophie tucked the postcards back in her purse and began zipping it up.

"I have another favour to ask you."

"Name it."

"I didn't mention that the police gave me the keys to Steve's apartment. I really need to go over there, but I'm a little …"

"I'd be happy to come along for moral support."

"Thanks," she said, glancing at the shops below them. "You can help me pick out a pair of gloves first."

Charlie squinted at the street sign affixed to the stone building at the far corner of the intersection. He had checked the address before leaving his office and he knew they were in the right vicinity, but he still found translating the Cyrillic alphabet a challenge.

"I think that says 'Golovin.'"

Sohie looked the building over and grimaced. "It looks like a real dump."

"Good location, though," Charlie offered. It was true that the second-floor apartment — located above what looked like a dentist's office, from the oversized picture of a molar hanging in the ground-floor window — was only a few blocks from the Sukharevskaya Metro station, which itself was only a few stops from the Kremlin. From what he had heard, apartments inside the Boulevard Ring road were hard to find, and for that reason, often overpriced and undersized. He found Sophie's impression accurate when they set foot inside the cramped lobby, which smelled vaguely of a mix of alcohol and urine. He led the way to the dimly lit staircase and up to the second floor, where a single door barred any further progress. Above the tattered plaque bearing the Cyrillic equivalent, someone had affixed a yellow sticky note with "2A Golovin" scrawled on it.

"That's Steve's writing," Sophie said, removing the note and holding it as though it were made of precious stone. "I'd recognize his chicken scratches anywhere."

"I thought it was doctors who had the messy handwriting."

Sophie gave him a look that suggested appreciation at his attempt to lighten her mood as she inserted the key in the lock, paused for a moment, and then turned the handle. Charlie's first instinct on entering the tiny apartment was to search for a window, so oppressive was the stale air that met them. Finding one on the other side of the room, he fumbled with the latch and tugged at the ancient frame, managing to jerk it open a few inches before it squeaked to a halt. Pulling back the curtains, the room was cast in the bright sunlight of the cold Moscow day.

"I was wrong," Sophie said, swinging the door shut behind her. "It's not a dump. It's a shithole."

"It's not so bad." Charlie's remark prompted a raised eyebrow from across the room. "I mean, it's just a little ... untidy, that's all." As he glanced around the room, maybe twelve feet by twelve and adorned with a battered sofa, an ugly chair, a large bookcase that seemed to list on the uneven floor, and a coffee table with a surface largely obscured by clutter, he tried to decide whether they were looking at the apartment as Steve Liepa had left it, or whether it had been turned upside down by the militia, or maybe the FSB.

"I know Steve was a slob, but this is ridiculous," Sophie said, after they had both done a preliminary scan of the room. "Someone's obviously been through the place."

"Doesn't look like a break-in," Charlie said, looking back to the door. "Door was locked and intact. Could've been the cops or the FSB."

"Yeah, I think keys are kind of just decorative in this environment, don't you?"

Charlie nodded and looked around the corner into the tiny alcove that served as a kitchen. There was a little bar fridge that was making the kind of strained hum that precedes complete electrical failure and a hot plate on a corner counter, next to the smallest, and possibly the dirtiest, microwave Charlie had ever seen. As he flipped the wall switch, a single fluorescent tube flickered overhead and he saw something small and black scurry under the little curtain that covered the open area under the sink. Stepping gingerly forward, he noticed a pile of dirty dishes half immersed in sludge at the bottom of the sink and realized it was the source of the low-grade funk that had sent him to the window when he first stepped into the apartment and now made him turn back to the main living area. Sophie was in the doorway of the only other room in the apartment, which he assumed was the bedroom. He decided to inspect the bookcase while she stepped inside. The top shelf was devoted to technical manuals and a pair of enormous, dog-eared Russian-English dictionaries. The next was filled with a mixture of novels and works of non-fiction. Pulling out a couple, Charlie found a smattering of works on Russian history mixed in with what appeared to be mostly mysteries. He plucked a thick, hard-bound book from the shelf and looked at the cover.

"I know he liked Hemingway," Sophie said from over his shoulder, causing him to spin around and lose his grip on the collection of Hemingway's novels, which fell with a thud on the cracked linoleum.

"Sorry. I didn't mean to startle you."

"No problem." Charlie stooped to pick up the book.

"Steve always said Hemingway was the only serious novelist he liked. He said he identified with him, though I don't know what that meant ... and don't say it's because he committed suicide."

"Nothing in the bedroom?"

"Unless you're interested in examining his dirty socks," she said with a sigh. "What's in these?" She pointed at the three cardboard boxes on the middle shelf, then pulled one out, opened the lid, and began rummaging through a stack of papers. Charlie pulled out a second box and did the same. "Looks like stuff he was working on," she said, putting the lid back on the box.

Charlie was staring at a Russian manual of some kind with a series of loose-leaf sheets inserted in the middle. At the bottom corner of the box were a half dozen business cards, which Charlie carefully retrieved. The first was Liepa's, indicating him as a technical translator for Technion. The next four were the same, but the last one had a different name embossed in the centre: Nikolai Shakirov, who was also described as a translator. Charlie pocketed the last card, as well as one of Liepa's, before returning to the document in his hand.

"Looks like a translation in progress, of a ... building-management system," he said, reading the heading of the translated document.

Sophie opened the third box only to find it empty. Next she pressed the power switch on the decrepit-looking desktop computer that sat on the second shelf, which Liepa had apparently used as an improvised desk; a lawn chair sat in front of the monitor.

"How could he ... how could *anyone* work like this?" she said as the CPU whirred and the monitor blinked reluctantly to life. "He said he was making decent money. I just don't underst —"

Charlie followed her fixed stare to the monitor, where an image of a smiling Liepa gazed back at them both, his arm around an equally happy-looking Sophie. The backdrop showed trees and sparkling water.

"Our aunt's cottage up in Muskoka," Sophie said after a prolonged silence. "I always loved that place ..." She turned toward the door. "I've got to get out of here."

Charlie followed her out into the hall and saw her leaning against the wall, clearly trying to compose herself.

"I know this must be awful for you," he said, wishing there were something he could say or do to lessen her pain. She took a deep breath, then Charlie watched as her eyes, clouded with tears, suddenly sharpened and the familiar resolve returned.

"You check his computer," she said when they returned to the apartment. She inspected the closet by the bedroom.

Charlie sat in front of the computer and began clicking around. The hard drive wasn't password protected, so he was free to search through the various directories. Other than translations and other work-related material, though, he found nothing. The computer didn't appear to be connected to the internet and the email software was unused. He recalled Liepa's mention of a phone — he said the police had taken it.

"Did you get Steve's phone with his personal effects?"

"There was no phone," Sophie said from across the room, where she was rummaging through a shoebox she'd found. "I think we can guess what happened to it," she added, standing up and discarding the shoebox. "Anything on there?"

Charlie shook his head. "Just work stuff."

"Then let's get out of here."

"You didn't find anything either?"

She gestured to the door. "Come on, there's nothing more to learn from this place."

They descended the rickety stairs to the street, filling their lungs with the crisp, raw air outside before setting off for the Metro.

"What is it you're not telling me?" Charlie said quietly after they had gone a few steps.

They walked on in silence for a few minutes before she replied, and when she did, her voice was barely more than a whisper. "There was no laptop."

Charlie shrugged. "How can you be sure he had one?"

"Because I gave it to him, last Christmas. He told me it never left his side, which means either someone took it," she said, as they reached the steps to the Metro, "or it's still out there somewhere."

CHAPTER 15

Charlie was sitting at his desk on Monday morning, trying to concentrate on an email from Ottawa. All he had been able to think about since getting up this morning was Sophie Durant and the suspicions she had revealed to him over the weekend. It was true that she was distraught, and that had to influence the way she confronted her brother's death, especially given what she had told Charlie about their relationship while Liepa was alive. On the other hand, Sophie was a medical doctor, and Charlie could only take her word for the explanation of the strange mark on Steve Liepa's shoulder. Then there was the mysterious meeting at the Conservatory. Did it actually prove anything, or could it be written off to journalistic paranoia? Charlie had only to remind himself of the recent cases involving the harassment and even murder of Russian journalists to realize that the danger of asking the wrong questions was real, but what could Liepa have been working on that put him at risk, when he had spent his days translating technical manuals? And what did this Alexander Surin have to do with anything?

Charlie took a sip of coffee and tried to refocus on his email. He was still adjusting to the reality of working seven or eight hours ahead of Ottawa, which made him feel constantly out of synch. At least the usual bombardment of

messages wouldn't begin until late in the day. He was reread-
ing the same paragraph for the third time when he noticed a
message from the ambassador reminding a dozen people on
the circulation list of the reception to be held at the official
residence at seven. Charlie groaned at the thought of another
mandatory schmooze-fest. He got up and looked out the
window into the crowded courtyard, watching the cloud of
snow descend from the darkened sky and accumulate on the
ground. He saw one of the drivers emerge from the garage
and start the ambassador's Volvo, before meticulously brushing the snow off the windows. The chill in Charlie's feet, still
damp from his morning walk to work from his apartment,
reminded him that he was going to have to get new boots.

Returning to his desk, he pulled Steve Liepa's file from
a tray and flipped the folder open. He paused at the sight
of the phone number he had tried the week before, for the
friend Liepa had mentioned at Charlie's last interview with
him — Sergei Yermolov. He thought it odd that he hadn't
received a response to either his email or the call he had
made to the number he'd found for Yermolov on his employer's online directory, though he was learning that business
was done very differently in Russia. He brought up UPI's
website, and something about the logo seemed familiar. It
only took a moment to place it: on the side of a building near
a restaurant he had been to a couple of weeks before, just a
ten-minute walk from the embassy. Charlie glanced out the
window at the falling snow, then down to the sodden boots
under his desk. Sophie Durant clinched it for him, particularly her uncharacteristically forlorn expression across the
table the other night. He owed it to her to find out whatever
he could about her brother's arrest. He would spend the
next couple of hours cleaning out his inbox, then head over
to Yermolov's office to see if he could catch him there. In

the meantime he pulled the pair of business cards he had taken from Steve Liepa's apartment from his pocket and examined Nikolai Shakirov's for a moment before reaching for the handset of his phone and dialling the number. After a few rings, Charlie expected a receptionist or a recorded message, but he was surprised to hear a young man's voice just after the fifth ring.

"Is this Nikolai Shakirov?" Charlie said, guessing that Shakirov was used to working in English — probably translating from English to Russian.

"Yes, who is calling?" The voice was lightly accented.

"My name is Charlie Hillier. I'm calling about Steve Liepa."

Charlie waited through the silence at the other end before adding. "I just wanted to ask you a few questions about Steve. You're aware he recently … passed."

"You are a member of the family?"

"Sort of," Charlie lied. "I'm calling on behalf of his sister," he quickly improvised, sensing the hesitation on the other end of the line. "Sophie Durant."

There was a short release of breath on the otherwise silent phone line. "Steve talked about her a great deal. What did you want to ask?"

Charlie glanced at the business card and read the address, recognizing it as one of the few main streets he was familiar with. "Can we meet? I notice you're on Tverskaya. I could meet you at your office."

"No," Shakirov responded abruptly, and Charlie expected the phone to slam down. Instead there was a brief pause. "There's a coffee shop on the north side of Pushkin Square. I can meet you there in thirty minutes."

"I'll be there," Charlie said to the dead line at his ear.

Charlie walked into the busy coffee shop and stamped his feet before making his way to the back of the line of people queuing for coffee. He was scanning the right side of the room when he sensed someone at his left, turned, and saw a man in his mid-twenties looking him over.

"Mr. Hillier?" The young man approached him tentatively.

"Charlie. You're Nikolai?"

"I ordered coffee already — over there," he said, pointing to a table with two chairs overlooking the square. Charlie followed him over. There was a tray in the middle of the table with a steel coffee pot surrounded by a pair of mugs, a little jug of milk, and a sugar bowl. Shakirov gestured to one of the chairs.

"Please."

"Thanks," Charlie said, taking a seat as Shakirov poured coffee into both mugs. "I appreciate you making time to meet with me on such short notice."

"You are Sophie's ... husband?"

"Uh, I'm a friend ... of the family. I'm helping Sophie with some of the logistics."

Shakirov looked at him over his coffee mug, as though trying to figure out whether he could be trusted.

"You can imagine," Charlie continued, "Steve's death was a real shock, and she's just trying to come to terms with her loss and maybe find out if there was anything odd about Steve's behaviour recently." He wondered if he was succeeding at putting Shakirov at ease or making him more suspicious. From the young Russian's inscrutable expression, it was hard to tell. "Did you two work together for long?"

Shakirov sipped his coffee leisurely, glanced out the window, and then appeared to settle some internal debate.

"I have been working for Technion these past two years, so I know Steve since he joined the company."

"Did you work together closely?"

Shakirov shrugged. "Generally we worked on different texts, but sometimes we ... collaborated. Steve's Russian was very good, but he needed help with some of the technical terms, and he helped me with my English grammar."

"Your English is excellent."

"Thank you." Shakirov gave a thin smile and pushed the wire-rimmed glasses back up the bridge of his nose. "It was not so perfect six months ago, so I should thank him for that. We had many lunches together."

"So you both did the same kind of work?"

"Yes and no. I did more of the English-to-Russian translations and German-to-Russian. Steve did Russian-to-English, some Russian-to-French also. His French was also excellent."

"And what are you normally translating?"

"Depends on the client." Shakirov shrugged. "But usually it's technical manuals. Building-management systems, fire alarm, and other electrical systems — we get a lot of work from construction companies, Russian and German mostly. We worked on some appliance manuals, as well."

"And it's interesting work," Charlie said, more as a question than a statement — he couldn't imagine anything more mind-numbing, and he had suffered through some pretty boring jobs in Ottawa. Shakirov looked at him as though wondering whether there was a challenge in the question, then took a sip of coffee and shrugged again.

"It is not so bad. Once you build up a vocabulary of technical terms, it is ... predictable."

"And did Steve seem to enjoy the work, as well?"

"Yes, I think so."

"Did you notice if he was unhappy or particularly stressed lately?"

Shakirov gave a curt shake of his head. "Steve was a very happy person. Why do you ask?"

"I was just wondering if he mentioned anything going on in his life. Financial troubles, problems with a girlfriend, that sort of thing."

"You think he killed himself, yes?" Shakirov's matter-of-fact tone made Charlie think he was putting it forward as a plausible explanation, until Shakirov let out a rough laugh. "Not Steve. He was not the unhappy type. Impossible."

"Did you know Steve socially … outside the office, I mean?"

Shakirov scratched his wispy goatee and shook his head. "I don't socialize much, so my experience of Steve is at work and many lunches, as I mentioned. But Steve was very, how do you say the word … I don't know, but he had many friends."

"Gregarious," Charlie offered, which seemed to please Shakirov.

"Yes, I think so." His smile faded and he looked down at his coffee cup. Charlie had a sudden image of him sitting alone at a computer terminal in a dingy room full of technical manuals. He imagined it was located in his parents' basement, though, unlike Liepa's grubby, if well-located bachelor pad.

"You should ask Tania about his social life," Shakirov added. "She knew him much better outside the office."

"Tania?"

Shakirov's raised eyebrows conveyed his surprise at Charlie's lack of knowledge. "Ivanova. His girlfriend."

"Do you have a phone number or an address for her?" Charlie asked, trying to conceal the excitement he felt at finally making some progress.

"I have it at the office.… Wait." He pulled out his phone and scrolled through his contact list. "Yes, here she is."

Charlie took down the contact information and they continued to chat for another ten minutes, then Shakirov drained the last of the coffee in his cup, and set it on the table. "I should be going."

"Me, too," Charlie replied, thinking he had just enough time to make it to Sergei Yermolov's office, which was a short Metro ride away, before lunch. "Thank you very much for meeting me."

"My pleasure. Please, pass on my regrets to Sophie. I didn't meet her but Steve talked about her often. She is a doctor, yes?"

"Yes. And I'll be sure to tell her. I'm sure she'll appreciate the thought."

CHAPTER 16

Charlie hustled up the steps of Belorusskaya station. When he reached street level, he glanced around and immediately spotted the onion domes of the church he had seen on Yermolov's website, next to the modern office complex known as White Square.

Stepping into the lobby, Charlie stamped his feet before the snow had a chance to seep further into the worn leather of his boots. He dusted his shoulders and made his way over to the reception desk, where he inquired after Yermolov. He continued to brush the melting snow off the sleeves of his coat as the young woman called upstairs. He listened as she spoke to someone, understanding enough of what she said, together with her direction for him to take a seat, to know that Yermolov was in. Charlie declined the seat, preferring to stand in the waiting area and let the warmth penetrate his boots. He watched as a stream of secretaries left the building for lunch, noticing how they bundled themselves in coats, hats, and scarves, but refused to abandon their thin-heeled boots. Was it just a question of practice, or did Russian women really possess superior equilibrium? Charlie watched as a young man in a snug shirt and bold tie emerged from one of the elevators and looked in his direction, his annoyance barely concealed. He strode over to the waiting area and greeted Charlie tersely in Russian.

"Do you speak English?" Charlie sincerely hoped he wouldn't have to resort to his rudimentary Russian to communicate. The other man looked at him warily before answering.

"Yes. Who are you?"

"I'm a friend of Steve Liepa's," he said, stretching the truth. He wondered whether Yermolov knew Liepa was dead, and guessed he didn't.

"What do you want?" From Yermolov's defensive body position, Charlie didn't get the impression he was going to be invited up to the office, so he gestured for them to sit in the leather chairs. Yermolov remained standing.

"I just wanted to talk to you about Steve," Charlie said, also still on his feet.

"What about him?"

"Look, I know you were with him the night he was arrested. I'm just trying to help."

"You're from Canada?"

"Yes."

He waited as Yermolov seemed to assess the truth of his statement. Charlie purposely avoided mentioning that he worked at the embassy, lest his inquiry be construed as official, which it was not.

"You are a lawyer?"

"No," Charlie lied, hoping his hesitation hadn't been noticed, even though the fact that he hadn't actually practised law in years made the statement essentially true. "I'm a friend of the family. I was hoping you could tell me what happened that night."

Yermolov paused and glanced around the lobby. Apart from the woman behind the counter and a bored-looking guard kicking at something stuck to the floor, it was empty. "It was a raid." Yermolov shrugged. "We were just having fun — it was a party that some girls I know were having at their apartment. The police came in and broke it up. That's it."

"Did the police question you?"

"Not really. They talked to everyone for a while, then they let us go."

"Except for Steve."

"He was the only one without a Russian passport."

"So they took him."

Yermolov nodded, then shot another glance at the guard, who was looking their way now. "Why are you asking me these questions? You should go to the police."

"I've been to the police," Charlie said, becoming frustrated with Yermolov's intransigence. He obviously had no idea that Liepa was dead, but he hadn't even asked after him — some friend.

"Is he still there?" The question was asked like an after-thought, as though Yermolov was suddenly aware of an underlying current of danger.

Charlie ignored the question and countered with another of his own. "Did the police say why they were taking Steve to the station, other than because of his passport?"

Yermolov shook his head.

"These friends of yours who were having the party. What are their names?"

"I don't remember. I heard about the party from someone at work."

"Can we go and ask them?" Charlie said, gesturing upstairs. But Yermolov was done, and Charlie knew it by the way he looked at his watch and began backing away.

"I have to go back to work, Mr. —"

"Steve said you were a friend, Sergei. Was he wrong?"

"Tell him hello for me," Yermolov said, turning to leave. Charlie held his tongue as he watched the man retreat to the elevators. He watched the doors close before he swore and began buttoning up his coat for the walk back to the embassy.

"I wish I could," he muttered as he walked toward the door.

Charlie was still shaking off the cold as he stood at the cafeteria counter in the basement of the embassy, ordering what would be a hurried lunch before Sophie showed up in advance of the afternoon meeting. He had just taken a seat at one of the empty tables when an athletic man in his mid-thirties sat opposite him.

"Mind if I join you?" he said, setting his tray down on the table.

"Please do," Charlie replied.

"I'm Ed Torrance, RCMP liaison. Welcome to Moscow."

"Thanks." Charlie hadn't had much contact with the RCMP officers posted to Moscow, or the handful of others who occupied the mysterious labyrinth behind a coded access door in one of the embassy's secure zones, other than seeing the acronym for their positions on the floor plan.

"Settling in?"

Charlie nodded. "Trying to. Still getting used to Moscow traffic, and the language … well, you know how it is. How long have you been here?"

"Came in last summer. Are you downtown or out in the Hills?" Torrance asked, referring to the group of single-family homes located in the suburbs near the American school, for use by embassy personnel with families.

"I'm a few blocks away. I'm solo."

"Makes life a lot simpler," Torrance said. "In terms of the commute, I mean."

They chatted for a few minutes, exchanging notes on their accommodations and discussing the best place to buy fresh produce, before the conversation led to Charlie's consular workload.

"I heard about the guy who died in detention," Torrance said. "That's a hell of a file to start out with. Any idea what happened?"

"They say it was suicide, but the sister thinks that's bull-shit."

"She's probably right." Torrance paused, seeing Charlie's expression. "I just mean they tend to say that a lot, whether it's because they're trying to cover up the shitty conditions in their prisons … or something else."

"Say," Charlie said, as a thought occurred to him, "you guys can't check on passport activity, can you?"

Torrance shrugged. "Depends on the situation, but that's generally CIC's bailiwick," he said, referring to the immigration program operating in the embassy.

"Right," Charlie said, his dejection obvious.

"But if you get me a passport number, I could probably find out for you."

"Really?"

"My wife's a CIC officer," Torrance said with a smile.

"I'll get you the passport number," Charlie said.

Just as he spoke he saw his assistant walk through the cafeteria doors, wide-eyed. Spotting him, she rushed over and Charlie sensed his lunch was over.

"Mr. Hillier, I've been looking all over for you!"

"What's the matter, Irina?"

"Something terrible has happened. They called from the morgue."

Charlie put down his spoon, trying to imagine what bad news could come from the morgue. He knew Steve Liepa's body was to be transferred into embassy custody later in the day, in preparation for transport back to Canada.

"There was a mistake," Irina continued, wringing her hands as though she was personally to blame for whatever had occurred. "They cremated him."

"They *what*?"

"They sent the wrong body for cremation — Mr. Liepa's body."

He looked up at her, and they seemed to share the same thought.

"His sister ..." Irina began, but Charlie was already on his feet. He excused himself from the table, then hurried after Irina, thinking there might be time to talk to someone at the morgue before Sophie arrived for the meeting at the Ministry of Foreign Affairs.

As they left the cafeteria, Irina's worried chatter over the unfortunate mix-up faded into oblivion as Charlie was struck with a far more sinister possibility. Cremation was certainly an effective way of ensuring that no one, including Liepa's sister, had the opportunity to pursue any theories of his having died in any other way than by his own hand. Charlie's mind was swimming with the possibilities as they stepped into the snow for the quick dash across the courtyard, and he saw the van pull in through the front gate. As the driver emerged and opened the door to let Sophie out, Charlie froze. Her smile of recognition faded as she read his eyes. He managed to unglue his feet and make his way slowly to her, the look of incomprehension and fear on her delicate features was almost unbearable as he grasped for words to convey the news, but found none.

CHAPTER 17

Charlie sat at his desk, his phone at his ear as he listened to another apology from the protocol officer on the other end of the line. As tired as he was of hearing the platitudes, he could only imagine how hollow they would sound to Sophie. The news that her brother's body had been cremated had been the final straw, and she had refused to attend the meeting scheduled for the day before. Instead, she had gone off to interview a private investigator. Charlie had reached her at her hotel in the evening and convinced her to attend a rescheduled meeting today at the MFA with the wrongful cremation added to the agenda, but he could hardly blame her for her skepticism. Nor was he any more hopeful that the meeting would yield anything useful. Still, they had to try to get answers. He was wrapping up the call when he sensed someone in his doorway and looked up to see the RCMP liaison officer he had met in the cafeteria the day before.

"Hi, Ed," he said, after he'd hung up. "Come on in."

"I'm on my way to a meeting," Torrance said, with a wave of his hand as he stepped inside Charlie's office. "I just wanted to drop this off for you." Charlie watched as Torrance slid a single sheet of paper onto the corner of his desk. "I hope this is useful." He turned to go.

"Thanks. I appreciate it." Charlie gave him a grateful nod and then Torrance was gone. Leaning back in his chair, Charlie perused the paper — a printout in an odd-looking font with Steve Liepa's name and passport number at the top, above a series of lines representing passport entry points over the past six months. The first six lines were in the spring, when Liepa's passport was logged going into Frankfurt, then back into Moscow, the sequence repeating itself three times in a two-month period. Each stay was about a week, and Charlie remembered Sophie's mentioning that Steve spent a lot of time in Berlin, having lived there for some time. More interesting were the later entries, when Liepa's passport was logged going into Astana a month before his arrest. The return date to Moscow indicated he was in Kazakhstan for less than forty-eight hours. Charlie paused as he considered the dates, as well as possible reasons for going to the Kazakh capital. He then turned his attention to the last entry line — the last time Liepa's passport was logged outgoing from Russia, at Charles de Gaulle Airport in Paris. Liepa had spent three days in France before returning to Moscow less than a week before his arrest. It occurred to Charlie that Liepa could actually have gone to any number of places before returning to Moscow, given the freedom to move within the European Union.

Charlie sat back and pondered the new information. The Berlin trips made sense; after all, Liepa had lived there before taking the Technion job and moving to Moscow, and he would have established a network of friends and put down some roots, even if he had been there for only a year or so. He recalled Sophie's comment that her brother enjoyed the atmosphere in Berlin. As for the last two trips — especially the one to Astana — Charlie wondered whether there was anything to them. He sat there for a few minutes, then rummaged in his top drawer and pulled out Nikolai Shakirov's business card and called the direct line. He waited a few rings and then Shakirov's familiar voice answered.

"Hello, Nikolai. This is Charlie Hillier. We met the other day for —"

"Of course, I remember," he said in the same detached tone that Charlie had noticed at the coffee shop. "What can I do for you?"

"I forgot to ask you whether you or Steve ever travelled for work. Did you?"

There was a slight chuckle at the other end of the line. "Not usually. Our work doesn't really require it, and then there's the cost — Technion's always looking for ways to cut costs, not increase them."

"Right," Charlie said, undeterred. "You mentioned you had some big German and Russian construction companies as clients. Do you have any in Kazakhstan?"

Shakirov paused. "Yes, I believe we have a few. I myself worked on a translation for a company based in Almaty. As for Steve, it's possible, but I don't know for sure."

"But you're saying that even if he did, it's unlikely he would have gone there for work-related purposes?"

"Of that I can assure you."

"I see. Did Steve mention to you that he was going to Kazakhstan — this would have been late July, early August?"

"I was on holiday for most of August and only started work again a week before Steve returned from Paris."

"So you knew he'd been to Paris, but not Astana."

"That's right."

"Did he say why he had gone to Paris?"

"It was a short trip, just a few days, so I assumed it was a little holiday," Shakirov said. "I didn't really see him that much after he got back."

"Did he mention whether he had gone with anyone — Tania, for example?"

"I don't recall."

"Well," Charlie said, as he saw the red light for his other phone line flashing, "it was probably just a little vacation, like you said. I don't want to keep you, so thanks for your time."

He hung up and then punched the button for the other line. It was Irina, telling him that Sophie Durant had arrived. He scanned an incoming email and, noticing the deadline for a response, made a mental note to come back to it later, after the meeting at the MFA. He straightened his tie and headed out into the hall, and was almost at the stairs when he heard his name and retraced his steps back to Rob Brooker's open door. The property officer was seated behind his desk.

"Hi Charlie. I was wondering if you had some time today to discuss the property file. I just wanted to pick your brain about a couple of options the brokers have come up with. But you look busy …."

"It's just that I have a meeting this morning," Charlie replied, surprised at how impatient he felt at the property officer's interruption. He hoped it wasn't obvious. "But I'll have time this afternoon, if you want."

Brooker glanced at his monitor. "After lunch, say, two-ish?"

"Sure," Charlie said, checking his watch and realizing that Sophie was fifteen minutes early. He stepped inside Brooker's office, though he stayed away from the chair. "You've got some prospects?"

Brooker nodded. "Oleg faxed over some stuff this morning on a couple of options, including that big development he was talking about at the reception — Petr Square." He tapped his pen on the unruly pile of paper in front of him. "I think Oleg's pretty keen to get the commission."

"They'll be tripping over each other trying to get a piece of this one, I'm sure," Charlie agreed, glancing at the paper, as Brooker turned the top sheet so he could see it. "What is it, anyway?"

"Info sheets on Petr Square, and the developer, BayCo. You familiar with them?"

"No, I don't think so." Charlie shook his head, but something about the letterhead seemed familiar. Perhaps he had seen it on a billboard or at a construction site. Or maybe he remembered it from the brochure Oleg had given him at the reception a couple of weeks ago. "Anyway, I'd better get going. We'll talk this afternoon."

He made his way downstairs and found Sophie waiting there, looking elegant in a dark coat and a colourful scarf. The cold outside had left her cheeks pink, giving her face a healthy glow.

"We've got about twenty minutes before we have to leave for the MFA meeting," he said after she had been through security and surrendered her cellphone. He led her upstairs to his office. "Before we talk about the meeting, though, I wanted to ask you a couple of things about Steve."

"Shoot," she said, slipping out of her coat and draping it across the back of a chair.

"Did he mention anything about a girlfriend?"

"Here in Moscow? No, but Steve always had plenty of female company. And Moscow women are supposed to be beautiful."

Charlie just nodded, unsure if he was supposed to answer or comment. It was true that he had seen many beautiful women on the streets of the city he now called home, though Sophie was no slouch herself.

"Who told you he had a girlfriend?" she asked.

"Nikolai Shakirov — the co-worker at Technion whose business card was on Steve's shelf."

Sophie grinned. "Doing a little moonlighting as a PI? Did you get a name?"

"Tania Ivanova."

"That sounds pretty Russian. I'll bet she's a knockout."

"I've got an address, too, but no phone number. If you want, we could drop in on her later."

Sophie shrugged. "Not like I'm doing anything else." She fiddled with the scarf she had set on top of the coat. "Sorry. I don't mean to sound ungrateful. It's just that the investigator I hired seems to be sitting on his ass, whereas you ..." She smiled. "Anyway, yes, I would like to meet Steve's girlfriend. In fact," she added, her expression turning serious, "I'd like to talk to anyone who can provide some kind of explanation for why he died, other than this bullshit suicide theory."

"I understand you're frustrated, but don't lose hope."

"Never." The determined look that had become her hall-mark returned.

"There's something else. Did you know anything about a trip Steve took to Paris a couple of weeks before he was detained?"

Sophie shook her head.

"Or another one to Astana in early August?"

Her surprise turned to pure befuddlement. "Where the hell's Astana?"

"Kazakhstan."

"Did this Shakirov guy tell you all this?"

"Sort of." Charlie got up and walked by her to close the door. "I just know he spent three days in France — starting and ending in Paris — and less than forty-eight hours in Astana."

Sophie frowned. "No, he didn't mention either place to me, but then I'm not even sure exactly when I last talked to him." Her eyes narrowed slightly. "If the co-worker didn't tell you, then how do you know?"

"I checked his passport activity, so there's no doubt he was in both places within weeks of being detained."

"Shit, Charlie, maybe I should fire my PI and hire you full-time."

"I told you not to lose hope."

Charlie and Sophie waited in the reception area of the Russian Ministry of Foreign Affairs office. Housed in one of the seven identical and enormous spired monstrosities commissioned by Stalin to dominate the Moscow skyline — known as the seven sisters — the MFA building was only a couple of kilometres from the Canadian Embassy. Sophie had been game to walk it, especially when Charlie informed her that Moscow traffic could often make the drive thirty minutes or longer. He thought she seemed surprisingly well rested when he saw her sitting in the waiting area at the embassy, though he knew it was more reflective of her desire to focus on getting answers than any lessening of her grief over her brother's death. They had floated some theories about Steve Liepa's puzzling itinerary on the walk over. A fresh dusting of overnight snow intensified the brightness of the winter morning and made the walk down to the Moscow River relatively pleasant, spoiled only by the odour of gasoline that seemed to permeate everything in the city's congested core.

He was trying to think of something to break the silence that had descended on them as they sat there waiting when a stern-looking woman approached, greeted them perfunctorily, and beckoned them to follow her down the hall from which she had just emerged. Turning a corner beyond the reception area, they emerged at the foot of a wide staircase,

which led them up to the next floor, past enormous paint-
ings depicting a procession of scenes, from pastoral to
military, and ending with a nineteenth-century painting of
St. Petersburg. At the top of the landing, their guide paused
and pointed to a small meeting room with an elaborate fire-
place and gleaming parquet floor, centred by a cherrywood
table with two chairs on either side. A man and a woman
stood inside the doorway and stepped forward to greet them.

"Mr. Hillier, Dr. Durant. I am Anatoly Federov, from the
Protocol Department," the man said, shaking their hands,
then stepping aside to let them in. "And this is Dr. Nikulin,
from the legal branch."

Charlie and Sophie shook hands with the lawyer, whose
severe expression didn't change much despite what might have
been an attempt at a smile. Her blond hair was pinned back so
tightly that it seemed to stretch the skin of her cheeks. After
some awkward initial banter, Federov gestured for them to take
a seat. When they were all settled, Federov got down to business.

"Allow me first of all to express our deepest condolences
to you, Dr. Durant, for your loss," he began. His English was
excellent, and other than an occasional harsh edge, Federov
could have passed for a Briton. Charlie guessed he had been
educated at Oxford or Cambridge. Sophie acknowledged the
statement with a brief nod.

"Thank you."

"And we must also apologize to you both, on behalf of
the state medical authority, for this most unfortunate error."

"We appreciate that, Mr. Federov ... May I call you
Anatoly?" Charlie asked.

"Of course."

"We appreciate that, Anatoly, and we understand that
accidents happen." Federov bowed his head in acknowledgement and allowed Charlie to finish his thought. "But

as you can imagine, Dr. Durant has some questions about what actually happened in this particular case."

"I can tell you that an investigation has already been concluded, and the finding was of a very unfortunate, but essentially simple, error. A matter of a form being improperly completed. Steps have been taken to ensure this doesn't happen again, naturally."

"You've completed your investigation already?" Sophie looked across the table, first at Federov, then at the lawyer. Whereas Federov was smiling, Nikulin was not, and her expression seemed to chill a few degrees with every second that she returned Sophie's gaze.

"We are nothing if not efficient, Ms. Durant," Federov said cheerily. A little too cheerily.

"Oh, really —" Sophie began, before Charlie cut her off, sensing a heated exchange that could only result in stonewalling from across the table.

"I think we're both a bit surprised," he said, "at how quickly your investigation has concluded. We're used to a ... different process in Canada." He tried a disarming smile. "It would be very helpful if we could have a copy of the findings for our files."

Federov's smile remained unaffected as he and Nikulin exchanged a quick glance. "I can certainly request the report, although this is not usually disclosed."

"We would appreciate it," Charlie said. "We also requested Mr. Liepa's entire file from the correctional authority and the prosecutor's office, but were told we would have to make an official request."

"Again," Federov said, "those files are not usually disclosed, but I can ask my colleague, Dr. Nikulin, to make inquiries on your behalf." Charlie wondered whether he would ever stop smiling. Nikulin scribbled something on her pad and looked up, stone-faced.

"I still don't know why he was even in jail in the first place," Sophie said.

"Detention," Nikulin corrected her. Her own accent was harsher and matched her demeanour perfectly.

"Whatever you want to call it," Sophie continued. "He was locked up for a week without any charges. We have this thing in Canada called due process —"

"We were wondering if you could tell us more about the charges pending against Mr. Liepa," Charlie interjected, seeing Nikulin's features hardening. Even Federov's smile was beginning to show signs of cracking.

"I can assure you that he would not have been held if charges from the prosecutor's office were not imminent," he said.

"What charges?" Sophie was staring at Nikulin again.

"Drug-related."

"What — smoking a joint?" Sophie scoffed.

"Your brother was a regular drug user, then?" Nikulin smiled for the first time, but it was limited to her mouth. Her eyes remained icy.

"Maybe we should wait until we get the report." Charlie put his hand on Sophie's forearm. She brushed it off.

"No, I want to know *now*."

"Perhaps some answers are better not known," Nikulin said.

"What the hell does that mean?" Sophie was leaning over the table now.

"Though," Nikulin continued, unfazed by the menace in Sophie's tone, "we will, of course, endeavour to assist you in your inquiries. I will contact a colleague about your brother's file as soon as I return to my office."

Charlie turned to Federov. "We would really appreciate your help, especially since Dr. Durant's time in Moscow is limited."

"We will do our very best," the protocol officer said, his smile restored to its full wattage.

CHAPTER 18

Back at his embassy desk, Charlie was reading through the search criteria for the new embassy site that he and Brooker had discussed. He glanced up at the clock, as though doing so might cause it to hit five sooner. His mind kept replaying the meeting at the MFA and Sophie's reaction afterward. He had to admit, it didn't look promising. What were the odds that the Russians would give full disclosure of what was in the files of the prosecutor's office or the correctional authorities, even if they were dealing with an unfortunate accident, not some cover-up? This was Moscow. If he and Sophie were lucky, they might get a heavily edited report before her visa ran out and she had to get on a plane back to Canada with nothing but a jar of her brother's ashes. She'd told him she understood the way the system worked, but he could tell he had disappointed her at the meeting. He knew she had wanted to bound across the table and wipe that smirk off Federov's face the whole time, and he couldn't blame her. Worse than that, his own playing by the rules just made him feel part of the problem for her, not the solution. They had parted on the steps of the MFA building and promised to meet up after five to go pay a visit to Tania Ivanova.

Charlie sighed and flipped the piece of paper he had been reading on top of the property file on his desk and was sorting the documents back into the folder when he noticed the letter from BayCo describing the Petr Square development. Something about the letterhead had seemed familiar when he'd first noticed it on Brooker's desk, and it struck him again as he stared at it, trying to place where he had seen it before. He was still staring at it when he called Sophie's hotel and got connected to her room.

"Hi Charlie." She sounded flat.

"I'm just wrapping up here. I've located the address, just on the other side of the Garden Ring — we can take the subway, but I'm thinking we should give her time to get home from work, assuming she works."

"Makes sense. Why don't we meet in the hotel bar here. I don't know about you, but after today, I could use a drink."

"I'll meet you there in half an hour," he said, eyeing the property file on his desk. "And bring Steve's postcards."

"His postcards — why?"

"I'll see you soon."

Charlie had no trouble spotting Sophie as soon as he walked into the lobby bar, sitting alone in the corner in jeans and a roll-neck sweater. He felt the rush of attraction, then reminded himself why he was here.

"How are you?" he asked as he sat opposite her.

"I'm okay." She tried a smile, but he could tell she was still angry with him. Maybe disappointed was the better term, and that felt even worse. "I've already ordered," she added as a server approached. Charlie ordered a beer and took off his coat.

"Did you bring the postcards?"

She reached into her purse and brought out the postcards from her brother, then laid them on the table in front of him. He sifted through them and plucked out the one Liepa had sent from Astana, showing the city skyline at night. He looked at it again and pulled a copy of a letter from his jacket pocket and laid it on the table next to the card.

"What's that?"

Charlie turned the letter around so the text was facing her. "It's a letter from a property developer, wanting to rent us space for our embassy in their new development. I thought I'd seen it somewhere before."

"The logo on the building? Yeah, I guess it's the same. So what?"

Charlie turned the postcard over and reread the conclusion of the note from Liepa to his sister aloud. "'Sometimes the answers are right in front of you.'"

Sophie reached for the postcard, glanced at the words, then flipped it over. "You think this means something?"

"I don't know. You said Steve could be cryptic. This was the last postcard you got from him, right?" He watched her nod, but she didn't seem to share his enthusiasm. Maybe he had been reading too much into it, but he wasn't prepared to give up just yet. "You said he wanted to be a journalist, right?"

"Well, I think I said writer or a novelist, or both." She laughed, then her smile faded. "You think he might have been writing something about this —" she turned the letter around to read the name at the top "— BayCo?"

"You knew him a lot better than I did. What do you think?"

"You want to know what I *really* think?"

He nodded, though he had the sense he may not.

"I think I'll never find out what happened to my brother. I think they'll give me the runaround until my visa expires, and then they'll send me back to Canada."

Charlie considered the statement and interpreted the look on her face as blaming him as much as the Russians. "Look, Sophie, I know you're frustrated with the process, but you have to understand —"

"I know, this is Moscow, and you're supposed to smile and say thank you while they fuck you over, but how could you just sit there and accept being lied to like that?" Her anger had made its way into her voice now and her cheeks were flushed with emotion. He could tell she was biting back the stronger words he deserved.

"We haven't finished with them yet, I promise you," he said, though he knew that if they stuck to the protocol playbook, they would get nowhere. As they sat there in silence, Charlie vowed he would not let that happen. He didn't know what he was going to do exactly, but he knew he had to do *some*thing.

CHAPTER 19

Charlie led the way up out of Baumanskaya Metro station and started heading north. An icy rain had begun since they got on the subway near Sophie's hotel, and the dimly lit streets didn't make the unfamiliar neighbourhood any more inviting. As they got further from the Metro station and into an area with one high-rise apartment building after another, the side streets looked more and more ominous.

"Cheery place," Sophie muttered as they passed a trio of men standing on a street corner chugging beer from litre bottles. The men eyed the pair as they walked past, but did nothing more. Charlie felt some relief when he recognized the name of Ivanova's street on a sign affixed to a wall and saw from the number on the corner that they weren't far away. After a few minutes they were in front of a building of about eight storeys, with a directory out front by a locked main entrance door.

"This is it," he said, walking up the steps and scanning the directory until he found the button he was looking for and pressed it. They waited in silence as the rain intensified.

"Maybe she's not in," Sophie suggested, pulling the collar of her raincoat tight to her throat. Charlie hit the button again, already working on Plan B when a crackly voice came over the speaker and said something unintelligible in Russian.

"Tania Ivanova?"

"What do you want?" The voice was lightly accented and tentative. She'd obviously recognized Charlie's voice as that of an English speaker.

"I'm a friend of Steve's — Steve Liepa."

Charlie looked at Sophie in the silence that followed. The distorted voice returned.

"What do you want?" it repeated.

"I understand you knew Steve. I was just wondering if we could talk about him, if you have a couple of minutes."

"I'm very busy." The woman's tone suggested the end of any discussion, not the beginning. Sophie stepped up to the microphone and pressed the button.

"This is Steve's sister, Sophie," she said. "Please ... we won't take up much of your time. I've come all the way from Canada."

Sophie waited by the door, staring at the little square of cross-hatched steel that covered the speaker. Charlie looked on. Then they were both jolted by the sound of a buzzer and a loud click as the front door opened. Charlie grabbed the handle and pulled the door wide open, and they stepped in out of the rain. They shook the water from their coats and took one look at the elevator before opting for the stairs. On the fifth floor they entered a grubby hallway and walked down it until they found Ivanova's apartment number. Charlie rapped on the door. He wondered if Ivanova had been toying with them when after a full minute, there was still no sign of life, but then he heard faint footsteps on the other side of the door and it opened slightly, still on the chain.

"Ms. Ivanova?" Charlie said, seeing only an eye, a fair-skinned face, and blond hair. "I'm Charlie, and this is Steve's sister, Sophie." He stood aside so Ivanova could see her, and as he looked at her himself he realized for the first time the similarity of her features to Steve's: the same aquiline nose and oval eyes. If Ivanova had any doubts, the sight of Sophie Durant seemed to remove them. The door shut and reopened a moment later, after the chain had been removed. Ivanova was almost as tall as Charlie, with long, blond hair and slender limbs. She was dressed plainly in jeans and a sweatshirt, but she was elegant nonetheless.

"Come in," she said, stepping aside and glancing out into the empty hallway. Charlie let Sophie go first, sensing Ivanova's willingness to open her door came either from her trust of another woman or from a sense of obligation to Steve's sister. The apartment was small but tidy, and though the furnishings were cheap, the room conveyed a feeling of warmth and that its owner took pride in the comfort of guests. Ivanova pointed to the sofa, while she sat in an adjacent armchair.

"Thank for you seeing us," Charlie began, searching Ivanova's face for signs of comprehension. "Is English okay?"

She nodded and Charlie continued. "We apologize for dropping in on you like this, but I didn't have a phone number, and we're also a bit short on time."

Ivanova turned to Sophie and gave her a look that was somewhere between compassion and guilt. "I just heard about Steve a few days ago. I am very sorry."

"Thank you. How well did you know him?" Sophie asked, getting right to the point.

Ivanova smiled demurely. "We met through work about three months ago. Steve hadn't been in Moscow very long."

"Do you work at Technion?" Charlie asked, flipping open a little notebook he had brought from the office.

Ivanova shook her head. "I work for a different company — office supplies. I was making a delivery to Technion when I first met Steve." She smiled, seeming to recall the occasion well. "He was very … charming and funny." She stopped and looked guiltily at Sophie, who urged her on.

"Were you in a relationship with him?"

"Yes, we began seeing each other. Not serious … I mean, we just enjoyed each other's company very much. We went to dinner and some parties. I introduced him to some of my friends."

"Were you at the party where he was arrested?" Charlie asked, prompting an emphatic shake of her head.

"I was not feeling well. Steve tried to convince me to go, but I didn't. I heard from a friend who was there what happened. I tried to visit Steve when I heard …" She looked at Sophie, who was doing a good job of reining in her emotions. "They wouldn't allow anyone to visit. Then the other day, I heard he had died." She stopped and her eyes welled with tears. "I just don't understand."

"What did your friend tell you about what happened the night of the party?" Charlie asked, more aware than ever of Sophie's struggle to maintain her composure.

Ivanova reached for a tissue and dabbed at her eyes. "The police raided the party. They said they were looking for drug traffickers, and they took everyone downstairs and threw them into their trucks. But then they let everyone go. Except Steve."

"Did they say why they were keeping him?" Charlie prompted.

"No … I don't know. Nobody knew. It was so stupid that the police would even come."

"Why?" Sophie asked.

"It was a nice party, just some friends. A couple of people had some marijuana, but it was not a drugs party, you know?"

"Do you know if Steve was smoking marijuana that night?"

Ivanova shrugged. "He usually had a joint — at a party, I mean," she added quickly.

"Look Ms. ... Can I call you Tania?" Sophie was leaning forward on the edge of the sofa.

"Yes, of course."

"I know Steve smoked the odd joint. All I'm interested in is anything that could explain why he was the only one who was taken away that night, apart from being a foreigner."

Ivanova was shaking her head. "No, it makes no sense."

"Were there any other foreigners at the party that night?" Charlie asked.

"I don't know. There could have been, but I wasn't there. I'm sorry."

He glanced at Sophie before moving on. "Did Steve mention a trip he made to Kazakhstan?"

Ivanova seemed to perk up at the mention of it. "Yes, he went to Astana — in August. He seemed very excited, but I don't really know why."

"Astana's nothing to get excited about?"

Ivanova shrugged again. "I have never been, but no, I don't think so. But Steve was very eager to go."

"He didn't say why?"

"Not really. He said it was important for something he was working on."

"What was he working on?" Sophie asked, eager to get back into the exchange and sensing they were entering new ground.

"I asked him a few times. I told him I could tell he was very ... excited, but he would just smile and say he'd tell me later, when he got back."

"And did he?" Sophie was practically falling off the sofa by now, but her hopes were dashed by another of Ivanova's shrugs.

"No, he was very different when he returned. As though he had lost something." Ivanova paused and looked at Sophie, then at Charlie before continuing. "I don't think he was ever the same again after he got back from Astana. Whenever I asked him what was wrong, he would just say no —"

"No biggie?"

Ivanova looked up at Sophie and smiled. "Yes, exactly."

"One of his favourite expressions," Sophie said, then a pall of silence descended on the room.

"What about Paris?" Charlie said, restarting the conversation. "Did Steve mention going there? It would have been a couple of weeks after he got back from Astana."

Ivanova looked puzzled. "Paris? No, he never said anything about Paris. Did he go there?"

"We think so, yes," Sophie said.

"It must have been around the time I was very busy at work. I didn't see Steve for about a week. What was he doing in Paris?"

"We were hoping you might tell us," Charlie said, then flipped over a page in his notebook. "Back to the night of the party. Is there anyone else we could talk to who was there? What about Steve's friend, Sergei Yermolov?"

Ivanova's face hardened. "I wouldn't call him a friend."

"No?" Charlie looked up from his notes. "Steve gave me his name as someone I could talk to. I got the impression they were friends."

"Sergei thinks only of Sergei," Ivanova said in a tone that made her feelings about him clear.

"But they knew each other."

"Yes, and I wouldn't be surprised that Sergei was there. There were a lot of girls there — girls he would have been interested in."

"Do you mean ... party girls?" Sophie asked.

"Yes, that kind of girl is Sergei's specialty," she said with a frown. "Girls he can impress with his fancy clothes and expensive clubs. No friends of mine."

"You don't like him," Charlie said. "Why not?"

"He is very full of himself — arrogant. And like many other things and people in this city," she added, her eyes narrowing with contempt, "corrupt."

Charlie prompted her and tried to tease out more information, but it was clear Ivanova had little else to add. Fifteen minutes later he and Sophie were back out on the street, where the rain had turned to icy pellets of sleet.

"Well, she wasn't much help," Sophie said as they set off for the Metro station.

"Maybe, maybe not. I'm curious about this trip to Astana, especially since Steve's co-worker didn't seem to think it had anything to do with work."

"So why the hell would Steve go to Kazakhstan? And why was he so excited about it?"

"Why indeed," Charlie said as the bright light above the station beckoned to them from down the busy street. One thing was for sure, he was going to have another chat with Sergei Yermolov.

CHAPTER 20

Charlie gave the text of the diplomatic note one more glance before signing it and putting it on top of his out tray. He continued to stare at it for a few seconds, in some fruitless attempt to render it more meaningful. But he knew that it would elicit a very polite response from the Russian Ministry of Foreign Affairs to the effect that he could take his request for an extension of Dr. Sophie Durant's visa and shove it up his ass. Despite his assurances to Sophie the evening before, he knew he was virtually powerless to extend her stay beyond the end of the week, even with a well-placed call from the ambassador.

Since the meeting at the MFA, Charlie had been receiving not-so-subtle hints that the Russians didn't like Sophie's line of inquiry. For starters, he had been informed upon his arrival at the embassy this morning that the release of the official police report was going to take a few more days. As for the report on the internal investigation at the prison — if such a document actually existed — it seemed to have fallen into the same bureaucratic black hole. Charlie was beginning to wonder if Sophie would have either of the reports in hand before she was forced to leave the country. She was due to call in around mid-morning, and the thought of breaking this unhappy news added to the gloom he felt each time he looked out the window at the grey morning sky. If his performance at the MFA meeting the day before had left her with the impression that he was an inept and ball-less bureaucrat, this latest development would do little to improve her impression of him, not to mention his own self-esteem.

Charlie sipped the tepid coffee at the bottom of his cup and scanned the papers on his desk, settling on the BayCo logo. After staring at it for a few seconds, he clicked open his email address book and typed in a name, then an alternative spelling, before coming up with his counterpart in Astana. He dialled the number and tapped the letter with a pencil while his call rang through. Charlie had never been to Astana, although he had been on a conference call with someone in Almaty — the former capital, before the Kazakh president had decided to relocate it to what twenty years before had been a frozen wasteland.

"Doug Cullen."

"Charlie Hillier, from Moscow. How are you?"

"Not bad, not bad," Cullen replied, in a friendly tone. "Though the weather's taken a turn for the worse here. How's Moscow?"

"Not too bad so far. Getting cold there?"

"Went down to minus twenty last night and it's only November. Makes Ottawa seem like Florida."

Charlie laughed. He knew Cullen was into the second year of his posting to Kazakhstan, having arrived the summer before, and he had the distinct impression that Cullen was looking forward to the end of his two-year stint. "Hope you brought your parka."

"Yeah, but I wasn't planning on breaking it out until after Christmas. Anyway, what can I do for you?"

"I wanted to ask you about a company — a property developer, actually. It's called BayCo."

"They looking to build us an embassy in Moscow?"

"So you've heard of them."

"I guess so. They sold us the official residence here and wanted to build us a new embassy last year, but HQ couldn't make up its mind."

"I didn't realize the Department had dealt with them before."

"Oh, yeah. Dmitri Bayzhanov's quite a character. A real schmoozer, and he can put the vodka away like you wouldn't believe." Cullen sighed, as though recalling an awful hangover. "I heard he was getting into the Moscow market. He might as well — he's already built half of Astana."

"So he's a big player there?"

"He owns half the city, literally. Close friend of the president's, too."

"And how'd the residence work out?"

"It's all right. It's got a few leaks, but that's par for the course around here. The building standards leave a little to be desired, but he's probably the best of the local builders. Are you looking at a new build or to rent?"

"I'm not sure. It's actually Rob Brooker who's in charge of the property file, and it's early days. I was just curious about the company, generally. Whether they're legit."

"I'd say they're legit, to the extent any developer can be in this neck of the woods," Cullen added with a chuckle. "I'm sure Moscow's even worse."

"You mean corruption?"

"I wouldn't even call it that, really," Cullen continued. "It's so ingrained in the system, it's just a normal part of doing business."

"So BayCo's no better or worse than any of the others?"

"You could talk to the property guys in Ottawa if you want a better sense of what BayCo's like. They had some preliminary discussions about a new building with a few local developers, including Bayzhanov. Like I said, they ended up leasing something shorter-term, until we can figure out what we're doing with the Almaty office."

Charlie tapped his finger on the BayCo letter, eyeing the logo again. "And you figure these guys are pretty new to Moscow, then?"

"Pretty sure. But it makes sense that they'd move into that market. I hear it's on fire, and Astana's overbuilt now."

"Yeah," Charlie said, remembering what Brooker had said about Moscow's commercial real-estate market recently surpassing London and Paris on a cost-per-square-metre basis. "It's pretty crazy around here. And now word's out that we might be looking to buy, they're starting to come out of the woodwork."

"I'll bet. Listen, I'm gonna be in Moscow for meetings later this week. I'll do a bit of digging on BayCo before I come, if you want."

"Sure," Charlie said. "I'll buy you lunch if our schedules match up."

"Sounds like a plan."

Charlie hung up the phone and was still staring at the letter in his hands when he sensed someone at his office door. He looked up to see Rob Brooker standing there, an excited look on his freckled features.

"What is it?"

"Petr Square got the green light. Oleg just called."

"So he wasn't bullshitting us at the reception."

"Apparently not. They officially got their permit and construction's supposed to resume tomorrow. Oleg wants to set up a meeting."

"I'll bet he does," Charlie said, as his assistant appeared at the door.

"The MFA called," Irina said. "That report from the prison that you've been waiting for is ready. Do you want them to send it or shall I have a driver pick it up?"

"Let's have it picked up for sure," Charlie said, not wanting to wait three weeks for it to be delivered. "Thanks."

"I've got to deal with this right now," he said to Brooker, fumbling through the papers on his desk for the Marriott's number. "But let's talk about Petr Square later," he added, picking up the phone as Brooker disappeared with a nod. He dialled the number and was soon connected to Sophie Durant's room.

"Hello?" She sounded groggy. He checked his watch and hoped he hadn't interrupted a sleep-in.

"It's Charlie. I wanted to let you know the report from the Ministry of Corrections is ready." He heard a sneeze at the other end of the line.

"Excuse me. I think I'm coming down with a cold, on top of everything else."

"I'm sorry to hear that. I'm going to have it picked up this morning, and we'll do a rough translation right away. If you wanted to come by to go over it ... or I can just drop it off at the hotel."

"My Russian's kinda non-existent," Sophie said. "I'm meeting with another investigator at three for an hour, and I'm told it's a bit of a hike from here, so I might not be back until after five."

"You arranged a hotel car?"

"You think I'm going to trust a cab in this town?"

"Just making sure." He paused to consider options. "Well, I can have my assistant make a translation and take you through it when you get back."

"That would be great. Do you want me to drop by the embassy, or ..."

"Why don't you call when you get back and I'll swing by."

"Are you sure?"

"Of course. As for this investigator, I thought you already had one."

"I did, but he was useless. I did some research online and found a firm that looks legit. I'm meeting with an investigator named Povetkina — Natalia Povetkina."

Charlie frowned but said nothing. "All right. Good luck."

"I'll call you later. And thanks, Charlie. I appreciate this."

He hung up the phone and sighed, looking from the file sitting in the middle of his desk to the one on top of the pile at the far left corner, trying to figure out which was more pressing. Neither was particularly interesting, but both had the potential to bite him in the ass if he didn't spend some time on them. He opted for the one in front of him, and as he looked up at his monitor for the latest email traffic, he noticed an information bulletin sitting unopened in his mailbox. Clicking on it, he saw that it was a reference to the same story that had been circulating for the past couple of weeks, about the massive and anonymous online deposit of information exposing the offshore holdings of thousands of Russians. He read the summary update, which covered far more than just Russia, with millions of electronic files detailing various tax-shelter schemes around the globe, some legal but most not. Most of the Russian money was apparently being stashed in Cyprus or Panama, whereas the Cayman and Cook Islands seemed more popular for Western European and North American tax dodgers. The more he read, the more interested he became, especially when a link redirected him to a list of companies and individuals whose shareholdings had been leaked. He scanned the list for a minute, finding himself in the Bs and realizing there were literally thousands of listings. He was about to close the link when a name caught his eye — Bayzhanov. He leaned forward in his chair and focused on the list. There were actually three Bayzhanovs, and working his way up the list, he made out Bayzhanov, Oleg; then Bayzhanov, Fedor; and finally, Bayzhanov, Dmitri. He stared at the name for a moment, holding the cursor over the column to the right of the name that listed the number of shares Bayzhanov purportedly held in a Cyprus company called Kvartal.

He stared at the screen for a few more minutes, then made some scribblings on a pad and headed out the door with a sheet of paper. He was on his way to the other building when he bumped into one of the trade officers on his way to the cafeteria.

"Bill, I had a question for you — sort of trade-related."

"Shoot," the other man said. In his mid-thirties and always well-dressed, Bill Halston was the prototypical foreign-service officer, designed for the easy banter of trade fairs and other events aimed at facilitating Canadian business contacts with the Russian market.

"I'm looking for shareholders in a particular company."

"Russian company?"

"Russian and Cypriot, actually."

"You can probably find out all you need about the Cyprus one online, what with the big tax-haven fiasco," Halston said, smiling.

"I did find some of what I was looking for there, but not these two particular companies." Charlie held out the sheet of paper.

Halston took the sheet. "BayCo and Kvartal, eh? Sure, I can give it a try. I've got a contact at the main corporate registry. I'll be seeing him tomorrow on something else and he owes me a favour, so you might get lucky."

"Thanks, I appreciate that."

Charlie was at the top of the stairs when Irina called out.

"The prison report just arrived," she said, waving an envelope at him.

"Can you make a quick translation — a rough one?"

She nodded. "Give me twenty minutes."

Charlie frowned as he finished his scan of the mangled translation of the report. As difficult as it was to make sense of the stilted text, one thing was clear — the document was a whitewash. According to what he was reading, the result of the "interior analysis" of the circumstances surrounding the death of Stephen Liepa was that his death was accidental and that the prison officials had followed every conceivable procedure correctly. This, despite the fact that prisoner 421 had somehow managed to conceal on his person the shoelaces for the makeshift noose despite repeated searches. He had also managed to hang himself during an incredibly short time window, according to the report, which indicated that his cell had been visually inspected every five minutes. The report went on to praise the prison staff, who had apparently gone to heroic lengths in a fruitless attempt to save said prisoner 421.

The more he read, the less Charlie believed. The idea that the guards had conducted a cell inspection every five minutes was pure farce, but from what Charlie had seen of Butyrka Prison, privacy and personal space were not high on the list of priorities. How, then, could Liepa have hung himself without anyone raising the alarm, even if it was only his neighbouring cellmates cheering him on? The medical portion of the report was as thin on details as the rest, and no more plausible. Liepa had died of asphyxiation. Conveniently there was no toxicology report, nor any mention of the puncture wound that Sophie had noticed on her preliminary, and only, inspection of her brother's body.

Charlie threw the report on his desk in disgust. He had been foolish to allow himself even the slightest hope that the report might actually shed some light on what had happened to Liepa. The prison had seen to it that it would not, and now all Charlie could feel was disgust — at the system that had killed Liepa, but also at himself, for being equally powerless in its face. At the sound of his phone, Charlie glanced at the clock, surprised that it was already past five o'clock. He registered the unfamiliar number and picked up the phone.

"It's me. I'm in the car. About twenty minutes away." Sophie's tone had regained some of its conviction.

"Oh, hi," he said, which led to a brief pause on the other end of the line.

"What's wrong?"

"What? Nothing, I —"

"Is it the report?"

Charlie hesitated, considering a glossier facsimile of the truth, then decided not to go down that road.

"It's not very helpful."

"You were expecting something else?" Her tone was lighter than he had anticipated, almost positive.

"How did your meeting go?"

"Better than I thought. Do you want to meet at the hotel bar in half an hour? I'll tell you all about it. And I'm going to have to ask you for another favour."

CHAPTER 21

Charlie sat at a table in the corner, sipping his beer and trying not to feel self-conscious under the occasional, amused glances of the two leggy blondes at the bar. Probably high-end prostitutes, he decided with a quick look in their direction. When he turned back, Sophie was standing on the opposite side of the table.

"Am I cramping your style?" She gestured toward the bar.

"Oh, please," he said with a little laugh. "I couldn't afford them even if I wanted to."

"You might get a diplomatic discount, no?"

"Very funny."

She smiled and took a seat. "So, let me guess. My brother's death was self-inflicted, and that in spite of the prison and its officials following every rule and procedure to a T. And as for the cremation, we already know that was just an unfortunate accident."

He nodded. "I'm afraid that's the gist of it, except the report doesn't actually get into the accidental cremation."

Sophie raised an eyebrow.

"Beyond the scope," Charlie said.

"Of course it is."

"I'm sorry. I had hoped —"

"Don't be. That's exactly what Natalia told me they'd say."

Charlie looked away as the server arrived to take her order. Whether she had intended it as a barb or not, he couldn't help thinking he should have known what was coming. So much for his consular expertise.

"So your meeting went well?" he said after the server had left.

"I'm going to get some answers, finally. Natalia's got a source at the prison she's sure will be able to tell me what really happened."

Charlie nodded. "By the way, I noticed Natalia's name wasn't on the list of Katya Dontseva's referrals. Moscow private investigators don't have the best reputation, generally. They also tend to be very expensive."

Sophie whistled. "You can say that again, but money's one thing I'm not short of, thanks to my ex-asshole and the shark I hired to squeeze him dry after I found out he was screwing his residen —" She put her hand over her mouth, then removed it, to reveal a guilty grin. "Sorry. Forgot, you told me you're a lawyer. Or used to be."

He considered her description and wondered whether it was accurate. Had he ever been a lawyer, or was he simply someone with an expensive education? "It's all right," he lied. "I have a thick skin."

"You're too nice to be a lawyer."

He knew she meant it as a compliment, but he quickly changed the subject, anyway. "I'd just hate to see you taken advantage of," he said, realizing how foolish it sounded coming from him. Sophie was more than capable of taking care of herself. Just ask her ex-husband.

"My main concern is timing. I'm not sure how much she's going to be able to uncover this week." Sophie took a sip of her drink before continuing. "Which is why I was wondering if there was anything you could do about extending my visa?"

Charlie's heart fell at the optimistic look in her eyes. It had occurred to him, after she had mentioned the meeting with Natalia Povetkina, that if there was one way to ensure that the MFA refused her request for an extension, it was to hire a private eye to make trouble. This was Russia, after all, and the odds that they already knew about this afternoon's meeting were pretty good — about as good as the guy sitting alone in the corner being with the Ministry of the Interior, or the Federal Security Service, or whoever it was that handled domestic surveillance these days, Charlie thought as he returned his focus to Sophie. With a face like hers, he could hardly blame her for assuming any man would move mountains to help her, and he was no less susceptible than the average Joe. Maybe a little more.

"I've already sent a diplomatic note and I'll do whatever else I can. I wish I could give you more, but I don't want to promise something I can't deliver."

"I appreciate it, Charlie. I appreciate everything you've done for me." She smiled. "You probably can't wait for them to kick me out, so you can get back to your work."

He laughed, but just the thought made Moscow seem unbearably dreary. Sophie watched as a server delivered a tray of food to a nearby table. "Have you eaten yet?" she asked. "The least I can do is buy you dinner, but I'm not sure the food here's any good. We could go to the restaurant next door."

"What kind of food do you like?"

"I like all kinds, but to be honest, I'm sick of eating here. Maybe you know somewhere nearby?"

"I usually only eat out at lunch, and I'm not that familiar with the options in this area. Plus, I'm trying to expand my culinary skills...." He stopped when he noticed her smiling, unsure why he thought she would give a shit about what he had learned in the couple of cooking classes he'd attended since coming to Moscow.

"You a decent cook?"

"I try." He hesitated only for a moment before committing himself. "I'd be happy to cook you something Russian, if you'd like."

Sophie sipped her wine, then set down the glass and shrugged. "That sounds great."

Charlie scanned the back of the fridge, looking for the bottle of white he was sure was back there somewhere.

"It's a lovely apartment," he heard Sophie say from the living room.

"Yeah, it's okay," he muttered, moving a large jar of mayonnaise just as he recalled that he'd taken the Chardonnay to a dinner party. "Shit."

"Everything all right?" Sophie appeared as he closed the fridge door.

"I thought I had a bottle of white wine in there," he said just as he saw her eyes rest on the bottle of red sitting on the counter, unopened. "I've got red, or there's beer."

"Either's fine," she said, scanning the kitchen with an appraising eye. "You eat in a lot?"

"I'm trying to get in the habit of cooking more," he said, noticing with alarm that the wine was Ukrainian. His one previous experience with Ukrainian wine was not good — it had tasted more like vinegar than wine. How could he not have noticed that on the label? Still, it had been expensive, as far as Russian corner-store wine went. "I joined a cooking class at the embassy, though I've only been to two classes so far."

"So you're saying I'm your guinea pig?"

"Don't worry, I'll keep it simple tonight," he said, uncorking the wine and pouring two glasses. He handed her one and discreetly sniffed at the other, relieved that it didn't smell pickled. "Cheers."

They both sipped and he was pleasantly surprised not to see her spit it back out — it actually wasn't bad. He set the bottle back on the counter and turned the label in as he pulled a head of lettuce out of the fridge.

"Now, I want you to go and relax in there while I take care of this," he said, trying to shoo her out of the kitchen, but she stood her ground, a determined smile on her face.

"No, let me do something. I'm not much of a chef, but I can certainly wash lettuce."

Charlie shrugged and handed her the salad spinner, while he pulled a bag of beets from underneath the counter.

"You like borscht?"

Sophie nodded.

"That's really the only Russian thing I know. I was thinking we'd have chick —"

"I'm not a picky eater, Charlie. I'm sure whatever you have in mind will be just fine."

As she washed lettuce and he peeled beets, they chatted about Russian cuisine, weather, and people, and anything else that had no remote connection to why she found herself in Moscow. She seemed keen to switch to slicing the beets, as Charlie turned his attention to the only edible recipe for chicken breasts in his repertoire. As the meal preparation advanced, he refilled their glasses and began to relax.

"So tell me about Cuba," she said as he crushed garlic for the salad dressing.

"Amazing place. Wonderful people. Have you been?"

"No, I could never convince my … It's on my to-do list."

"So what kind of surgery do you do?" he asked brightly, trying to move off the minefield he had stumbled into. "I've always wondered what it must be like to have that sort of ability — power, really."

She smiled. "Are you mocking me?"

"No, not at all. I mean, you literally have people's lives in your hands."

"Don't get carried away. I do mostly cosmetic surgery."

"Oh."

"Exactly."

"I didn't mean —"

"It's all right. I'm under no illusions. I'm in it mostly for the money, though not all cosmetic surgery is about the money. Reconstructive surgery, for example." She was smiling, but he could see that he had hit a nerve, and he was eager to change topics again.

"Excuse me for a sec. I'd better stir the borscht."

It was on his way back to the kitchen that he first noticed the smell. Like something burning. Like beets burning, actually.

CHAPTER 22

"Well," Charlie said, tossing his napkin onto the table, "my apologies for the meal. Not exactly my finest hour."

"Don't be silly," Sophie said. "I'm pretty sure neither us will end up with botulism."

They both laughed. Gun-shy after having let the borscht burn on the bottom of the pot, he had so undercooked the chicken that he'd had to put it back in the oven before they could eat it. Fortunately, Charlie had used the delay for a toast with a shot each of iced vodka, à la Russian, and they were both smiling despite the culinary shortfalls.

"Can I interest you in some dessert?" he said, taking her plate. "Don't worry — it's from a nearby bakery. An apple torte I've had before, and I can vouch for it being edible."

"Sure," she said, starting to get up, but he insisted on her staying put. He returned a few moments later with the dessert, along with a bottle of cognac he had picked up on his last trip through duty-free.

"I don't know if I should," she said, though she made no move to stop him pouring her an ample dose of the amber liquid.

"Nonsense. It's not like either of us is driving anywhere," he said, quickly adding, "And I can do the subway ride to the Marriott with my eyes closed. Promise."

"Oh, look, it's snowing out," she said, pointing out through the tall windows into the night sky.

"I heard we're in for a dump of snow later in the week. Maybe this is the beginning."

They ate their dessert, then brought their drinks to the living room.

"This has been really nice, Charlie. Thank you so much."

"Sorry about the food."

She smiled and gave him a dismissive wave as they sipped their drinks and watched the fat flakes of snow drifting by the window. Sophie sat back on the sofa, one leg tucked up under the other and her hands cradling the snifter to her chest. In the soft light of the living room — or in any light, for that matter — she was beautiful. Usually Charlie didn't bother fantasizing about women who were so far out of his league, but he couldn't help himself.

"So what happened, anyway?" she asked, bringing him back to reality. "With your ex?"

"I found her with another man in a broom closet at a Christmas party," he said almost automatically. Maybe it was the combination of wine, vodka, and cognac, or the realization that there would never be anything between him and this beautiful creature that made him unconcerned about how he sounded.

"No, seriously."

"I'm serious," he said.

She put a hand over her mouth. "I'm sorry. That's awful."

"It's all right," he said with a wave of a hand. "Ancient history. Best thing that could have happened and all that, right?"

She gave a grim nod. "Mine was cheating, too. A surgical resident. And now they plan to get married, no less."

"How long ago did you find out?"

"About a year and a half."

He nodded as though this explained a lot. "It took me a while before I really started to feel normal again. But you do get over it."

"Oh, I'm over it," she said, visibly straighter in the chair for a moment, before slumping back just a little.

"Have you started dating again yet?" he asked her.

"Not really."

"You should. Good for the psyche."

"That's what my therapist keeps telling me, but I'm just … I don't know. I keep inventing reasons not to. Like getting so bitchy that no one in their right mind would want to go on a date with me."

Charlie laughed. "I think it's normal to be hesitant."

"What about you? I wouldn't think it's easy to find dates." She paused, realizing how that sounded. "I meant, because you're in Moscow and it mustn't be that easy to meet people — what with the language," she added for good measure as she hid her face in her snifter.

"Right," he said.

"It's not like you couldn't get a date," she said, continuing to backpedal. He did nothing to stop her. "I mean, you're certainly charming and …"

He let her off the hook with a laugh. "It's okay, I know what you meant."

She smiled and they sipped their cognac in silence, before Charlie moved on to another topic.

"Did you hear about this tax-haven stuff online?" he said, thinking it was an awkward segue into an area Sophie seemed, by her expression, to care little about.

"I saw something on CNN in my hotel — kind of a WikiLeaks for tax dodgers?"

"Right." Charlie set his cognac on the coffee table. "I was just skimming an article and I noticed Dmitri

Bayzhanov's name among the people exposed for sheltering money in Cyprus."

Sophie looked puzzled. "Who's that?"

"He's a real-estate developer. His company's the one
doing Petr —"

Charlie was struck by a thought, and he abruptly fell
silent.

"What's the matter?" she said.

"Do you have that USB stick with the spreadsheet on you?
I left my copy at the office."

"The one Steve's journalist friend gave me? Yes, why?"

"Where is it?"

She reached for her purse and rummaged around, as
Charlie got his laptop out of his work bag.

"I'm thinking I might know what that spreadsheet's all
about," he began. Both sat on the sofa and he positioned
the laptop on the coffee table and waited for it to fire up.
It seemed to take forever to open the file, but as soon as it
popped open, Charlie pointed at the screen.

"*OS* stands for offshore, and *RU* is for Russian," he said,
pointing to the top of the columns. "This is a list of Alexander
Surin's stock holdings in Russian and offshore companies,
and I bet the offshore companies are all registered in Cyprus."

"Do you recognize any of them?" Sophie asked, scanning
the letters under each column, which looked like abbrevia-
tions or acronyms for corporate names.

Charlie shook his head and opened the web browser on
his laptop, searching for the same news story he had been
looking at in his office. "Here it is," he said after a few seconds of clicking around. He looked at the list under Dmitri
Bayzhanov's name and compared it to the Surin spreadsheet.

"They don't seem to match," Sophie said, looking from
one window to the other.

"Shit."

"You're thinking there's a connection between Surin and Bayzhanov?"

Charlie nodded. "Maybe I was getting ahead of myself, but I thought it might explain why Steve was given — maybe even asked for — information on Surin. Bayzhanov's a big fish in real estate and is sure to have some skeletons in his closet. What if Steve was looking into crime or corruption? Bayzhanov might be of interest. It might also explain why Steve went to Astana."

"How so?" Sophie looked puzzled. She was sitting on the edge of the sofa, next to Charlie — both of them poised at the edge for a better view of the laptop screen. He could smell her perfume mingled with the fruity smell of the cognac on her breath.

"Because Bayzhanov's company started out there, before he moved into the Moscow market."

"And the connection between Surin and Bayzhanov?"

Charlie sighed. "Maybe there isn't one."

"The Bayzhanov thing makes sense, though. Maybe you're on to something."

Charlie sat back on the sofa and Sophie reached for her cognac before doing the same. Suddenly they were very close together on the little sofa. She put her arm over the back and curled her legs up under her as she sipped from her glass. The background music switched to soft jazz as the snow continued to fall outside.

"I don't know what I'd do without you, Charlie," she murmured. "I'd be lost."

Charlie couldn't help but consider the irony of her statement. It was Steve Liepa who had saved his ass in prison, not the other way around. Charlie had managed to do absolutely nothing to get Liepa out and hadn't even managed to ensure the safe repatriation of his body. Yet his sister was sitting here thanking him. He looked at her as she leaned forward and set her glass on the coffee table. The gesture brought her face close to his and he could almost feel the heat of her skin....

"A penny for your thoughts," she said suddenly.

Not for a million bucks, he thought, trying to bring his focus to the investigation. "I was just thinking about the BayCo angle."

"So you think there's something to this Bayzhanov guy?" she asked, smoothing the front of her shirt. Her manner seemed totally at ease, whereas Charlie was in turmoil.

"It's a possibility for sure," he said, regaining some composure. "I'm going to have lunch with my counterpart from Astana this week — he's in town for some meetings. I might talk to Katya Dontseva, too. See if she knows anything about Bayzhanov."

Sophie nodded, then glanced at her watch. "My God, is that the time?"

Charlie looked at his own watch and realized it was almost midnight. Waving off her protestations that she should help him with the dishes, they set off into the snowy Moscow night. The accumulation over dinner softened the sounds of the street and gave the city an unusually bright feel as they made their way back to the Metro. Charlie did most of the talking on the ride back to her hotel, and they both seemed surprised at how quickly they found themselves at the front steps.

"Well, here you are."

"I feel like I could walk for miles," she said, taking a deep breath of the cold night air. "It must be your cognac."

"Warms the insides, doesn't it?"

"I want to thank you for a wonderful evening, Charlie. It was just what I needed."

"You're welcome."

She paused just a tick, then smiled and disappeared through the revolving door, leaving him there in the snow. It had grown suddenly cold, but as he turned and headed back up Tverskaya, the image of her curled up on his sofa, a glass of cognac in her hand and a smile on her face, kept him warm.

CHAPTER 23

Charlie sat at his kitchen table, sipping a coffee and reading the newspaper spread out before him. Despite the late hour, he had been unable to sleep upon his return to the apartment the night before, and he had awoken half an hour earlier than usual. He told himself it was the cognac, as he yawned and flipped to the next page and scanned the articles. The Russian markets had taken another turn for the worse, but that hadn't prevented one of the former state-owned oil companies from achieving a record quarterly profit. He was about to head off to the shower when an article at the bottom of the page caught his eye.

It was about the Petr Square development and cited the removal of a long-standing planning obstacle as the principal reason the development was now proceeding full steam ahead, and how, when it was complete, it would dwarf any other commercial development in the city. He read on with interest as the article noted that the anchor tenant alone would take over a hundred thousand square metres of the new space. He paused when he read the name — United Pharma International. It took him a few seconds to make the connection that he knew lay somewhere in the recesses of his sleepy mind.

Then it came to him. Sergei Yermolov worked for United Pharma, and Charlie recalled the meeting in the lobby of the firm's current premises. Charlie returned his attention to the article and the summary of United Pharma's operations in Russia and worldwide. It soon became clear that the pharmaceutical firm was a behemoth, with annual sales in the billions and a stable of subsidiaries that it had gobbled up over the years, including some familiar drug companies. Charlie thought back to Yermolov's attendance at the same pot party as Steve Liepa and wondered how his employer would feel about his dabbling in recreational narcotics. Maybe that explained the curt reception, he thought as he flipped the paper shut and downed the rest of his coffee. He paused as he caught sight of last night's dishes still in the sink, lingering over one of the wineglasses — a faint trace of lipstick around the rim — before setting off for the shower.

Charlie was on hold, waiting for the clerk at the Ministry of Foreign Affairs to let him know whether his sole contact was available. Charlie had met her at one of the first functions he had attended after arriving in Moscow, and she had been somewhat helpful in getting Sophie's visa processed quickly. He didn't hold out much hope that she would be able to do much to extend it, but he figured it was worth a try. As he sat there, the phone at his ear, he recognized a familiar voice in the hall, and he stepped out the doorway just in time to see a dark-haired man in his thirties rounding the corner with one of the immigration officers.

"Doug?" he called out, his hand over the receiver by his chin. The other man stopped and made an about-face.

"Charlie, hi," Cullen said, extending his hand as he approached.

"On hold with the MFA — could be a while," Charlie said, gesturing to the phone as he shook hands. "You gonna be around at lunch?"

Cullen nodded. "We just wrapped up the morning session. I was going to come find you but you saved me the trouble."

Charlie looked at his watch. "Let me finish up here and I'll come get you downstairs. There's a little Moroccan place nearby where we can grab a quick bite."

Twenty minutes later they were sitting in a restaurant just around the corner from the embassy. The low red couches were covered with brightly coloured cushions.

"It's a bit smoky in here," Charlie said as they settled in. "But the food's pretty good."

"No worries," Cullen said.

"So how's Astana?"

"I can't complain. It beats the hell out of Ottawa." Cullen grinned. Charlie assumed Astana had a higher hardship rating than Moscow, and thus the incentives were greater. For a young guy like Cullen, a two-year posting went by quickly, and with nowhere to spend the extra money, it made saving easier. "But to be perfectly honest, this is my second winter, and I'm not really looking forward to the next few months. How about you?"

"It's pretty good so far, though the bureaucracy's awful."

"That's nothing compared to the corruption, I'm sure. The scenery's nice, though," he added quietly, as a striking brunette tottered by on stiletto-heeled boots.

A server appeared just then and read off the lunch special, which they both ordered.

"So I did a bit of digging before I came," Cullen said when they were alone again.

"And?"

"I didn't find out much about Bayzhanov, at least nothing that makes him any different from any other successful developer in Eastern Europe. He's well connected, probably got half the local officials on his payroll and always willing to bend some rules, but that's about it. He's new to Moscow, though, and apparently this Petr Square is a big deal."

Charlie nodded, trying to conceal his disappointment. "It's the largest commercial development in the city, from what the brokers tell me."

"His brother, though, is another story," Cullen said, his voice lowering as he leaned forward on the red velour couch.

"His brother?"

"He's been in jail for the past couple of years," Cullen said, taking a sip of his water and grimacing at the taste. "Shit, I forgot to ask for still."

"It's safer if it's carbonated," Charlie said, which prompted a shrug and another tentative sip. "If Bayzhanov's so well-connected, why can't he get his brother out of jail?"

"'Cause he's not in jail in Kazakhstan. He's in Tajikistan."

"Tajikistan?"

"It's right next door, but apparently not as susceptible to Bayzhanov's influence, or maybe he hasn't found the right palm to grease yet, who knows."

"What's he in for?"

"That's the funny thing," Cullen said. "No one's really sure. I heard corruption, sort of. Everyone I talked to seemed to think he was guilty, but no one knew what of."

"Is the brother in construction, too?"

"Not that I could see. He might have had some role, unofficially, but it seems he was a bureaucrat."

"You mean he was responsible for finding the right people for big brother to pay off?"

Cullen smiled. "Government liaison, I think it's called."

"So how did he end up in a cell in Tajikistan?"

"That's the question no one seems to have an answer for, and from what I can tell, he's not getting out anytime soon, either. Are you guys looking at Petr Square for the new embassy here?"

"Not really, although I'm only loosely involved in that file. I had heard that there were a lot of problems with Petr Square, though apparently they just got their building permit, so who knows. Rob Brooker's more in the know — he's been working on that file for a while."

Cullen nodded. "Rob's a good guy. We were at HQ together for a while, before he got posted here."

They continued to chat as their lunch arrived, and when they were done, Charlie insisted on paying the bill, despite a mild protest from Cullen.

"So how long are you here for?" Charlie asked as they stood on the front steps of the restaurant and zipped up their jackets. The air had grown colder over the past hour, and fat snowflakes had begun to fly on a brisk wind.

"I head back tomorrow. I'll keep digging and see what I can find out about Bayzhanov and his brother — let you know if anything turns up."

Charlie returned to his office, his conversation with Doug Cullen still on his mind. The fact that Bayzhanov's brother was in jail was interesting, but without knowing the reason, it didn't seem all that helpful or relevant. Charlie decided to do a quick search on BayCo and was immediately directed to a page advertising space available for rent in Petr Square. A bright banner across the top of the web page announced that the plans had been granted. He clicked on the link that led him to a full-page article on the Petr Square development and he read it with interest, looking for some reference to Bayzhanov but finding only a quote from the chair of the planning committee that had given the project the green light. Charlie froze when he saw the name of the planning committee chair — Alexander Surin. He stared at the screen, going back over the Russian text to make sure he had understood it properly, but there was no doubt — the Petr Square project had been approved by a committee headed by Alexander Surin. It had to be the same Alexander Surin that Steve Liepa's journalist friend had given him information on. He was still staring at the monitor when his assistant appeared at his door.

"Hi Irina."

"This just came for you," she said, handing him a couple of envelopes.

"Could you translate something for me?" he asked, pointing to the monitor and turning it so she could view it from the other side of the desk.

"Of course," she said, leaning forward to view the text as Charlie scrolled down to the article on Petr Square. "It is talking about the Petr Square office complex that is being built near the Belorusskaya station." She went on to summarize the article. When she got to the quote, Charlie pointed to the name onscreen.

"And this Alexander Surin is the chair of the planning committee?"

Irina nodded. "Yes, he is talking about the importance of the project to the Moscow market and also of the need for transparency and certainty in the planning process."

"What else does it say?"

Irina continued. "It talks about the fact that the development had been stalled for almost a year for lack of a permit, but ongoing discussions with the city's planning committee and mutual co-operation resolved the issue. It goes on to say that the developer has lost a lot of money as a result of the delay." She looked up again. "That's about it. It's a short article."

"Thanks, Irina. That's very helpful. "Oh, I almost forgot," he said before she had reached the door. "Has there been any word from protocol about our request to extend Dr. Durant's visa?"

"No. I was waiting a couple of minutes to call over. My contact usually starts late. I will find out if there are any developments."

"Thank you." Charlie turned the monitor back to face him and considered the article for a moment before turning to the two envelopes that Irina had neatly deposited on the corner of his desk. He tossed the first into the recycling bin without even opening it, recognizing it as a subscription form for a magazine he didn't need. Glancing at the second, he noticed his name was handwritten on the cover. Intrigued, he opened it and slid the contents, two sheets of paper, onto his desk. There was no cover letter, and the first sheet was a photocopied obituary in Russian for a man called Mikhail Krasnikov who appeared to have died about a month ago. The second sheet was a copy of a photo of a meeting room with a dozen severe-looking Russian men seated along a conference table, a red circle drawn around the man seated in the middle of the group.

Charlie scanned the text under the photo and tried to make out the names, but they were barely legible. He counted the number of people from left to right until he got to the man circled in red felt pen, then did the same count of the names captioned below. The resolution was fuzzy and he had a hard time making out the name, but he was pretty sure the sixth from the left was "M. Krasnikov." He retrieved the envelope from his recycling bin and checked it again for a return address, finding none. He would check with Irina, but the postmark looked like Moscow. He sat back in his chair and wondered who could have sent him this and why? He typed the name into his search engine and sighed when a dozen links appeared in Russian, and he realized making any sense of it at all would take him hours. He moved his cursor over to close the browser when his eye caught a familiar name in the fourth entry. He clicked on the entry, then leaned forward in his chair as the link opened and a couple of paragraphs of text appeared. He struggled with the text for a few seconds, then called out to Irina.

"I'm sorry to bother you again," he began when she entered, "but I was just reading this article and I don't think I've understood it properly."

She came over and leaned toward the monitor. "It is a short biography on Mikhail Krasnikov, an official with the Moscow City Architect's Office and chair of the main planning committee."

"But I thought Alexander Surin was the chair of the planning committee."

Irina frowned. "You're right. That's what the article we read earlier said. Let me go to my computer and I will find out for you."

She was only gone a few minutes before she reappeared with a smile. "Mr. Krasnikov was replaced by Mr. Surin two weeks ago." Her smile faded. "It appears Mr. Krasnikov was killed in an accident abroad." She paused, seeing Charlie's reaction. "Does this clear up the confusion?"

Charlie gave her a quick smile. "Yes, I think you've cleared things up nicely," he said, his smile evaporating as soon as she turned to leave. His head was swimming. The message was clear enough — a picture of the chair of the committee blocking the Petr Square development, and his obituary. The question was, who had sent the message and why? Suddenly an overdue meeting became all the more urgent. He walked out to Irina's desk.

"Could you try to get me a home address for Sergei Yermolov?"

Charlie checked the number on the building before climbing the steps to the entrance just as a young couple was leaving. He smiled and slid through the door behind them into a lobby that smelled of a mixture of stewing meat, cabbage, and dirty socks. Walking over to the elevators, he pressed the button and waited, wondering how Yermolov would react to an unexpected visit at his home. He had tried to get in touch with him, but had been unable to reach him either at United Pharma or at the phone number Irina had dug up for his apartment. Hopefully he would understand, once Charlie told him Steve Liepa was dead — that is, if Yermolov didn't already know. And besides, his reception here couldn't be much worse than the one at Yermolov's workplace.

He rode the elevator to the seventh floor and got off onto a dimly lit landing. At least the smell was better here. He followed the sign on the wall toward Yermolov's apartment door, and as he approached it, he noticed a thin ray of light outlining the door frame. He checked the number again, then knocked on the door, his light rap causing it to open an inch, its hinges creaking in protest.

"Mr. Yermolov?"

Other than the faint sound of a radio from somewhere within, there was no response. He called out again, a little louder. From where he stood, he could see a sliver of the hallway and a doorway to one of the rooms. He gently pushed the door open a few more inches before putting one foot inside.

"Sergei?"

Halfway in the doorway now, he hesitated, but before turning to leave, he peeked into the living room, which was off to the right. And then froze at the sight of a foot on the floor. When Charlie leaned forward, the full body came into view — Sergei Yermolov, lying on his back. It wasn't the awkward angle of his legs that struck Charlie, but rather the dark puddle that had formed by his head from a blackish wound on the side of his skull.

"Christ," he uttered as he recoiled. His first instinct was to bolt, but curiosity overcame him, and instead, he stepped fully inside and pushed the door shut behind him, then moved gingerly into the living room. He forced himself to look at Yermolov's face, and from the vacant stare of the open eyes, it was clear he was dead. Charlie stood there for a few seconds, his mind spinning. At last he realized there was nothing to gain from his continued presence and potentially a lot to lose if someone walked in on him standing over the dead occupant of an apartment in which he was trespassing. He returned to the hallway and pulled the door almost closed, the way he'd found it, then walked briskly down the hall to the elevator. It wasn't until he was back outside that his heart rate began to return to normal. He was on his way toward the lights of Tverskaya when his cell went off, startling him.

"Hello?"

"Charlie. This a bad time?" In his current state of mind, Sophie's voice was like a warm blanket.

"No. Not at all. I was just … heading home."

"I was just wondering if you'd heard anything about my visa. I know you're busy …"

"I'm, uh … Actually, can you meet me at the embassy? I can tell you the latest, but it's not great news."

"Sure." A little sigh. "I'll get a car from the hotel."

"I'll be there in fifteen."

"You sure everything's okay?"

"Yeah," he said, hanging up. He had fifteen minutes to collect himself and decide what to do next. One thing he was sure of, though — everything was far from okay. He walked under the arch that led out onto the main boulevard, drawing a sense of safety from the bright lights.

CHAPTER 24

"Oh, my God." Sophie's hand was over her mouth as she sat on the other side of Charlie's desk, having just heard his description of his visit to Yermolov's apartment and what he had found there. "What are you going to do? I mean, did you call the police?"

Charlie just sat there for a moment, stunned by the simplicity of the remark.

Why didn't I think of that? I'm only the fricken consular officer ...

"Not yet. I ... I guess I'm still sort of shocked."

"Of course you are." She slid a hand across the desk and laid it on his arm. "And you're sure he was dead?"

Charlie nodded. "There was a hole in the side of his head, a pool of blood on the floor, and his eyes were staring up at the ceiling. I'm no doctor, but I'm pretty sure he was dead."

"I didn't mean ..."

"I'm sorry. You're right, though, I need to get a hold of the police right away." He paused as he tried to imagine how his call to the police would play out. Why had he been visiting Yermolov at his home? In response to an anonymously sent article and photograph suggesting ... What exactly did they have to do with Yermolov?

"What were you going to see him about, anyway?" Sophie asked, as though Charlie's internal debate had been spoken aloud. He hadn't mentioned his discovery that United Pharma — Yermolov's employer — was the main tenant at Petr Square. "What is it, Charlie?"

He was still trying to piece things together in his own mind, and he decided that airing his jumbled thoughts might help. "Look, we know that Yermolov was with Steve the night he was arrested."

Sophie looked puzzled. "Yeah, and you said you already tried to talk to him and he didn't have much to say."

"Right, but what I haven't had a chance to tell you yet is that Yermolov's employer, United Pharma, is taking almost a full building in the Petr Square complex."

"UPI?"

"You've heard of them?"

"Are you kidding?" Sophie shook her head. "They're only the biggest player in international pharma — not to mention a bunch of unethical scumbags. They throw money at doctors to push their pills. Send them to conferences in Maui, that sort of thing. They're more aggressive in the U.S., but they target Canadian docs, as well. I can only imagine what they get up to in a place like this."

"It was in the papers this morning." Charlie paused as he watched her digest the information and go through the same thought process he had when he'd learned of the connection.

"So Steve was looking into this Bayzhanov guy, or Petr Square, maybe both," she said. "You think Yermolov is connected to Bayzhanov somehow?"

"I don't know. That's one of the things I wanted to talk to him about," Charlie said.

"Sounds like he's not going to be doing much talking now ... Wait a second," she said. "What if Steve was looking into United Pharma, not Bayzhanov? And Yermolov found out and had Steve framed …"

"But why's Yermolov dead, then?"

She sighed. "Good question."

"There's something else." Charlie reached into his desk drawer and pulled out the envelope that had arrived earlier. He opened it and slid out the two sheets of paper. "This came this morning."

"What is it?"

"It's a copy of a newspaper obituary and a photo, sent anonymously."

"Of who?"

"A man called Mikael Krasnikov," Charlie replied.

"Who's he?" Sophie was frowning.

"He chaired the planning committee that was holding up the Petr Square development by denying the crucial building permit … until he died."

"Whoa." Sophie held up a hand. "You mean this guy dies and then presto, the Petr Square development gets its permit?"

He nodded. "And guess who the new chair of the planning committee is?"

She shook her head.

"Alexander Surin."

"What the *fuck*?" Her eyes were wide as saucers. "That's the guy —"

"I know," Charlie interrupted. "And the guy he replaced died in an accident abroad." He turned the obituary toward her before realizing that she didn't read Russian.

"This is really starting to stink," she said, sitting back in her chair and crossing her arms. "I'm assuming you think maybe it wasn't an accident?"

Charlie nodded again. "And I get the sense that whoever sent me this sure didn't think it was, either."

They both sat in silence for a while, their minds whirring with the possibilities.

"But who would have sent you this and why?"

Charlie sighed. "I have no idea."

"So, what are you going to do?"

He looked at her vacantly.

"About Yermolov, I mean," she said.

"I don't know. What am I supposed to tell the cops?" Charlie said, making a helpless gesture with both hands. "I went to see him because of this stuff?" He pointed to the two sheets from the envelope. "It's ridiculous. Besides, they're liable to think I had something to do with it. But I can't just leave Yermolov lying there, and if I call from here …"

"I'm meeting Natalia later this evening at the hotel," Sophie said. "What if she made an anonymous call to the police?"

"I don't know. Maybe I should talk to the embassy's security guy …"

"What did Tania say Yermolov did at UPI?"

Charlie shrugged. "I think she said he was in sales. Some kind of junior executive."

"You think Yermolov might have suffered the same fate as this planning guy?" Sophie pointed to the photo of Krasnikov.

Charlie nodded. "And I'm not sure I want to announce my own connection to any of this."

"What do you mean?" Sophie's eyes widened as she arrived at his line of thought. "My God, you …"

"Don't want to be next. Exactly."

"You know more about how things work in Moscow than I do," she said. "But I don't get a warm fuzzy feeling from all this."

"I agree, but I don't think this is something we can just go to the police with — not if we hope to get to the bottom of it. Besides, I'm not sure how much protection they'd be able to provide even if we did."

"But we have to do something." She looked at her watch. "Come with me to meet Natalia."

"I'm not sure that's such a great idea."

She shrugged. "You got a better one?"

He stared at the picture of Krasnikov for a moment, then glanced at his obituary before looking up at Sophie. "Can't say that I do."

Charlie, Sophie, and Natalia Povetkina sat huddled around the little table in the lobby bar.

"You're sure this man is dead?" Povetkina asked, prompting a nod from Charlie. "And you say the apartment door was open when you arrived?"

"That's right, just a crack."

"What's the address?" she asked, pulling out her cellphone.

"What are you doing?" Charlie asked.

"I'm going to call my police contact, see if anyone else has called it in."

Charlie nodded, realizing that would make his own report of the death, and whatever complications that might go with it, unnecessary. He gave her the address and she punched a number from her speed-dial list, as Charlie and Sophie sat in silence. Povetkina spoke with someone on the other end for a few minutes, then hung up.

"Well, your first problem is solved. There's already a team on-site. A neighbour found him and called it in."

"So what do we do now?" Sophie said.

Povetkina looked at Charlie. "What do you know about this Yermolov?"

"Not much really, other than that he attended the same party on the night Steve was picked up."

"And why were you going to see him tonight?"

"I was curious about how well he and Steve knew each other, and to see if there was anything he might not have already told me about that night the first time I talked to him."

"You already spoke with him? When?"

"A week ago I dropped by his office, but he wasn't very … forthcoming, and I was hoping he might be more comfortable talking to me at his home." Charlie could sense Sophie scrutinizing him, no doubt wondering why he was holding back on Povetkina. He hoped the private eye didn't get the same impression.

"Can you find out more about him from your police contact?" Sophie asked.

"Of course, but I'm not sure what I'm looking for." She glanced at Charlie.

"Did you find out the address of the party?" Sophie continued.

"Yes, from my contact. I wasn't able to contact the owner yet, though, to ask about that night."

"But once you do, you can ask him or her about Yermolov. Maybe pick up a lead that way?"

Povetkina frowned. "Yes, but for you, the most critical thing is time, with your visa expiring in two days. I assume you have not had success with the Foreign Ministry?"

Charlie shook his head. "I'm not hopeful we'll get an extension by tomorrow." He looked at Sophie and saw her disappointment. It was the first time he had admitted as much directly. "We need to discuss your options. If we don't get an extension during the day tomorrow, you really need to be on a flight tomorrow night."

Povetkina broke the silence that followed. "Well, I've got a lot of work to do if you're only here for another twenty-four hours," she said, getting to her feet. "I'll try to get in touch with the owner of the party apartment again tonight, and I'll find out as much as I can about what happened to Yermolov."

"Thank you, Natalia."

"I will call you tomorrow, or earlier, depending on what I find out. Goodbye, Mr. Hillier."

"Goodbye," Charlie said. "And good luck."

Sophie waited for her to leave and stirred her half-empty martini glass. "So, what was all that about?"

"All what?"

"Why so coy with Natalia? You didn't mention the obituary or the photo. Why not? I don't have the luxury of time, as you know."

"I'm not sure how much I can trust a Moscow PI, Sophie. I know you've got your hopes pinned on her, but ..."

"Please don't patronize me, Charlie. I really don't need that right now on top of everything else. Natalia's been a valuable resource already."

"I'm just saying —"

"I'm sorry, Charlie, but I'm having a hard time with them kicking me out of the country in twenty-four hours." She sighed. "Are you really sure there's nothing you can do about my visa?"

"I've been thinking, part of the problem is bureaucratic. Extensions are always more problematic than a new application — don't ask me why. What if we were able to get you a new visa on an expedited basis?"

"You mean I have to go back to Canada and wait for permission to return?"

"What if you just left Russia?"

"And go where? Ukraine?"

"Actually, that's not such a bad idea. Canadians don't need a visa to go there. But I was thinking more Frankfurt or London — somewhere you could hop back on a direct flight on short notice."

"I can't believe I'm going to have to leave as early as tomorrow night." She put her head in her hands. "These bastards kill my brother and then won't even allow me to stick around long enough to find out what really happened. Not to mention 'accidentally' cremating his remains."

"I know it's frustrating. I wish there was something I could do."

"I don't blame you, you know," she said after a moment, but it didn't make him feel any less helpless.

CHAPTER 25

Charlie adjusted his woollen scarf to cover the bottom half of his face as he hurried toward the stairs down to the underpass. The mercury had been dropping all day, and he guessed it was now well below zero, accompanied by gusting winds. As an icy blast stung his eyes, he turned away to adjust his scarf higher, and for an instant, he found himself locked in a glance with a thickset man in a long leather coat twenty feet behind him. The man was looking up after shielding himself from the same blast of wind, and when his eyes met Charlie's, he looked away and changed course toward a tobacco stand. Charlie didn't know why, but he couldn't resist watching the man proceed to the stand and ask for something. With his scarf up to his eyes, Charlie turned and continued on to the steps, taking them two at a time as he descended to the relative warmth of the busy underpass. Halfway through the tiled corridor, he glanced back for the man in the leather coat but saw nothing amidst the moving crowd. He continued on and considered calling Sophie again. He hadn't heard from her since early afternoon, despite their agreement to meet for a final drink this evening.

Since the meeting with her and Povetkina the previous evening, nothing had changed. He hadn't heard whether Povetkina had made any progress in her inquiries about

Yermolov's death, or about the owner of the apartment where Steve Liepa had been detained. If anything, Sophie's situation had gotten worse. As expected, the Ministry of Foreign Affairs had refused her request for an extension of her visa, meaning she would be on a flight out tonight, or at the latest, tomorrow morning. Charlie had already started the process of applying for a new visa and was even hopeful that he could get it issued within a week, but that didn't change his sense of failure at being unable to keep her here.

Sophie had been pragmatic about the whole situation. She'd considered the possibility of using the opportunity to return her brother's ashes to Canada and make funeral arrangements before returning to Moscow. Charlie looked around at the sea of faces, somehow less friendly now, and felt an emptiness at the thought of Moscow without Sophie's presence. He pulled his cellphone out of his pocket and considered another call, but decided against it. He had left a message less than an hour ago. Maybe she didn't want to return it. Maybe she felt he had let her down. Maybe she was right.

Charlie's mind was in a grey fog as he came up out of the underpass on the south side of Ostozhenka and made his way southwest. He was contemplating the empty fridge in his apartment and debating a stop at the nearby deli when he felt a shove from behind, then a sharp pain in his head as his world went dark for a moment. He felt his arms being pinned behind him and his feet leave the ground as he was tossed sideways to land on a cold, hard surface. His muffled shout was overwhelmed by the sound of a metal door slamming shut and an engine revving, as he slid back in response to the sudden forward motion.

Light returned with a blinding flash when the hood that had shielded Charlie's face was whipped off. After a short drive, he had been shuffled out of the vehicle and down a steep set of stairs. The descent and the dank air told him he was in a basement somewhere not too far from central Moscow. They might have been driving long enough to have reached the Garden Ring, but not much further. His eyes darted around instinctively, but his view was obscured by a desk lamp shining in his face, virtually blacking out the rest of the room, including the men he could sense lurking in the shadows. He had heard unintelligible snippets of conversation on the journey here, he wasn't entirely sure they were in Russian.

"What do you want?" he said to the shadows. There was no reply, but after a hushed exchange from the other side of the room, Charlie made out the shape of a man of average size on the other side of the lamp. He heard the screech of metal chair legs on the concrete floor as the man sat down.

"Good evening, Mr. Hillier." The English was clear enough, though heavily accented.

"Who are you?"

"That doesn't concern you. You are here to answer my questions."

Charlie swallowed and tried to peer past the light, but succeeded only in creating floaters in his field of vision. "I'm a consul with the Canadian Em —"

"We know who you are!" the man snapped, continuing in a normal tone only after his authority had been acknowledged by Charlie's silence. "And your embassy will be of no help to you here. But if you answer our questions, you can be home again soon, yes?"

Charlie allowed himself to accept the sliver of hope that had been offered and nodded.

"What were you doing at the apartment of Sergei Yermolov last night?"

Charlie's heart began to race at the mention of the name. The reference to Yermolov, now deceased, didn't give him a warm feeling, since the only other people he could think of who might know he'd been there were the killers. But the Russian's use of the collective "we" gained a new significance as Charlie contemplated the possibility that he was being interrogated by the police or, possibly worse, the FSB.

"Who's asking?" he said, though he regretted it instantly, as he felt the air at the side of his head displaced a split second before something hard contacted with his ear, rendering him temporarily deaf.

"Take it easy!" he protested, though he could only hear himself though one ear, and he was unable to raise his restrained hands to protect himself from any further blows. As his head continued to ring, he got his breath back and said, "All right. I was there. I went to see him, but he was already ..."

"Why did you go to see him?"

"I wanted to ask him about a consular case. A Canadian citizen, who died in police custody. Yermolov knew him and was with him on the night he was detained."

"And what did you talk about last night?"

"We didn't talk about anything. He was dead when I got to his apartment."

"How did you get in?"

"The door was open — unlocked." Charlie strained to see the form behind the light. The effort was futile.

"Did he know you were coming to talk to him?"

"No. I tried calling him at work but didn't get an answer."

"Did you leave a message?"

"No. Look, if I knew what this was all about, maybe I could help you ... give you the information you're looking for, but —"

"What do you know about Steven Liepa's death?"

"That he died in custody, that's about it," Charlie said, unprepared for the blow that came from the opposite side this time. The stunning effect was the same.

"What was *that* for?"

"Liepa was a Canadian citizen. You're the Canadian consul — you must know something!"

"I swear I don't. He died of asphyxiation in his cell, apparently as a result of hanging himself."

"Apparently? The sister doesn't believe that, does she?"

Charlie froze at the reference to Sophie, and his interrogator noticed the reaction

"You like her, yes?" A guttural laugh.

Charlie tried to compose himself in the pause that followed. "Steve Liepa had no reason to take his own life," he said, hoping to steer the conversation away from Sophie and rein in the horrific possibilities his mind was conjuring up.

What if they have her, too?

"So why was he killed?"

It was a simple question, but one that Charlie honestly couldn't answer. He shook his head. "I don't know. I wish I did, but I don't."

"What about Krasnikov? Did Liepa speak to you of him? Did Yermolov?"

Charlie shook his head and squinted, still trying to see beyond the bright light in his eyes. "No."

"Perhaps you should consider another line of work, Mr. Hillier." Charlie tensed for another blow as the screech of metal on concrete announced that his interrogator had stood up from his chair. "I should kill you for being useless." Charlie could see the shadowy figure retreat toward the far side of the room, then come back. "By the way," the man continued, "I hope you didn't leave any fingerprints at Yermolov's apartment, or you can expect a visit from representatives of the Moscow prosecutor's office." Charlie experienced a sudden chill in his spine and quickly replayed the scene from the previous evening. Had he been wearing his gloves when he pushed the door open? What about when he left?

"They're very thorough, if a little slow," his interrogator said. "I'd say you've got about twenty-four hours before they find out you were there. If I were you, I'd start working on my answers to their questions right away, otherwise you could end up like Mr. Liepa."

"Did you kill Yermolov?" Charlie called out as the shape on the other side of the light began to move away, then seemed to merge with another, much larger figure. The voice that he heard next was different, an octave deeper and gravelly.

"Your lack of information is disturbing, Mr. Hillier, not to mention dangerous, to yourself and your lovely friend. If I were you, I would get her out of here as soon as possible."

"What do you mean? Why would you —"

"You should be more careful about who you choose to confide in. If the people who killed Yermolov find out about your social call to his apartment, you are both in grave danger."

Again Charlie tried to make out who the speaker was, but it was pointless. "Who are you?"

The voice was further away now. "Consider me your guardian angel, Mr. Hillier," it said, before barking an order in Russian to its cohorts and disappearing.

CHAPTER 26

Charlie heard the rough, metallic sound of the sliding door and felt the blast of cold air through the hood that still obscured his vision. He braced himself as a knife ripped through the tape that bound his hands behind his back and then, with a single shove, he was out on the sidewalk, barely able to stay on his feet as the van sped off. It was around the nearest corner in a squeal of tires before he was able to remove the hood and draw in a lungful of the exhaust-infused air and look around. He was on a quiet, residential street, but as he started walking and rounded the first corner, he made out the sound of heavier traffic a few blocks east. He breathed a sigh of relief when he reached the main thoroughfare and realized it was the familiar Tverskaya Street.

Having gotten his bearings, Charlie's next impulse was to reach for his BlackBerry, but a quick search of his pockets turned up nothing. He swore, wondering how he would explain the loss of his second BlackBerry in as many weeks. The IT department was going to flip out, but that was the least of his worries, he knew, as he made a quick assessment of his location and raced off toward the Marriott Grand. He was in the lobby in under ten minutes and gasping to regain his breath as he approached the house phone and dialled

Sophie's room. When a dozen rings got no response, he hurried to the reception desk.

"I'm trying to get hold of Dr. Sophie Durant. She's in room 605."

The woman tapped a few keys, then said, "Dr. Durant has checked out, sir."

"What?"

"She checked out. Fifteen minutes ago."

"Fiftee — I need to reach her urgently," he said as beads of sweat formed on his forehead. "Did she book a hotel car to the airport?"

"I'm sorry, sir …" The girl was eyeing him as though he were an exotic reptile.

"Forget it," he said and turned to make his way out toward the waiting line of gleaming black Benzes and Bimmers. He was almost at the door when he heard his name called. He swivelled around to see Sophie standing near the entrance to the lobby bar.

"Thank God," he said as relief washed over him. He felt an overwhelming urge to hug her tight to his chest. Instead he just stood there, still sweating from his run over.

"What's the matter? You look like you've seen a ghost."

"Where are you going?" he asked, avoiding her questions.

"I've been trying to reach you for the past hour. I decided there was no point staying until tomorrow, so I got a flight tonight."

"Back to Canada?"

"No, Berlin."

"Why Berlin?" His first thought was that it sounded too close.

"I took your advice. In case my new visa comes through, I'll just be a few hours away." She looked at him in confusion. "What's going on?"

"Nothing. When's your flight?"

"Eleven-thirty. I was just about to leave for the airport."

"I'll go with you. We can talk in the car."

"There's obviously something going on. I wish you'd just tell me," Sophie said. The car had passed the outer ring road and the purr of its V8 morphed into a low growl as it accelerated into the fast lane.

"It's not safe here anymore," he said quietly. The driver seemed absorbed in his job, and the radio provided enough white noise that he felt safe talking to her in the back seat. "I don't know if you should be thinking about coming back next week."

"You're starting to freak me out. What happened?"

"Nothing." He shook his head. "You sure you shouldn't go back to Toronto until we figure out your visa?"

"I got an email from a girlfriend of Steve's in Berlin sending me her condolences. I don't know how she found out or got my coordinates, but she did. I'm meeting with her tomorrow."

Charlie said nothing for a minute as he looked out the window at the blur of lights from a truck they were passing. He replayed in his mind his earlier interrogation — the mysterious outline behind the desk lamp, the second gravelly voice, and the dire warnings it had issued. Was a police team going through his apartment at this very moment? Was it possible that in the shock and confusion over his discovery of Yermolov's corpse that he could have left fingerprints or some other telltale sign of his presence at Yermolov's apartment? It was too late now, anyway. He could hardly call up the police and admit that he had walked away from a murder scene the night before and not bothered to tell anyone. There were only two people he had told — and he had a pretty good idea who had leaked it to whomever had grabbed him.

"You didn't mention going to Berlin to Natalia, did you?" he said at last.

"Not yet. I was going to send her an email. You think I should call her?"

"No. I don't think you should tell her anything."

"But she needs to know in case she finds out —"

"Keep your travel plans to yourself," he said with a force he hadn't intended. Sophie looked stung. "You have to trust me on this one," he added, trying to soften the message with a smile. "By the way, do you know if there's any room on your flight?"

They were at thirty thousand feet, seated together in the sparsely populated front of the plane, each with a drink in hand, before he told her what had happened. She listened without interruption.

"Oh, my God," she said when he was finished. "It's ..." Words seemed to fail her. "How does that happen in this day and age?"

"I'll tell you how it happened — Natalia."

"You think she told ... But who, and why?"

"The *why* is easy — cash. It's the *who* I wish I could figure out." Charlie downed the last of his scotch, then caught the eye of the attendant and pointed to their glasses. "At first, I thought maybe it was the police ... maybe even the FSB — but that doesn't make any sense. Besides, they seemed to be more interested in Steve than Yermolov. They also asked about Krasnikov. I would have thought the FSB would have all the information they need without having to abduct me."

"So who, then?"

"Whoever it is, they knew all about Steve's death. They also knew about you."

"They mentioned me?"

"They said you were in danger if you stayed in Moscow."

"Are you kidding?"

Charlie shook his head. "Listen, threats from people who can pluck you off the street and beat information out of you at will should be taken very seriously, in my book."

"My God, did they hurt you?"

"Nothing serious — just a couple of swats. It was more for intimidation than to do physical damage."

"That's awful. I'm so sorry …"

"It's not your fault. Anyway, they let me go. That's the main thing."

"I don't believe it was Natalia." Sophie was shaking her head.

"Maybe not." Charlie's tone conveyed little conviction.

"Thanks for warning me," she said as their drink refills arrived. He stared at his scotch as it occurred to him that his abductors could easily have followed him straight to the hotel, then the airport.… He looked out into the aisle and scanned the few other faces in the business-class cabin — a couple of executive types and an elderly couple who looked pretty harmless. Whoever had grabbed him seemed to know all about Sophie, anyway, including which hotel she was staying at, if they wanted to follow her.

"Why didn't you call me after they let you go, instead of running to my hotel?" she asked.

Charlie sighed as he remembered the lost BlackBerry. "They must have taken it, unless it fell out when they grabbed me. Either way, I'll have to get a replacement on Monday. Assuming I'm back at the office on Monday."

"What are you going to do? You can't stay in Berlin indefinitely."

Charlie was wondering the same thing. He was due at the office on Monday morning, but for all he knew the cops might already be looking for him. Why hadn't he called the police when he left Yermolov's apartment? Or after he had been snatched off the street, instead of rabbiting to Berlin? How was it that he always found himself alone?

You can't run forever.

"I don't know what I'm doing anymore," he said after a long silence. "All I wanted was to escape to a nice, quiet career in the Foreign Service. See a bit of the world, do some good and put in my time for the pension. I don't know how everything got so fucked up." He was feeling the effects of the scotch as he finished his second glass. "I'm sorry."

She put her hand on his arm. "What about the Canadian Embassy in Berlin? Surely you can talk to someone there."

He nodded, feeling suddenly exhausted. "That's what I'll do," he said with little conviction as he tried to imagine a plausible explanation for his actions.

"We've got another couple of hours," Sophie said, putting her seat back. "I might try and get some shut-eye."

"Sweet dreams," he said, closing his eyes and trying not to think about his status as a fugitive, imagining instead that he and Sophie were on a vacation together. But try as he might, he couldn't shake the feeling of dread as he looked over his shoulder again and scanned the cabin behind him. Sophie had pulled the thin, blue blanket over her shoulders, and he envied her as she dozed peacefully.

CHAPTER 27

Charlie skewered the last of a syrup-covered sausage and popped it into his mouth before setting the fork down and pushing the plate away. He had made a pig of himself at the buffet, but he didn't care. The flight had been ahead of schedule, and with the time change, they had made it to the hotel before 1:00 a.m. He'd been able to book a room for himself.

Despite the nap on the plane, Charlie had slept for a good seven hours before showering and heading downstairs for breakfast. But if he was hoping a good sleep would change his outlook, he was wrong. In the light of day, his situation seemed even worse. So much so that he had briefly considered checking out and getting on the next flight back to Moscow. He sipped the strong coffee and looked out the window at all the Mercedes, BMWs, and Porsches sliding by on Ebertstrasse, the morning sun glinting off their high-gloss metal skins. He noticed the thin layer of white on the ground from an overnight snowfall as he glanced across the street toward Leipziger Platz and the Canadian flag flapping from the top of one of the newer buildings. There was no avoiding the chat he was going to have to have with the embassy's security officer.

"Deep in thought?"

He looked up to see Sophie standing over him, her auburn hair tied back in a tight ponytail. She had traded in her jeans and sweater for form-fitting athletic wear that made her even more attractive, if that was possible. He tossed his napkin over the remnants of his fatty breakfast and waved to the chair opposite him.

"Morning."

"Sleep well?" she asked, taking a seat as a server appeared with a fresh carafe of coffee.

He waited until their cups were filled, then replied, "Yes. You?"

"Like a baby." She looked out the window to where Charlie had been staring and spotted the flag. "Is that the Canadian Embassy?"

He nodded.

"Are you going to go talk to someone there?"

"Maybe later," he said, sipping his coffee.

"I don't want you to get into any trouble, Charlie."

"I'll be fine. Any word from Steve's girlfriend here?"

"She wants to meet at noon. She lives near Friedrichstrasse station, if you know where that is."

"Not sure, but I think it's pretty central. We can get the S-Bahn over there." He motioned across the street to the Metro station. "It's probably only a couple of stops."

"What is it?" he asked, sensing her sudden preoccupation.

"Did Steve mention her to you at all?"

"The German girlfriend?" Charlie asked, sipping his coffee. "No, why?"

"I was just wondering. It feels kind of awkward given we just talked to another girlfriend in Moscow. I can't say I'm surprised. I just hope he wasn't misleading anyone."

"Maybe they weren't exclusive," Charlie said, trying to sound knowledgeable about current dating practices.

"I guess dating isn't what it used to be."

Charlie laughed.

"What's so funny?"

"Nothing," he said. "You make it sound like you're eighty or something."

"I guess it could be worse," she said with a grin. Charlie said nothing as he finished his coffee, thinking the statement sounded ridiculous coming from her — young, beautiful, and a successful surgeon to boot.

"What are you smirking about now?" Sophie asked.

"What?" Charlie set his cup down, wondering if his expression had somehow betrayed what he was thinking.

"You have this ... look." Something about the way she was staring at him made him laugh again. Her severe expression broke into her own smirk, followed by a full-blown smile that lit her face. "You're pretty chipper for a guy who's off the reservation," she added.

"I'm just a guy enjoying a weekend in Berlin," he said, maintaining his smile. "Until Monday, that is — then I'm officially AWOL."

She nodded. "You're right. All we have to do is figure this all out over the weekend and we're golden." She raised her glass of orange juice in a salute before taking a sip.

They took the S-Bahn from Potsdamer Platz and got off at Friedrichstrasse. Walking down from the upper platform into the central part of the station, they were overwhelmed by the smell of coffee and pastries. Outside, the sun was shining on a beautiful fall day as they made their way east over the river Spree and toward the address. They found it in a side street a few blocks past the river — a four-storey building connected on either side to buildings whose facades were much better maintained. The rack by the front door, overflowing with bicycles of every description, gave the impression of a student dorm, but Charlie remembered that lots of people rode bikes in Berlin, not just students. They scanned the directory outside the front door, and Sophie pressed the button next to "Donner, H."

They waited for a response, but when it came, it wasn't from the little microphone, but from somewhere over their heads. They stepped back and looked up to see a woman's dark hair waving in the wind as she leaned over a little balcony on the fourth floor.

"Hello?"

"Heidi?" Sophie looked up. "I'm Sophie Durant, and this is my friend Charlie," she said as he gave the young woman his most reassuring smile. "Can we come up?"

Heidi disappeared above the rail and a few seconds later, the entrance door began to buzz. The four flights of stairs took them a couple of minutes, during which time Charlie tried to focus on his breathing and avoid staring at Sophie's Lycra-clad backside as she gracefully took each step with ease. As they reached the fourth-floor landing, a door opened and a young woman in her late twenties appeared in jeans and a hoodie, her wavy black hair tied back in a hurried ponytail.

"Come in."

"Thanks for meeting us on a Saturday," Sophie said as she and Charlie made their way inside.

"It's no problem," Heidi said, her English enveloped in the singsong edge of her native German. "Come, let's sit down." She led the way past the cluttered entrance into a small living area that brought to mind an IKEA display after an especially hectic Saturday. Sophie and Charlie sat on a couch as Heidi took the chair opposite, curling her legs up under her. "I'm so sorry to hear about Steven."

"Thank you," Sophie said. "Did you know him well?"

Charlie sensed the unspoken communication between the two women as Heidi hesitated. "We were friends," she eventually said. "At one time, we were more than that, but when Steven decided to move to Moscow, we ... well, you know how it is."

Sophie gave a sad smile, and Charlie wondered if it was because her brother had never told her about Heidi. It seemed to Charlie that there was a lot the brother and sister didn't know about each other.

"He never told you about us," Heidi continued. "But he talked about you often. He was very proud of you."

Sohie's words seemed to catch in her throat as she spoke. "How did you ... hear about Steve's death?"

"One of his former colleagues here in Berlin is a mutual friend. He was in touch with the Moscow office where Steven worked. He thought I should know." She changed position on the couch. "I knew you were a surgeon in Toronto, so I found your contact information online so I could offer my — how do you say? — condolences. I hope you don't mind."

"Of course not," Sophie said. "It was very kind of you."

"I have a younger brother myself and ..."

A silence descended over the room for a few seconds before Heidi sprang to her feet. "I made coffee. Would you like some?"

They accepted, and she returned a few minutes later with a tray laden with an assortment of brightly patterned enamel mugs, a French press full of rich-smelling coffee, and a little plate of biscuits.

"Do you know what happened to him?" Heidi asked as she pushed the coffee plunger down slowly.

"Just that he died in police custody. He had been picked up at a party on some trumped-up drug charge."

Heidi snorted in disgust as she poured the coffee into the mugs and passed them over. "That's ridiculous. Steven was no drug dealer, and he would have known better than to get involved with them in Moscow, of all places."

Sophie nodded. "How did your friend say he died?"

"He didn't, really." Heidi sipped her coffee and looked at them both before continuing. "The Moscow office said his death was under investigation, but that it seemed like an accident."

"The official line is suicide." Sophie drank from her coffee. "Which is total bullshit."

Heidi nodded. "I think we both know Steven would never do that. He was so full of life." She reached for a tissue and blew her nose.

"When was the last time you saw Steve?" Charlie asked after giving Heidi a moment.

"About three months ago," she said, nodding again as she recalled the time frame. "I saw him in a coffee shop around the corner. He was sitting there, in the corner, working on his laptop. I almost didn't want to interrupt, he looked so ... intent, and we hadn't seen each other since we split up. But he saw me and gave me that big smile of his." She seemed absorbed by the scene as Sophie and Charlie looked on in silence. "I should have known he would be as kind as he always was. I really loved him, do you know?"

Charlie noticed that Sophie seemed to be struggling to maintain her own composure, so he decided to pitch in again.

"Did he say what he was doing in Berlin?"

"He said he was working on something, but he didn't really say what. I got the impression it was outside of his regular work in Moscow, though."

"Why do you say that?"

"I don't think he enjoyed his work very much. He always said technical writing and translation was boring."

"It's the last thing I would ever have thought he'd be doing," Sophie said with a smile.

Heidi smiled back. "Exactly. Steven was much more of a free spirit, and it showed. But he seemed very passionate about whatever he was working on that day. We were together for months and I don't ever remember him working on the weekend or bringing work to a coffee shop. He used to make fun of people who did that."

"That's Steve," Sophie said, then her smile faded. "You said he had a laptop?"

"Yes." Heidi paused, as they both looked on in anticipation. "What is it?"

"It's just that there was no laptop among his things, either at his apartment or office," Charlie said. "It's possible he sold it or it broke, I suppose."

"I don't think he would have sold it," Heidi said. "He loved it. He stored all his music and work on it."

"He didn't say if he was writing anything, did he?" Sophie asked. "He was always going on about wanting to write a novel."

"He told me the same thing, and I wondered if that was what he was working on, but he really didn't say. We chatted for a while, laughed, and then I left him there, after we promised to stay in touch. Now I'll never see him again." Her eyes glistened with tears. The three of them drank their coffee and talked for another fifteen minutes or so, Charlie and Sophie asking questions and not learning much of particular interest.

"Thank you for meeting us on such short notice," Sophie said at last, rising to her feet. "We really appreciate it."

"Of course. If there's anything I can do ... well, you know how to reach me."

At the door, Sophie asked, "When you saw Steve in the coffee shop that day, he didn't say where he was staying, did he?"

"In Berlin? No, but you might want to check with Gunther."

"Gunther?"

"He and Steven used to work together, before your brother went to Moscow. They were good friends, and I'm sure if Steven was in town, he would probably have stayed there."

"I don't suppose you have his contact information?"

"Just a minute," Heidi said, disappearing back into the kitchen and returning after a few seconds of rustling noises. "Here's his card. His mobile is on the back." A frown creased her brow. "I probably should have called him. I don't know if he knows that Steven ..." She trailed off.

"Don't worry," Sophie said. "I'll tell him. It was really nice to meet you, Heidi. I can see why Steve liked you."

The two women shared a brief hug at the door, and Charlie waited until they were back outside before looking at Sophie.

"Are you okay?"

She nodded. "I just need some air. Let's walk down to the river."

They walked in silence back toward Friedrichstrasse, then down along by the water. The bright sunlight was enough to take the edge off the cold, and the walking path was full of strollers.

"You sure you're all right?" Charlie asked when Sophie came to a stop and leaned up against the rail. A tour boat glided by, a smattering of tourists snapping pictures from the top deck.

"I could ask you the same thing," she said, fixing him with those green eyes. "We're quite a pair. Me trying to find out what those bastards did to Steve, you trying to figure out whether you can go back to Moscow without being arrested." She gave a grim laugh and looked back out over the water.

"You're thinking about the laptop?"

"I'm thinking how little I knew about my kid brother. I wasn't a very good sister."

"Don't do that to yourself. You had separate lives. Steve was the one who chose to roam around Eastern Europe. You can hardly blame yourself if you didn't know every detail about his life."

"That's true," she said. "I was the one who stayed close to home. I did all the family dinners, attended all the functions, pretended to be happily married — but in the end it didn't matter, and why should it have? Everyone loved Steve."

"He loved you, too, Sophie. Didn't you hear what Heidi said? What they all say."

They stood in silence for a while, leaning on the rail.

"Well, there was clearly something on that laptop that Steve, or someone else, didn't want anyone to see," she said.

"Maybe it was stolen, taken by some unscrupulous cop or prison official who was only interested in pawning the laptop itself." He stopped when he noticed her expression. "All right. Suppose there *was* something on it?"

"I've got to find out what he was working on." She looked out at the river. "I agree with Heidi — it seems odd for him to be working on a weekend. Plus, he would have been in town for a few days. I would have thought he'd spend some time in his favourite beer hall."

Charlie nodded. "So let's talk to this Gunther guy."

"Maybe he knows something we don't," Sophie said, fishing out her cellphone and punching in the number on the back of the card. Charlie could tell from her expression that she had gotten his voice mail. After she had left a message with her number, she put the phone away and slipped on her sunglasses.

"Come on, let's keep walking," she said, turning away from the rail. "I don't know about you, but I could do with the exercise."

"Sure," Charlie said, thinking that *he* was the one who needed exercise. He had been breathless by the time she had floated effortlessly up Heidi's stairs. "The Tiergarten's this way. You game?"

"Why not?"

As they set off again, Charlie couldn't help a smile. He might be personally adrift, his career on the line and possibly wanted by the Moscow police for murder, but there still seemed no place he would rather be at that very moment.

CHAPTER 28

They were sitting in the glassed-in section of the restaurant, overlooking the green expanse of the Tiergarten, when Sophie's cellphone rang.

"Sophie Durant," she said, snatching it up from the table. Charlie looked on to see if it might be the anticipated call from Gunther and was surprised when she passed him the phone. "It's for you."

"Uh, hello?" he said, wondering who would be calling him via Sophie. His stomach sank as he heard the voice of Bob Rouleau, the head of security at the Canadian Embassy in Moscow.

"Charlie, where the hell are you? We've been trying to reach you all last night and this morning. Do you still have your BlackBerry?"

"I forgot I'd turned it off last night," he lied. "What's up?" He preferred not to mention his whereabouts for the time being.

"The Moscow police want to question you in connection with a murder that happened Thursday night — a man named Sergei Yermolov. They say they got a tip that you were at the crime scene." Charlie waited for more detail before saying anything.

"You need to come in right away so we can talk about this. We'll need to consult with Justice and arrange an interview with the police as soon as possible. When can you be at the embassy?"

"Uh, I'm not actually in Moscow," Charlie said, wondering how much he should be saying on a cellphone. Then again, the Russians, and Rouleau for that matter, had only to check his passport data or the GPS in Sophie's phone to find out where he was. "I'm in Berlin."

"Berlin? What are you doing there?" Rouleau said, and although his question followed a brief pause, he didn't sound surprised by the news, which made Charlie think he had checked his passport activity first.

"I just came for the weekend."

"With the Durant woman?" The tone said everything.

"I'll be back tomorrow evening. Can it wait until then?"

"No, it can't, and if we don't deal with this today, you'll be detained when you fly into Domodedovo tomorrow." Charlie waited while there was a rustling at the other end, then Rouleau's voice returned. "I'm going to give you the number for my counterpart in Berlin. I want you to call him as soon as you hang up and arrange to meet at the mission there this afternoon. We'll set up a secure conference call and deal with this."

"Okay." Charlie was nodding and apparently looking as worried as he felt, if Sophie's expression across the table was any indication. He took out a pen and scribbled the number on a napkin.

"Call him right away, Charlie. Understood?"

"Yeah, sure," Charlie said, wondering what Rouleau was thinking, or what he had been told by the Moscow police. Was it possible that he thought Charlie might actually have murdered someone? "Listen, Bob, I don't know what's going on, but I've done nothing wrong."

"I didn't say you did, but we need to straighten this thing out as soon as we can. The sooner you get in touch with the security head there, the better."

"You're making me nervous, Bob."

"That's not my intent, but you have to realize this is a serious matter. And we have to follow standard procedure."

"Of course. I'll call right away."

"And, Charlie?"

"Yeah?"

"Make you sure you turn your BlackBerry on."

He hung up the phone and handed it back to Sophie.

"Who was that?"

"The head of security for the embassy in Moscow. He doesn't sound too happy with me. He wants me to go to the embassy here and basically turn myself in. I think I might be ... fucked."

"You did nothing wrong, other than try to help —" She was interrupted by the ring of her phone.

"That's probably him again."

"Sophie Durant. Yes ... Gunther? Thanks for calling me back. I'm Steve Liepa's sister."

Charlie watched her as she answered the next question awkwardly. "He's ... well, I'm afraid he died last week, in Moscow." There was a pause as Gunther apparently digested this information. "I'm in Berlin and I wonder whether you could spare me a few minutes...." Another pause. Then, "I'm in the Tiergarten right now. The ... yes, well, I can find it. Prenzlauer Berg ... yes." She was scribbling furiously as she nodded. "I'll be there as soon as I can."

She disconnected and waved at the server. "He says it's about half an hour by S-Bahn. Did you want to call your embassy contact?" She held out the phone.

Charlie stared at it for a second before answering. What difference did it make if he turned himself in now or later this afternoon? "I think I'll come along for the ride, if that's all right with you."

Sophie and Charlie walked into the crowded restaurant and made their way to the bar. It was only mid-afternoon, but the clientele was mostly students, and the preferred order mostly beer, so it seemed like the sort of place that could really get hopping early on a Saturday and go long into the night. Sophie was looking toward the rear corner of the room when a tall, dark-haired man in his thirties approached her from the other end of the bar.

"Ms. Durant?"

"Yes?"

"Gunther Volkmann. I have a table for us in the corner."

"Charlie." Charlie extended his hand and the German shook it, then led them to a booth at the far end of the bar.

"I am very sorry to hear about Steven," Volkmann began, as they sat. "He was a good friend and will be missed."

"Thank you," Sophie said, slipping off her coat. Charlie did the same. The crush of young bodies filling the place made the air seem close and stuffy. "We appreciate your meeting with us like this."

Volkmann nodded. "Have you come from Moscow?"

"Yes. I'm on my way back to Canada, and Charlie …" She paused uncertainly.

"I'm with the Canadian Embassy in Moscow," Charlie supplied. "I'm assisting Sophie."

She brought Volkmann up to speed on the official version of her brother's death, at the end of which she said, "I gather you believe he was a drug trafficker as much as I do, but the Russian authorities are sticking to their official version."

"This, at least, is not surprising," Volkmann said as the server delivered their drinks.

"You've worked in Moscow?" she asked.

Volkmann shook his head. "Not personally, but I know several colleagues who have spent time there over the years — you hear things." He paused and then raised his glass. Sophie and Charlie took their cue and did the same.

"To Steven," Volkmann said, and his solemn toast was followed by an awkward silence. Charlie decided to break it first.

"We're trying to find out as much as we can about Steve's activities in the past few months, and we've noticed he spent a lot of time in Berlin."

"We were hoping," Sophie interjected, "that you might be able to tell us more about what he was doing."

Volkmann set his beer down and met her gaze. "I will tell you everything I know, of course, but I fear you will be disappointed."

"What do you mean?"

"I think ... I know Steven was working on something very important to him. I knew him for some time and yet I never knew that side of him. He seemed almost obsessed with whatever he was doing. But he never told me what it was."

"Was he writing a book?"

"He was writing something." Volkmann nodded. "He spent every moment with his laptop. Did he tell you he was writing a book?"

"No, but you're not the first person to mention the laptop," she said, looking at Charlie.

Volkmann followed her gaze and frowned. "What is it?"

"It's just that the laptop wasn't at his apartment or office," Sophie said.

"He preferred to leave it at my place, rather than bring it to Moscow," Gunther said, reaching under the table and bringing out a small duffel bag. "He said he didn't trust the locks on his apartment door in Moscow. He left some personal things, too. I brought them for you."

"You have his laptop?" Sophie said, with something close to disbelief. She hesitated before taking the bag.

"It's mostly clothes," Volkmann continued. "But he had a rucksack that he always carried his computer in."

Sophie opened the bag and looked inside, pulling out the little canvas bag with the laptop inside. Aside from it, the duffel contained mostly clothes — a sweatshirt, a couple of T-shirts, and a pair of jeans. There were a half-dozen books and some toiletries. She plucked a balled-up T-shirt from the bag and unfolded it, staring at the logo of the Toronto Maple Leafs.

"I bought him this," she said with a grim smile. "The last time he was in Toronto. It was around his birthday and I got us a pair of Leafs tickets at centre ice. We went out to dinner, took in the game, and I bought him this while he was lined up to get us a couple of beers. We had such a good time." She hesitated, the T-shirt held tightly in her hands as she stared at the crest, then rolled it up and put it back in the bag.

"I'm very sorry," Volkmann said. "I wish I knew more about what he was working on."

"Me, too," Sophie said, unzipping the canvas bag and retrieving the silver laptop from a padded case. She opened it and turned it on as Volkmann and Charlie looked on.

"Shit, it's password protected," she said with a sigh, flipping the laptop around so they could see.

Volkmann pointed to the screen. "I can get through that — if you want me to, that is."

"It's that easy?" Charlie looked at Volkmann, who smiled.

"If your job is computer security, then yes," he replied, and when Sophie nodded, he turned the laptop toward himself and started tapping keys. A few clicks later, he was on Steve's desktop, the background a photo of a sunset over water. He turned the screen to Sophie.

"I have that picture somewhere," she said. "Steve took it himself." She stared at the screen for a moment before turning it so all three of them could see. "Let's see what he had on here." She launched the explorer function and brought up the documents stored on the hard drive. She flipped through a series of folders, some of which contained what looked like technical manuals, others miscellaneous correspondence and emails. She paused as the cursor hovered over a folder entitled *MC*.

"Does that mean something to you?" Charlie asked.

She shook her head as she clicked it open. "No, but it's empty, anyway." She frowned and went back to the desktop and, after clicking around for a few more minutes, she gave up.

"Well, that's not much help," she said.

Volkmann looked at his watch. "I should really be going. If there's anything I can do, or if I find anything else of Steve's at my place, I'll let you know."

"Thank you, Gunther," she said. "I really appreciate this." She looked at the bag as Volkmann stood to go.

"And I'm very sorry for your loss," he added as he turned to leave.

Sophie and Charlie sat at the table in silence for a while after Volkmann had gone, then Sophie reached into the bag and pulled out the handful of paperbacks and spread them on the table. The first two were mysteries, but the rest were non-fiction — true crime and books about the drug trade, biker gangs, and the like. Charlie picked up one entitled *Global Mafia*.

"It looks like Steve had an interest in investigative journalism," he said, flipping through the book.

"I guess so," Sophie said, picking up another on the drug trade. "Interesting that none of these were in his Moscow apartment, don't you think?"

Charlie tried to recall what type of books they *had* found in Liepa's bachelor pad — mostly novels, apart from the technical manuals he was translating. "You think that's because he didn't want to give anyone in Moscow any clues as to what he was working on?"

"That's apparently why he left his laptop here in Berlin," she said, pointing to the computer. "Though there doesn't seem to be much on it."

Charlie frowned, then pulled the laptop closer. "Do you mind?"

"Be my guest."

Charlie scanned the desktop, located the icon for the word-processing program, and clicked on it. Sophie looked on as they waited for the program to open. Once a blank document appeared on the page, Charlie clicked around under the file button until a drop-down list appeared.

"What's that?"

"It's the list of recent documents — the ones Steve would have opened lately," he said, scanning the list of about ten names, most of which were files Sophie had already looked up on her search of the computer's file directories. The titles were everything from *groceries* to *itinerary*. He clicked on the link to the document entitled *itinerary,* but it came up blank. As did a document entitled simply *MC.*

"The same name as the empty folder on the hard drive," Sophie said, looking over his shoulder with interest.

"Except this is a reference to an actual file. The path is to the E: directory — must have been a USB. I'm curious about this itinerary. Look at the date."

"It's just before Steve went to Paris."

Charlie nodded, then right-clicked on the second path, which brought up the properties of the document entitled *MC.* He leaned closer to the screen.

"What is it?"

"Look at the size of this thing," he said, pointing to the line that showed the document was almost five hundred kilobytes. The shopping list, by comparison, was under ten. He clicked back into the main directory and pulled up a translation of almost thirty pages and checked its size — it was less than two hundred kilobytes.

"Whatever it was, it was fifty or sixty pages long."

"*MC* — it's got to be someone's initials, but whose?" Sophie reached for the canvas bag and searched inside. "I don't suppose we'd be lucky enough to find the USB stick in here."

"What about the duffel?" Charlie asked when her search turned up only a few pens, a pack of gum, and some Post-it Notes. She searched all the pockets and turned up nothing of interest, other than a four-inch, soft rubber bear with "Berlin" stamped across the belly. Charlie had seen them in the airport gift shop — the city's mascot.

"It's not in here," she said with a sigh, tossing the bear back into the bag. She was staring at the Maples Leafs shirt still on the table in front of her when Charlie put his hand on her arm.

"We'll find it, don't worry. And we'll get to the bottom of this, one way or the other, I promise."

She looked at him and gave a feeble smile before balling up the T-shirt and putting it and the rest of all that remained of her brother back into the bag.

CHAPTER 29

Charlie sat in the fourth-floor conference room, waiting for the return of the security officer. He glanced at the digital thermostat and was surprised to see that it was a couple of degrees below normal room temperature. He felt warm all over.

"Sorry about that, but I was waiting to print this off." Tom Edwards was younger than Charlie by at least a decade, and his loose-fitting fleece vest did nothing to conceal his athletic build. Charlie wasn't sure if Edwards was with Defence or RCMP, but he had no problem imagining him with an assault rifle or Mountie-issue Beretta in hand.

"This is the latest from Moscow," Edwards said, taking a seat opposite Charlie and pointing at the sheet of paper. "It seems the local police want to have a talk with you, and they're being pretty insistent. I understand you've talked to Moscow this morning, so you know what this is about?"

Charlie gave a nod.

"Before we go any further, you should know that if you were involved in the death of a local on Russian soil, the consequences —"

"I wasn't involved in anything. I just happened to show up at his place when he —"

Edwards put up a hand. "We'll get to that. I just want to make sure you understand the situation, that's all. You may want to consider hiring a lawyer."

"I appreciate the warning, but I'm a lawyer myself. I know my rights." There was an awkward pause, and Charlie knew he had sounded far too defensive. There was also the fact that what he knew about criminal law in Canada could fit on half a cocktail napkin and was out of date by about fifteen years. As for Russia ...

"You're a lawyer?"

Charlie felt the colour rising to his cheeks, as Edwards continued.

"I haven't seen your file, so I didn't know. Anyway, you obviously understand why we have to be careful."

"I do, so what's the plan for my return to Moscow?"

"We'll get to that. Can I ask you why you left?"

"I'm allowed to do what I want on my free time," Charlie said, feigning indignation and trying to stay away from the subject of his capture and interrogation the day before. "Last time I checked, it was a free country — Canada, I mean."

Edwards nodded. "It's just that, given your alleged attendance at a murder scene on Thursday night, it might look a bit suspicious ... to the Russians. Why didn't you mention any of this to the Moscow mission?"

"What am I supposed to say? I went to see Yermolov to ask him some questions about a consular case I'm working on and found him dead." Charlie sighed. "To be honest, I was a bit shaken up. I would have mentioned it to the mission in due course, but I thought a little break might be —"

Charlie was glad for the interruption of Edwards's BlackBerry, realizing how implausible his version of events sounded. Edwards answered the call and glanced at Charlie as he spoke, then read off the number for the speakerphone sitting on the table in front of them before hanging up.

"That was the head of mission in Moscow. She wants to talk to you ... to us."

Charlie felt his chest deflate. He was trying very hard to think of an explanation as the phone rang and Edwards answered.

"Charlie, are you there?"

"Hello, Brigitte. I'm really sorry if I —"

"You damn well better be!" she snapped. "Do you have any idea what's been going on here in the past twenty-four hours? I've been on the phone with the MFA all morning, trying to respond to their inquiries. Just what the hell do you think you're doing, running off to Berlin without telling anyone? And why haven't you been answering your phone?"

Charlie groaned. He was going to have to tell her sooner or later. "I lost it."

"You lost it? *Again*?"

"I know it sounds ridiculous, but I can explain."

"That's the least of your worries, trust me. I've talked to HQ and I think it's best that you don't try to return to Moscow until we've sorted this thing out. I've got to talk to the Legal branch, but frankly, regardless of what they say, I don't think anyone can guarantee anything when it comes to what the Russians have in mind for you if you return."

Charlie felt relief at the news that he might stay in Berlin for a little longer, though it really wasn't due to a fear of the Russians. Martineau seemed to guess his thoughts at the other end of the line.

"Where are you staying, anyway?"

"Just across the street."

"And the Durant woman?"

"Same hotel," Charlie replied quickly, wondering whether he should specify that they were in different rooms.

"Charlie, I hope you haven't forgotten this is a consular case. I don't need to tell you that —"

"Please. We're at the same hotel, but that's it. And I don't think I've done anything wrong, either in relation to the Liepa case or otherwise. The only thing I didn't do was report my presence at a crime scene, and I'm sorry about that, but I wasn't thinking straight. To be honest, I was pretty shaken. I promise you, I had nothing to do with Yermolov's death."

"Nobody is saying you did." There was a long pause while Martineau seemed to be collecting her thoughts and Charlie tried to avoid eye contact with Edwards. "Can we get Charlie a temporary BlackBerry, Tom? I want to able to reach him on an urgent basis."

"Not a problem," Edwards said. "I'll set him up before he leaves this afternoon."

"And you're going to give a statement now, Charlie, is that correct?"

"Yes," Charlie said.

"Good, that will be helpful in my discussions with HQ."

"And after I've given my statement? What do you want me to do?" Charlie glanced across the table but Edwards was giving nothing away.

"Stay close to your BlackBerry, though it'll probably be Monday before we know for sure what approach to take."

When the call ended, Charlie stared at the saucer phone in the middle of the conference-room table, as Edwards turned over a fresh sheet of paper and clicked his pen.

"Let's get started."

It was after five by the time Charlie walked out of the
embassy into Leipziger Platz and headed around the corner
toward the hotel. Anyone examining his posture could easily
tell he was carrying the weight of the world on his shoulders
as he shuffled along the sidewalk, his hands jammed into his
pockets and his collar pulled up against the cold wind. He
crossed the road by the S-Bahn station and made his way
into the lane leading to the hotel, his mind preoccupied with
deconstructing the statement he had just given, as well as
the conference call with Brigitte Martineau. Just how pissed
off was she, exactly? He wondered whether it was enough to
have him shipped back to Ottawa on the next available flight.

Then it occurred to him that even if his employer did
decide he'd done nothing wrong, that didn't mean the
Russians would come to the same conclusion. And if they
didn't, he would have no choice but to return to headquarters. Official status: early termination of posting. Actual
status: pariah.

He rode the elevator up to the fifth floor and headed for his
room. As he opened the door, he saw an envelope on the car-
pet just inside the entrance. He stooped to pick it up and made
his way over to the bed, where he tossed his coat. He was
opening the envelope when he noticed the message light on
his hotel phone flashing. He ignored it for now and focused
on the contents of the envelope, pulling out a sheet of hotel
stationery on which a message was scribbled in pen: *Come by
my room when you get back.* He stared at Sophie's signature
and for a moment, he imagined what it would be like to be
on the receiving end of such a message if the motivation were
for something other than the need to get to the bottom of
her brother's death. He moved to the phone and dialled the
message service to discover he had three. He went through
them one by one, all from Sophie and all saying basically the

same thing, with increasing urgency — get in touch with her ASAP. He dialled her room and she answered after the second ring, a distinctly frantic tone in her voice.

"Charlie? Where were you? My God, I was so worried."

"Why? I told you I had to go to the embassy for a meeting."

"But that was hours ago. I thought something had happened to you. Is everything okay?"

"That's a tough one."

"You're not in trouble for leaving with me, are you?"

"No, it's not that," he said, wondering what her reaction would be if she knew Martineau had suggested that the two of them might be intimately involved. "Is everything okay with you?"

"I found something in Steve's stuff that I'd like to get your take on. Can you drop by?"

"I'll be right there."

He hung up the phone and caught his reflection in the mirror as he passed it. He looked like shit. After a quick detour to splash some cold water in his face in the bathroom sink, he felt a little revived and set off for Sophie's room.

The first thing he noticed when she opened the door was that she had let her hair down. He was used to seeing it in a braid or a ponytail, and the effect was unfamiliar, though she looked no less beautiful. Quite the opposite, in fact. The second thing he noticed, as she led him into her room, was how big it was compared to his own.

"I was going through a couple of books that were among his things," she said as she sat on the edge of the king-size bed and picked up a book, "when I found this." She flipped the book open to the last page and pulled out a brochure with a picture of what looked like a Mediterranean villa. The caption was in French.

Charlie took the brochure and scanned it quickly.

"It's for a French school in a place called Villefranche," he said, remembering that someone at HQ had tried to get a six-month training stint approved there a few years ago. It was rejected out of hand because of the cost, a lot of which had to do with the location in the south of France. "I thought Steve already spoke French."

"He did." She shrugged. "Maybe it was a refresher course."

"Yeah," Charlie said, though it seemed unlikely. He couldn't think why else Liepa would have the brochure among his things, unless ...

"What?" Sophie seemed able to see the wheels turning in Charlie's mind.

"I checked my secure email account before leaving the embassy," he said. "There was a message from one of the trade guys I'd asked to look into some offshore accounts — you remember all that stuff that's been in the news?"

"The tax dodgers?"

"Exactly. I asked them to check out other shareholders of the companies that Dmitri Bayzhanov held stock in. It turns out that Alexander Surin had shares in one of the same companies — Kvartal."

"You mean the guy on the planning committee," she said. "The one that just approved Petr Square?"

Charlie nodded. "Which just happens to be Bayzhanov's project."

"That must be it. Steve must have found the connection between Bayzhanov and Surin and then ..." She paused, noticing his frown. "You don't think so?"

"Petr Square was only approved yesterday, so how could Steve have known if Surin was in Bayzhanov's pocket a month ago? Besides, it doesn't add up that someone would want to kill Steve for that — I mean, corruption's not exactly uncommon in Moscow."

Now it was her turn to frown. "But what does that have to do with this?" she said, gesturing at to the brochure.

"Maybe nothing," he replied, pulling out the new BlackBerry he had just been issued and searching the internal employee directory for Drew Landon, his former colleague in Havana.

"What are you doing?" Sophie looked on.

"Playing a hunch," he said, selecting Landon's email from the list and thumbing a quick message. He looked at his watch and noted the time. "What's your cell number?" Sophie gave it to him without asking why and he sent his message. "I'm asking a former colleague to give me a call. I'd rather it not be on this." He indicated his BlackBerry. "His name's Drew Landon. He's posted in Paris now."

They were still discussing the Surin-Bayzhanov connection a few minutes later when her cell rang and she snatched it up.

"Hello? Yes, he is," she said, passing the phone to Charlie.

"I figured you'd be watching your emails, but I didn't think you'd be back to me that quick."

"How the hell are you? I've been meaning to touch base with you." Landon's voice had the same enthusiasm Charlie remembered. "I knew you were in Moscow. How's it going?"

"It's going well," he lied. "How about you? Paris, eh? Sounds rough."

Landon laughed. "It's not all croissants and Côtes du Rhône, you know."

"I'm sure it isn't." Charlie continued the banter for a minute before broaching the subject of the call. "Listen, I was hoping you could do me a favour."

"Name it, and I'll do my best."

"Can you check passport numbers at French entry points?"

Landon paused to consider the question. "I'm pretty sure we can get that from the French, sure. This a consular case?"

"Yeah, the only wrinkle is it's a Russian national, not a Canadian."

"Oh," Landon said, and Charlie's spirits sank. "That might be different, but I'll give it a try. I'll have to talk to someone in immigration, but it's gonna be Monday now before I'll get a chance. When do you need this by?"

"As soon as you can."

"What's the name?"

"Krasnikov, Mikhail," Charlie said, noticing Sophie's puzzled reaction to the name.

"Leave it with me and I'll see what I can do. You want me to call this number back?"

"Yeah, that'd be best. I'm having some issues with my phone." He hated lying to Landon, but he didn't want to get into the details, or even the fact that he wasn't actually in Moscow at the moment. They said their goodbyes, disconnected, and Charlie handed the phone back to Sophie.

"Krasnikov?" she said. "The guy whose obituary and picture showed up at your office the other day?"

"He was in an accident abroad, but we don't know where. Maybe it was France."

"I guess it's worth a shot," she said, though she didn't seem convinced. "How did your interview go, anyway?"

"Looks like I'll be staying in Berlin, for a while, at least. They don't want me going back to Moscow tomorrow, after all. They say they can't predict what the Russians will do with me."

"That doesn't sound good."

Charlie laughed humourlessly. "I'm not sure what it means, to be honest. But the embassy here didn't lock me up, so I guess things could be worse."

"Well, I'm glad of that, at least." She looked at her watch. "I'm starving. Do you want to go get something to eat?"

"That's the best idea I've heard all day."

CHAPTER 30

"So, do you think you're in trouble?" Sophie asked as they sat in the corner of the bustling restaurant, the remnants of a heavy Bavarian meal on the plates in front of them, along with an empty bottle of a very nice red wine. Charlie swallowed the last bit of it from the bottom of his glass before answering.

"I don't see how," he said. "And, anyway," he added, perhaps emboldened by the buzz of alcohol, "I don't really care what they do to me for doing my job."

"What about the Russians?"

The question sobered him quickly. "That's different. Spending the rest of my posting, if not my life, in a Russian jail is not an option. There's no way I'm setting foot on a Moscow-bound plane unless this is sorted out."

"And how does it get sorted out?"

"We have to talk to Justice. We might arrange for my statement to be taken by the Russians here in Berlin. Assuming they're satisfied that I'm not their man, they could provide an iron-clad guarantee that they'll respect my immunity and I could go back."

She frowned. "That sounds like it could take some time."

He nodded as the server arrived and offered dessert menus, which they declined.

"I'm thinking a walk might be in order after that meal," Sophie said. Charlie nodded his agreement, though he thought she had barely touched her food. They settled the cheque after a brief dispute, during which she tried to pay for it all, and headed outside. It was still cool, but the wind had gone, and it was quite pleasant as they headed off toward a nearby park. They had been walking and chatting for about twenty minutes when they came upon a large white tent with the sounds of music and people coming from inside. As they got nearer, they noticed the colourful banner by the front entrance.

"Oktoberfest," Charlie said. "I guess it's that time of year."

"I thought that was only in Munich." Sophie shivered as the wind picked up.

"I guess this is the Berlin version. Appears to be on a much smaller scale. Want to check it out?"

"Why not," she said, rubbing her arms. "It's probably a lot warmer in there."

They entered the noisy tent, paid the small admission fee, and made their way across the uneven wooden floor toward the crowded main space. Two rows of long tables covered the whole floor area, apart from a large open area for dancing in front of the stage and the bar off to the left. The tent was three-quarters full, and a twenty-piece band was on stage, pumping out what sounded like German drinking songs. The crowd was a mix of all ages, with the only common theme being everyone seemed to have an array of enormous beer mugs on the table in front of them.

"Well, I guess I know what we're ordering," Sophie shouted over the music as they found a spot at the end of one of the long picnic-style tables. A woman in traditional dress walked by and said something in German. Charlie responded by pointing at the two full steins of beer she held in one hand and she was off, returning a few minutes later with their order.

"*Prost*," Charlie said, raising his stein. Sophie was wide-eyed at the size of hers, but she managed to hoist it without a problem. They sipped the cool, golden lager.

"Mmm, it's good," she said, wiping a thin ridge of foam from her top lip.

Charlie nodded his agreement, and they spent the next fifteen minutes shouting to each other across the table over the din of music, clinking glasses, and raucous toasts. Half of the crowd swarmed onto the dance floor in response to exhortations by the singer onstage. A few seconds later came the unmistakable first few notes of the bird dance.

"Come on," Sophie said, jumping up and grabbing Charlie by the hand. "We've got to give this a try."

Charlie went with her to the dance floor as the crowd did a pantomime of bird-walking. After an awkward first attempt, Charlie found himself catching on. Sophie seemed particularly adept, and they were both soon laughing and dancing in synch with the rest of the room. The dance went on for five minutes and concluded with an improvised conga line that weaved its way from the dance floor, between the tables, and toward the rear of the hall, then back again up the far side. When it was over, there was a roar of applause from the crowd and the band announced a short break.

"That was great," Sophie said when they returned to their table to gulp more beer. Charlie was amazed to see she was two-thirds done with her beer and he took a large gulp of his own to catch up. He put his stein down and sat back.

"Where'd you learn that dance?" he asked.

She laughed, and he saw her face in full glow, a broad smile curling the edge of her full lips and her eyes twinkling with genuine happiness.

"I had a boyfriend from Kitchener. He turned out to be a jerk, but he did take me to Oktoberfest one year. I guess I can thank him for that."

"You looked like a real pro up there."

"Not so bad yourself, Charlie. You're a quick study."

A passing server paused and looked at their glasses. Sophie glanced at Charlie before nodding at the woman.

"Why not?"

"I didn't know you spoke German." Sophie was giggling as they boarded the hotel elevator and the doors slid shut.

"I don't think I do," he said, referring to the garbled exchange with the smiling security guard out front. "Geez, is that the time?" He moved his wrist closer and squinted as the chime sounded to announce their arrival on the fifth floor. "I have a feeling I'm going to regret this in the morning."

"The night's still young," Sophie said, with a wave of her hand as they walked out into the hallway and headed to their rooms. They reached his first and he fumbled in his pocket for his key card. He didn't feel drunk — exactly — but he wasn't sure how many of those giant beers he had consumed. Whatever the number, Sophie had been his equal and she seemed pretty normal, if a little giggly.

"Well, good night to you." He tried an improvised bow.

"Don't be such a wimp."

"Wimp? What are you talking —"

"I'm going to explore my mini-bar. Least you can do is join me for a nightcap."

He watched as she moved to the other side of the hall and then slid her card in and unlocked her door. He shrugged and followed her inside. "What's with the presidential suite, anyway?" he cracked. "You could fit three of my rooms in this."

She chuckled. "Now, what do we have," she said, her head in the mini-bar, emerging a few seconds later with a couple of miniature rums and a can of Warsteiner. He accepted the beer and waved off her offer of a glass, watching as she poured the rum, then opened the fridge again and took out a Coke.

"That's probably a thirty-dollar rum and Coke you're having there," he remarked, prompting another giggle.

"Cheers." She tapped her glass off his can and then sat heavily on the couch in the little sitting area on one side of the room. Charlie took the adjacent chair, prompting a frown from Sophie. "I don't bite, you know," she said, sipping her drink. He laughed and moved onto the couch, next to her.

"Unless you're cornered."

"What's that supposed to mean?" Her back had straightened, but he could tell her outrage was feigned.

"I mean you're tough," he said with a smile.

"Just what every girl wants to be known as." She took another sip of her drink.

He nudged her arm with his elbow. "I mean it in a good way. You're … tenacious, and spirited," he added, noticing that she was looking at him as though trying to decide if he was screwing with her. "What?"

"Tenacious, spirited, and bites when cornered. You make me sound like a fucking wolverine or something."

He burst out laughing, causing her to do the same. "Okay, then," he said, "you're a big softie."

"That's no better."

"You see? You're impossible."

They shared another laugh, then she slid out of her soft shell jacket and kicked off her shoes before leaning back on the cushions. "Seriously, though. I really needed this ... tonight. It was fun."

He nodded, content to concentrate on the present, not what awaited him tomorrow. "Yes, it was." He watched as she slid one leg under the other and leaned forward. The base of her neck was slightly flushed and a silver pendant dangled over her chest, her blouse parting a little to reveal the black lace of her bra. She seemed to sense the attention and he quickly looked down at his beer and took a swallow. "I should go," he said, putting his beer down on the table. She set her drink next to his and edged closer. The scent of her perfume reached him and he could feel the heat of her body, though there was still a small gap between them.

"Thank you, Charlie."

"For what?"

"For tonight. For putting yourself on the line. For being there for me." She put her hand on his upper arm, sending shock waves down his spine, and then closed the gap between them. "I don't know what I'd have done without you."

"You don't have to —"

She put a finger across his lips to silence him, and then they were face to face and he was lost in those beautiful eyes, unable to move as she came closer and he felt her full lips press against his own, her intoxicating scent in his nose. He tried to speak, but all that came out was a groan as her hands pulled at his shirt and groped for his belt, his own travelling up the silky skin of her belly to the swell of her breasts. Before he knew what he was doing, he had hoisted her into his arms and carried her to the bed, their lips fused together as they tore away at clothes and collided in a frantic melee of flesh and hands, heat and urgency that consumed them both.

CHAPTER 31

Charlie knew he was dreaming, but it felt real nonetheless. He was bobbing in a lifeboat in stormy seas, peering over the crest of the nearest wave, squinting to see if he could spot land or another ship. He couldn't remember how he had gotten there or why he was alone in a lifeboat made for twenty. The sky was dark and unforgiving and his prospects looked bleak, but he wasn't afraid. In fact, he felt strangely at ease, as though he had come to the end of a very long journey and was ready for the peace that awaited him on the other side of the finish line.

He opened his eyes and a flash of white light made him slam them shut again. He was immediately struck by a throbbing in his head and a thickness in his sinuses, throat, and tongue that had him wondering whether he had ingested Drano. He tried opening his eyes again, fighting the light and the waves of dizziness that turned his stomach. He recognized the hotel furniture, but something wasn't quite right. The room seemed ... enormous. He turned his head slowly on the pillow and took a sharp intake of breath at the sight of Sophie Durant's auburn hair spread across the pillow next to him — and it all came back to him. He reached under the covers to confirm that he was, in fact, naked under them and, as he turned to look at her, he noticed that her back was bare.

Suddenly something shrill pierced the silence of the room and he recognized the sound of Sophie's phone. Bolting out of bed, he following the sound to the side table, grabbed the phone, and slid back under the sheet just as Sophie rolled over and opened her eyes a crack.

"It's your phone," he said, sensing she was coming awake in the same fog that he was still drifting through. She looked at him for a moment, then reached out for the phone.

"Hello?" she croaked. "Yes, just a minute." She put her hand over the receiver and handed the phone back to him. "It's your colleague in Paris."

"Drew?" he said, taking the phone.

"Charlie, I hope I didn't wake you," Landon began, sounding awkward, though it was nothing compared to what Charlie was feeling.

"No problem."

"You said you wanted to know ASAP and I have some news."

"Already?" Charlie glanced at the clock radio and realized it was after ten on Sunday morning. "But I thought you weren't going to even get a chance to look into this until Monday."

"I was out for drinks with one of my Aussie counterparts last night. Turns out he's dating someone at the French embassy who was able to get what you needed."

Charlie grinned. He remembered that Landon had a lot of friends among the Australian contingent in Havana, as well, not least because they knew how to party. "I see you're as resourceful as ever, Drew."

"It turns out your guy's passport was logged coming into Charles de Gaulle September third. No exit, though."

"You're sure?"

"Yeah, unless it was another Russian national named Mikhail Krasnikov," Landon said. "I suppose it's possible — the Côte d'Azur is crawling with Russians."

"Oh, yeah?"

"The ones with money, anyway. And there seems to be no shortage of them."

"And it was just the one entry in Paris, then?" Charlie frowned and rubbed his eyes.

"Yeah, so I assume it means your guy is still in France."

Or dead, Charlie thought.

"Listen, I've got to get going," Landon said. "We should keep in touch, though, and make sure you let me know if you're going to be in my neck of the woods."

"You bet. Thanks again, Drew." Charlie hung up the phone and set it gingerly on the night table, as though doing so might extricate him from what came next. He turned back toward Sophie, expecting to see her buried in the covers, waiting for him to slink off and never return. Instead she was propped up on one elbow, her hair tousled and her eyes a little bloodshot — neither detracting from her beauty.

"So?" she said.

"He confirmed that Krasnikov's passport was logged at the airport in Paris about a week before Steve's trip. There's no way to tell where he went from there, but there was no record of an exit."

"So your hunch was right," she said, pulling herself up and leaning back against the padded headboard, the sheet clinging to the tops of her breasts.

"Except we still don't know where … Wait a second." Charlie grabbed her laptop off the floor by the bed and opened it, clicking the browser into action and bringing up a map of the south of France, then zooming in on the stretch between Monaco to the east and Marseille to the west. "Where's Villefranche?" he asked, then spotted it — a little dot near Nice.

"That's the place on the brochure," Sophie said as Charlie opened a new search window and typed in *accident* and

Villefranche. He scanned the results and, seeing nothing of interest, he revised the search to include *Krasnikov,* again without success.

"Try taking out *Villefranche* and putting in the French word for *Russian,*" Sophie suggested. Charlie added *Russe* and they both scanned the results. Charlie went to close the browser and return to the map, but Sophie grabbed his hand.

"Wait!" She was pointing to the last in the series of search results. Charlie moved the cursor down and clicked on it. A few seconds later they were looking at an article from a paper called *Journal de Nice.* Charlie scanned the French text and realized it was describing an accident that had happened on the winding highway between Nice and Monaco. A sports car had gone through a roadside barrier and plummeted onto the rocks in the Mediterranean below. The sole occupant of the vehicle was pronounced dead at the scene and was later determined to be a vacationing Russian national, though no name was mentioned.

"That's got to be it," he said excitedly, translating the text as Sophie leaned in closer.

"Maybe Steve found something out down there that got him into trouble."

"Like, maybe Mikhail Krasnikov's death wasn't an accident?" She pointed to the screen. "Does it say anything in there about foul play?"

Charlie shook his head. "No, just that speed was the main reason for the accident, and that there was alcohol in the victim's system."

Sophie leaned back onto the pillows as Charlie finished reading the rest of the article, which included a request for anyone with any knowledge of the incident to come forward. He was in the process of closing the browser when his

BlackBerry went off. He fumbled to get it out of its holder on the nightstand before hitting the button to accept the call.

"Hello?"

"Charlie?" He recognized Tom Edwards's voice on the other end of the line, though his own still sounded groggy, even to him.

"Sorry if I woke you."

"No, I was just coming back from breakfast," he lied.

"I was wondering if you could come back in later for a supplementary to your statement. I got some preliminary feedback on your interview from Legal, and they had a couple of follow-up questions."

"Sure, what time?"

"No rush. How about after lunch — two-ish?"

"I'll see you then," Charlie said and closed the phone.

"Was that the embassy security guy?"

He looked at Sophie and nodded. "He wants me to come back in for a supplementary interview this afternoon."

"Are you gonna go?"

He sighed. "I don't think I have much of a choice."

"Well, I know where my next stop is going to be," she said, glancing at the brochure from the French school in Villefranche. "But I understand if you can't come with me." They sat in silence for a moment, Charlie's thoughts divided between whether he should go with her and how to actually address the fact that they were sitting in bed together.

"So," she said, rolling onto her back and flicking the hair back from her face. "Last night was fun." A tease of a smile appeared at the corners of her mouth that, along with her dishevelled hair and the fact that she was naked under the thin bedsheets, made her more alluring than ever.

"Yeah," he said, smiling. "I didn't know you were such an expert bird-dancer."

"I have hidden talents, but I was talking about later, back here."

"Right," he said, searching her face for some sign that she was toying with him, but saw none. "Are you okay with —"

"When do you have to go to the embassy?" she asked, craning her neck to see the clock on the night table.

"After lunch."

She leaned closer to him, and he could feel the warmth of her flesh on his as she moved over him.

"I was thinking, you're not in a rush and we're already in bed…."

Charlie was crossing Ebertstrasse on his way to his meeting at the embassy when his phone went off. His first instinct was to let it ring, but he pulled it out as he reached the opposite curb. Seeing the incoming caller ID, his heart caught in his throat.

"Ambassador?"

"I told you to call me Brigitte."

"Sorry. Brigitte."

"Where are you?"

"I'm on my way to the embassy. I'm just a few steps a —"

"Don't bother."

"What do you mean?" Charlie's mind was processing the possible reasons for this instruction, none of which were good.

"Take a few days off while we get this figured out."

"But I'm supposed to be meeting with the Berlin RCMP liaison."

"I know. I've spoken to his boss. It's all right. We all agree there's no need for another interview, but I can't have you coming back here until I can be assured of your safety, so take advantage of a few days off. Go visit the Reichstag or Museum Island."

"I don't understand."

"You told me you had nothing to hide. Has something changed?" Martineau paused before adding, "Because if there's anything else you want to tell me, now's the time, Charlie."

"No," he said quickly. "I did nothing wrong, I can assure you."

"Then we'll let this play itself out and see where we are in a couple of days."

Charlie stood there on the sidewalk, wondering if he should say something else or just think himself lucky he wasn't being fired for going AWOL. "Thank you," he said, but Martineau had already hung up. He continued to stare at the phone for a few seconds, then made up his mind.

"Fuck it," he muttered, crossing back and hurrying to the hotel. Sophie was just coming out of the shower when he knocked on her door.

"Did you forget something?" she said, towelling her hair as she stood aside to let him in.

"Pack your stuff — we're catching the first flight to Nice."

CHAPTER 32

It was early evening by the time they landed in Nice, after a short flight.

"Any preference for hotels?" Sophie asked as they made their way through the arrivals area toward the stand of waiting taxis.

Charlie shook his head. "I've never been here. You?"

"I was here once with my ex," she said as Charlie waved one of the cabs over. "Not good memories," she added. "But the hotel was great. It's right on the boardwalk."

Half an hour later, they checked into the Hotel Negresco.

"I'm just trying to be efficient," she said with a grin, after requesting a single room with a king-size bed.

"Can you tell us where we can find the main police station?" she asked the clerk as he swiped a room card. He cast her a strange look before referring them to the concierge. Charlie went over and got directions while Sophie finished up at the desk.

"It's probably too late to accomplish anything tonight," he said as they crossed to the elevators, then rode up to the fourth floor.

"We'll hit the police station first thing tomorrow morning," she replied, stepping off the elevator. Arriving at their room and swiping the key, she opened the door onto a spacious room with a large bed, a workstation, and a set of armchairs. Beyond the sheers was a view of the Promenade des Anglais and the reflection of light off the Mediterranean beyond.

"You want to go out for dinner or just get room service?" she asked, setting her small suitcase on the bed.

"I'm not that hungry." Charlie sat in one of the armchairs.

"Everything okay?" Sophie said, unzipping her bag, pulling out her brother's duffel, and setting it on the bed.

"Yeah, sure," Charlie lied. He had been in a state of inner turmoil ever since deciding to join her when she left Moscow. He was also pretty sure that he was violating the implicit understanding that laying low for a few days meant staying in Berlin.

"I'll order us something," Sophie said, perusing the room-service menu. After she had called it in, she pulled out the books from her brother's bag, leaned back against the headboard, and started flipping through the one on biker gangs.

"Pass me one," Charlie said, and she flipped him the next in the pile — a paperback on the international drug trade.

"I just can't see Steve as an investigative journalist," she said, shaking her head. "It seems far too serious for him." She was looking at the back cover of the book, which featured a picture of a professorial-looking journalist above the author bio. A moment of silence extended until Sophie broke it. "Earth to Charlie."

"Hmm?" He looked up from the chapter he had stumbled onto about the Asian and East European heroin trade. "I'm just looking at these passages that someone — I assume Steve — highlighted, about the value of confidential informants in dismantling drug-smuggling operations."

"Let me see?" Sophie pulled up the other chair and looked over his shoulder. "That's definitely Steve's writing," she said, pointing to something scribbled in the margin.

"It looks like *Zhibek*. It must be in central Asia — that's what this section of the book is on." He tapped the page. "It's talking about the heroin trade there. I saw a reference to Afghanistan earlier." He flipped back a page to confirm and to scan the contents of the chapter. Indeed, it covered the trade in heroin, beginning with production in Afghanistan and its distribution worldwide, following the old Silk Route into Asia and its transportation to major European centres beyond.

"I'm sure the Russian army shipped its fair share of the stuff back to Moscow during the Afghan war in the eighties," Sophie said. "Maybe Steve was doing a historical piece."

"Maybe." Charlie continued flipping through the rest of the book, finding several sections highlighted in similar fashion, with some scribbled handwriting here and there. The problem was, the highlighted sections seemed to have no logical connection. Heroin trafficking in Afghanistan, counterfeiting and commercial espionage in China, prostitution in Ukraine. The only common theme — the subject of the book — was the role of organized crime in the various illegal enterprises. It was consistent with the general theory they had been developing that Liepa might have been looking into Dmitri Bayzhanov, but it was hardly a smoking gun. That Bayzhanov and his company BayCo were connected in one way or another to the Russian mob was almost a foregone conclusion. Charlie tossed the book onto the bed.

"Maybe we'll catch a break tomorrow," Sophie said, picking up on the negative vibe that Charlie was trying to suppress.

"Let's hope so."

The main police station was in an ugly part of the city, north of the train station. After the luxury of the Negresco, it gave the impression of being on another planet, despite being less than fifteen minutes away by taxi. Charlie and Sophie had gotten up early and set off in a cab after a quick breakfast in the hotel restaurant. The bright sunlight on the sparkling blue Mediterranean had lifted Charlie's spirits when he had looked out the window of the hotel room, but the interior of the police station was starting to drag him down.

They had been sitting and waiting there for almost thirty minutes. Their request to talk to someone about Krasknikov's accident had been taken by a gruff desk officer in his late fifties — the kind who didn't like to be rushed. Charlie was debating asking him for an update when another man — a younger, fitter man in a light cotton jacket over a white polo shirt — appeared in front of them.

"Monsieur Hillier?"

"Oui, et Mademoiselle Durant," Charlie began, hoping his high school French, slightly enhanced by the few weeks of language training he had managed to squeeze out of a reluctant manager a few years back, wouldn't fail him.

"Inspecteur Sebastien Coron," the man said, his smile coming to life when he turned to Sophie. "You were asking about an accident that occurred some weeks ago on the Cap?" Coron continued, in lightly accented English. His expression conveyed a mixture of caution and curiosity.

"Yes, a car that went off a cliff, driven by a Russian national."

Coron frowned and shook his head. "What makes you say he was Russian?"

Charlie sensed that Coron was concealing something, but decided to play dumb. "Well, we understand the body wasn't identified, but that's partly why we're here. We were wondering whether you could tell us what happened, maybe let us see the scene, or the wrecked car?"

Coron's reaction was immediate. "This is not Disney World, Monsieur, and I am not a *guide touristique*."

"We're not here to waste your time," Charlie said quickly as Coron turned to head back to the door that separated the precinct from the waiting area. "In fact, we may have information that you will find useful."

"Perhaps in America this is how you conduct investigations, but not in France," Coron said with an arrogant sniff.

"We're Canadian," Sophie said, stepping forward. At first, Charlie thought it was the plaintive look in her eyes that stopped Coron in his tracks, but soon realized there was something else going on.

"More Canadians?" the inspector said.

"What do you mean?" Charlie thought he knew the answer.

"A month ago, another Canadian, a young man, was asking me questions about this accident."

Sophie rummaged in her jacket pocket and pulled out a wallet-sized photo and showed it to him. "Was this the man who was asking questions?" Despite his obvious reluctance to confirm anything, the look in Coron's eyes said it all. "That's my brother, Steve," Sophie said, putting the picture back in her pocket. "He died a few weeks ago, in Moscow, not long after returning from France." They stood in silence for a moment while Coron seemed to process the information. "I just want to know what happened to him, that's all. If you could spare us a few minutes."

Coron seemed to consider the request for a moment, then made up his mind.

"*Venez*," he said, motioning to the secure door and punching in his access code. They followed him in silence to a desk in the far corner of a bustling room. The sight of the palm branches gently swaying outside the grimy window was in stark contrast to the disarray of Coron's desk. He motioned to a tattered pair of mismatched chairs and took a seat in his own, its creak announcing that it, too, was approaching the end of its useful life.

"*Attendez, attendez,*" he said, tossing one pile of paper onto another and shuffling through a disorderly collection of files until he found what he was looking for. "*Voilà,*" he declared, pushing the loose papers off his blotter to make room. "This is my file. I'm afraid I haven't learned much since I met with your brother."

Charlie glanced at Sophie, sensing that Coron was assuming that Liepa had told his sister all about what he had learned on his visit a month ago.

"You still have no suspects?" she said, playing along.

"Why would I be looking for a suspect? It was an accidental death."

"But there was an article in the *Journal de Nice,*" Charlie said. "Asking for witnesses to come forward."

Coron nodded. "Yes, to provide information about the accident. Not to launch a murder investigation, Mr. Hill —"

"Call me Charlie, please. Do you mind?" he said, pointing at the file.

Just then someone across the room called out to him. "*Eh, Caron, une minute!*"

Coron replied, then slid the file toward them. "Please have a look for yourselves. I'll be back in a few minutes." He got to his feet and strode to the other cop, then started what looked to be a lengthy conversation. Charlie opened the file and spread its contents onto the desktop.

"My God," Sophie said, looking at the photo of a mangled red sports car, half in the water and half embedded in an outcrop of rock at the base of a cliff. The next photo was of the same scene, but taken from the road above.

"Here's the medical examiner's report," Charlie said, plucking the two-page form from the file folder and scanning the executive summary while Sophie flipped through the photos.

"Body was burned beyond recognition," Charlie said, translating as he read. "Identification impossible due to ... the state of the remains."

"What about dental records for identification? Does it say anything about that?" Sophie looked up from one of the photos. "Is that the body?" she said, pointing to a close-up of what looked vaguely like a skeleton, minus a skull.

Charlie continued to translate the medical report on the fly. "The head was ... missing."

"What do you mean *missing?*"

"Hang on," Charlie said, reading ahead. "It was likely severed on impact, and then lost in the sea."

"That's impossible, surely."

"That's what it says here. There's not much else of interest. Oh — what's this?" Charlie found another form in the folder and saw Coron's signature at the bottom. "This looks like some kind of summary of the findings. Let's see. Accident occurred at some point between midnight and 6:00 a.m. There was a ... storm that night with high winds. A *chaloupe* ... fishing boat noticed the wreckage in the morning. The body was badly ... disfigured and ... burned. The head had been remov — no, severed, and was not found despite ... despite the efforts of police divers. No identification, no sign of foul play ... preliminary finding of an accident."

"I'm still not convinced it was an accident," Sophie said, unaware that Coron had returned from across the room. He looked at her, glanced at his watch, and then smiled.

"*Venez.* I will show you."

They drove through the centre of town, then south along the Rue de Rivoli, past their hotel and onto the Promenade des Anglais. They went past the old port and fish market, taking the road west along the coast toward the Cap de Nice, gradually climbing as they left the city behind. The Mediterranean sparkled below, and Charlie noticed that the seaside road was bordered only by a low stone wall maybe a couple of feet high. As they navigated one twisting section of the road to another, he began to imagine a very different experience at two in the morning during a storm.

Coron was chatting as he drove and soon pulled over onto the narrow shoulder, just ahead of a break in the rock wall, marked by a pair of orange pylons. The three of them climbed out of the car.

"You see?" the policeman said, pointing to the cracked rock wall. Charlie noticed that the lower portion of the wall was largely intact, and the break point was edged with flakes of red. He realized on closer inspection that the red was probably paint from the car that had burst through the barrier.

"It was a red car?"

"Yes, a Porsche Carrera," Coron said, with a sombre nod, though whether it was out of respect for the victim of the deadly crash or the loss of a fine piece of automotive engineering, Charlie wasn't sure. He stepped up to the edge and looked down over the virtually sheer drop to an outcropping of sun-bleached rock below, a few square metres of which was still blackened.

"The car was travelling at a very high speed," Coron continued, pointing to the stone wall and the low curb that preceded it. "It was already — how do you say it? — airborne by the time it hit the wall, you see?" He pointed to the paint marks where the wall had been sheared off, then to the outcropping of rock below. "It landed there — probably exploding on impact, or soon after."

"And you say there were no witnesses?" Sophie glanced at the smattering of residences on the slope above the road.

"*Non, Madame*, it was a bad storm that night. Very noisy."

"And no skid marks?" Charlie asked, glancing at the road approaching from the east.

"The road was very wet." Coron shrugged and looked out over the water.

Charlie considered challenging the remark, but decided against it for now.

"And you were able to identify the victim through the registration of the car?" he asked instead, prompting a frown from Coron.

"*Non*. It was owned by a *société* — a company that rents to tourists. Rich tourists. They rent villas and cars."

"But surely the company is required by law to give you that information in a case like this," Sophie said, incredulous.

Coron gave a little snort. "Yes, and they were about to, when we received word from the *Ministère des affaires étrangères* telling us this identification would not be forthcoming."

Sophie and Charlie looked at each other. "The *French* Foreign Ministry?"

Coron nodded. "*Oui*."

"You mean, at the request of a foreign embassy?" Sophie asked, prompting another nod from Coron.

"Was it the Russian Embassy?"

The inspector shrugged. "They did not say, only that our inquiries into the victim's identity were at an end."

"And you were satisfied that it was an accident, so you didn't pursue it?"

Coron looked out over the Mediterranean and took a deep breath of the sea air. "We had no reason to believe otherwise, and even if we did, my power to pursue an investigation was …" He hesitated.

"Non-existent?" Charlie suggested.

"I have my orders to follow."

"So why bother to help us, show us the reports and the scene?" Sophie said.

"Maybe you have information I don't have." Coron walked back to the car and opened the door. "Or maybe not."

"Or maybe you don't think it was an accident any more than we do," Charlie said as the policeman got behind the wheel. Charlie held the door as Sophie got in the back seat, then followed her in. Their visit was apparently over. "Tell me this, then," Charlie persisted. "What did you do with the responses to your request for witnesses to come forward before your visit from the French Foreign Ministry? You must have had some, even if they were only a few cranks."

"Cranks?"

"Crazies … *des fous* … with nothing else to do."

Coron laughed, then started the car, his smile fading. "Nothing. We did nothing. There were not many, in any case."

"But there were some."

Coron put the car back in neutral and picked up the file folder from the passenger seat, then pulled out a sheet of paper. "A colleague spoke to this man — he was not a … crank," Coron said, passing the sheet of paper to Charlie. "Perhaps you can try him again, since I cannot." Coron put the car in gear and made a U-turn to point them back toward Nice. "He's a bartender at a restaurant in the *vieille ville*."

"What about the medical examiner — can we meet him?" Sophie leaned forward from the back seat.

Coron shook his head. "He is a very busy man, and very ... by the book."

"You mean he's not going to answer unofficial questions from a couple of Canadians," Charlie said.

"*Exactement.*"

"But if you came with us ...?"

Coron sighed and looked in the rear-view before making a sudden right. "I will introduce you, but I promise nothing."

CHAPTER 33

Charlie and Sophie waited in the basement hallway of the hospital, located in the northern part of the city, beyond the police station. Charlie tried to ignore the wave of nausea he felt at the smell of antiseptic and whatever else was up his nose. He hated to think what, given they were at the morgue. Sophie seemed perfectly at ease, which didn't surprise him since she probably spent a significant amount of time in hospitals.

"*Entrez,*" Coron said, emerging from a doorway and waving them into an anteroom, then stepping into the office beyond. A tall, thin man in his sixties stood on the other side of a cluttered desk. The windows behind him were stained with soot and covered by thick metal grates. Dust motes floated in the thin ray of natural light that filtered through. Sophie stepped up to the older man and extended her hand.

"Dr. Sophie Durant," she said, which seemed to relax him a little.

"Dr. Felix St. Jacques," he replied with a thin smile. "Coron tells me you are Canadian?"

"That's right," she said, introducing Charlie.

"I spent six months in Montreal several years ago, on an exchange in the pathology department at McGill."

"Your English is excellent," Sophie said, eliciting a slightly wider smile.

"I did some of my medical training in England, but that was many years ago."

They chatted for a couple of minutes more before St. Jacques got to the point. "Coron says you would like to ask me some questions about the victim of a car accident?"

"Yes, we read your report, and —"

"And your interest in this is?"

"We believe the accident could be connected to the death of my brother," Sophie said.

St. Jacques frowned as he listened, then appeared to soften his position.

"I'm sorry to hear about your brother. Your questions are ... unofficial?"

She nodded and St. Jacques looked at Coron, who gave his own barely perceptible nod before the pathologist pointed to the chairs on the other side of his desk. He took a seat himself in a creaking wooden chair.

"Very well. What do you want to know?"

"I was wondering about the cause of death," she said, as she and Charlie sat. Coron remained standing off to one side.

"Massive trauma," St. Jacques said with a shrug. "The car the victim was driving fell approximately thirty metres onto solid rock. On examination, we found the body severely damaged, as well as burned, the vehicle having exploded on impact."

"I assume you didn't inspect the body at the scene?" Sophie asked, prompting a rapid shake of the head.

"No, the examination was conducted here. A member of the police forensic services team did inspect the body on-site, and I was able to review his notes prior to my own examination."

"Did those notes give any indication of the location of the body?" Charlie asked. He heard a sharp inhalation of air from Coron.

"The location?" St. Jacques seemed puzzled.

"I mean, was the body in the driver's seat, wearing a seat belt, that sort of thing?"

"Ah." St. Jacques nodded. "The seat belt was not in use. As for the location of the body within the vehicle, it would have been difficult to determine, given the state of the car."

"Was a blood sample taken?"

"Of course. Alcohol was present in the victim's blood, enough that it had to be considered a factor in the crash, but it was just over the legal limit."

Sophie nodded and looked at Charlie before asking about some of the technical findings she had seen in the report. Charlie kept an eye on Coron, who was now leaning against the wall, rubbing a forefinger over his upper lip. He watched the cop stand straighter at Sophie's next line of questions.

"What happened to the victim's head?"

The pathologist paused, glancing quickly at Coron before answering. "As I said, the force of impact was very damaging — a drop onto solid rock from that height. The head was severed from the body likely on impact. Police divers dredged the water but were unable to locate the head. There are strong currents around the Cap."

Sohie nodded. "So, no possibility of identifying the victim with dental records."

St. Jacques shook his head.

"And fingerprints?" she persisted.

Coron gave a little smile. "They were sent to the national database, which links to international law-enforcement agencies."

"Which prompted the visit from the Russian Ministry of Foreign Affairs," she replied with her own smile. "No doubt at the request of the Russian Embassy in Paris."

The room fell silent for a moment. Then Coron looked at Sophie and Charlie. "Do you know the identity of the victim?" he asked, his tone detached, though it didn't conceal his underlying curiosity.

"We think his name was Mikhail Krasnikov," Charlie said. "Though why the Russian government was so keen to put a stop to the investigation is interesting."

"You have a theory?" Coron raised an eyebrow.

"I think it just became a bit more than a theory," Sophie said. "Thank you for your time, Dr. St. Jacques. You've been very helpful."

"Who is this Krasnikov?" Coron asked when they were back out in the parking lot.

Charlie didn't want to go into the details, but he felt they owed Coron something for his efforts. "He was a government official whose death coincides with something Steven Liepa was looking into."

Coron seemed about to ask something else, then looked at Sophie. "I hope you find justice for your brother, but there's little else I can do."

"Thanks for your help." She extended a hand.

"I wish you well in your search, but I fear you will be disappointed."

"There's still the bartender to talk to," she said as Coron nodded and turned to shake Charlie's hand.

"You don't really think it was an accident, do you?" Charlie watched Coron for his reaction.

"Instinct can be deceiving sometimes," the inspector replied. "But I think there is more to this case than — how do you say? — meets the eye."

After he had gone, Charlie looked at his watch. "We've got a couple of hours before the restaurant where the bartender works opens. Maybe we should get some lunch."

Sophie nodded. "Let's go back to the hotel. I need to get on the internet."

"Something St. Jacques said about the post-mortem?"

She frowned. "He didn't do a real post-mortem, although by the sounds of it, there wasn't much of Krasnikov to examine. And given the cops were presenting it as an accident from the get-go, there wouldn't necessarily have been a reason to do one."

"Over here," Charlie said, pointing to a row of taxis waiting at the hospital entrance. They rode south through the city, back to the palm-lined promenade and the hotel, stopping at a nearby coffee shop to get some sandwiches and cappuccinos to go. Back in the hotel room, Sophie ate a sandwich as she logged onto the internet with her laptop, while Charlie looked through the selection of Steve Liepa's paperbacks.

"Where's the one on the Asian drug trade?" he said, biting into his sandwich as she clicked away at her laptop.

"I put it back in the bag." She pointed to the collapsible duffel that held all of Liepa's effects.

Charlie found the book and started flipping through the pages as he ate. His sandwich done, he sipped the cappuccino and perused the book, concentrating on the highlighted areas but making nothing coherent of them. Abandoning the book, he closed his eyes and tried to piece together what they had learned from Coron, but other than a strong impression that Krasnikov's death was no accident, they were no further ahead. His thoughts turned to Moscow, and a wave of unease gripped him as he thought of what awaited him there. Would he even be allowed to return? And if so, to what?

CHAPTER 34

It was just after nine in the evening when their cab pulled up outside the restaurant in the old fish market on the east side of the city, just a few blocks from the waterfront. The outside of the building looked a bit rundown, but the inside was luxurious, with a soft-lit dining room to one side and a full bar to the other. A maître d' greeted them immediately and asked if they had a reservation, but Charlie shook his head and pointed to the bar.

They sat at the near end and waited for the bartender, a fit young man in his twenties, to finish the cocktail he was making for a woman at the other end of the bar.

"Un verre de vin blanc et une bière, s'il vous plaît," Charlie said when the bartender was free.

The man nodded and smiled. "American?"

"Canadian," Charlie replied, not the least surprised that he hadn't been able to pass for a native speaker. "You speak English?"

"Yes." The wattage of the bartender's smile increased as he got a closer look at Sophie. "I had an American girlfriend."

"They say necessity is the mother of invention." Sophie gave him a broad smile and offered her hand. "I'm Sophie and this is Charlie."

"Jean-Claude," he said, shaking her hand, then Charlie's, before turning to get their drinks. He was back a moment later and set the glasses down on the bar.

"Are you eating in the restaurant?" he asked.

"No, we're just having a drink," Charlie said, putting an assortment of Euros on the bar that covered the drinks and a very generous tip. "And we were wondering if we could ask you a few questions about that accident that happened up on the Cap de Nice a month ago." He saw the bartender's eyes narrow slightly. "We've already spoken to the police — Inspecteur Coron," Charlie said quickly, hoping the reference would put the young man at ease. "He mentioned you had called in with some information in response to the notice in the paper."

The bartender looked down the length of the bar. The woman at the other end was a third of the way through her martini and there was another handful of people in the adjacent booths, but it was pretty quiet. He gave a short nod.

"Yes, I called in, because of the car."

"The car?"

"The car in the accident was a red Porsche. I served a couple who were driving a red Porsche that night. I wondered ... well, I wondered if maybe it was them, but I understand it was a single victim. And anyway, the police said the case was ... closed."

"What did they look like?" Charlie asked.

He grinned. "He was older. Much older."

"Did he have an accent?"

He frowned with the effort of recall. "Maybe, but she did most of the talking. Her French was very good."

"What accent would you say the man had?"

"Eastern European, maybe Russian."

"But not her?"

"She was a tall blonde — very beautiful. She looked Russian, but she spoke excellent French."

"How did you know what car they were driving?" Sophie asked.

"I served them an aperitif here," he said, gesturing to the bar. "They had dinner, and then later, I went out back for a cigarette and saw them leave. Their car was parked around back."

"What about the man?" Charlie sipped his beer. "What did he look like?"

"A big man. Grey hair, big stomach. Too big for a girl like that," he added, with another grin.

"You think she was a hooker?"

The bartender looked puzzled.

"A prostitute."

"Ah," he said, recognition dawning. "Yes, maybe. She certainly was not his daughter," he added, chuckling. "I have a picture if you like."

Charlie looked at Sophie. "A picture?"

"We have a camera out back, to cover the parking lot," the bartender said. "We've had some thefts. When I saw the notice in the paper, I checked the tape and there were a few images — I printed a couple of the best shots, but the police didn't need them."

"You still have these photos?"

"Unless one of the staff threw them out," he said, rummaging behind the bar. He came up with an envelope, opened it, and pulled out a couple of sheets of paper. The first shot wasn't great, as the couple were both back-on. In the second, a man that could have been Krasnikov was side-on, but there was a good view of the woman as she stood by the passenger door. She was indeed tall and blond, with the high cheekbones that Charlie had seen in women all over Moscow.

What made his stomach clench, though, as he stared at her image, was the fact that he had seen her somewhere recently. Was it in Moscow? Or Berlin?

"They didn't say where they were staying or how long they were here for?" Sophie asked, apparently oblivious to Charlie's shock as he continued to stare at the woman's image.

The bartender shook his head. "We had some small talk, but they wanted to be alone."

"Do you mind if we keep these?" Charlie said, tapping a finger on the pictures.

"Please. But why are you so interested? The police told me the case was closed."

Charlie nodded. "The police investigation is closed, but let's just say we have a professional interest in finding out as much as we can about what happened." The bartender suddenly seemed more interested in responding to the empty martini glass at the other end of the bar than in asking for clarification, so Charlie thought it a good time for an exit. "Thank you for your help."

"My pleasure," the young man said, moving down the bar as Sophie and Charlie made for the door.

"What's wrong?" Sophie asked as they hit the sidewalk outside the restaurant.

"I recognize that blonde from somewhere."

"One of your conquests?" she joked, but she could tell from his reaction that Charlie was worried.

"I'm trying to recall if it was in Moscow or Berlin, but I definitely saw her somewhere recently."

"Well, I certainly didn't recognize her, and we spent most of our time together in Berlin, so it was probably in Moscow."

"Probably."

Sophie waved at a passing taxi, which slowed to pick them up. "So what now?"

"Back to Berlin, I guess." Charlie opened the back door for her to slide in. "For me, anyway."

"I guess there's not much else to be done here," she said, glancing at the dark sea beyond the lights of the promenade. "I was hoping we were on to something."

"Well, we confirmed our suspicions, at least."

Charlie tried to be upbeat, but he felt the familiar disappointment at being no further ahead. Yes, it looked as though Krasnikov could have had help in plunging off the cliff and that Steve Liepa had been here in September, asking questions. But the blonde remained a mystery. He pulled out his BlackBerry to check his messages, expecting nothing other than the routine stuff. He was surprised to see a message from Brigitte Martineau. Some "significant progress" had been made on his case during the day, whatever that meant. It concluded with a heads-up to expect an update tomorrow. She didn't ask where he was at the moment, but the subtext was that he should be back in Berlin by midday tomorrow.

"What is it?"

"It's a note from the head of mission. Seems they might be making progress."

"You mean you might be going back to Moscow, after all?"

"Uh-huh," Charlie said, tucking the BlackBerry back in his pocket. Two things ran across his mind. The first was the unhappy prospect of having to leave Sophie behind in Berlin if he were ordered back. The second was whether anyone could guarantee that he wouldn't be tossed into a holding cell at Domodedovo as soon as he stepped off the plane.

After the short cab ride, they were crossing the hotel lobby when Sophie pointed at the restaurant. "I don't know about you, but I could use a bite to eat."

"Might as well."

"I'm just going to run up to the room for a moment" —
she gestured to the elevators — "if you want to get us a table."

Charlie entered the busy restaurant and was seated at one
of the few remaining tables. A sliver of the boardwalk was
visible through the window to one side and a view of the lobby
on the other. There was a large table of business types behind
him. He noticed a mix of American and English accents, but
the theme of the conversation was universal — the number of
attractive women in the south of France. Charlie listened in
amusement for a few minutes as the young men traded war
stories, but when the server arrived with a pair of menus and
there was still no sign of Sophie, Charlie started to feel uneasy.
He was telling the server to come back in a few minutes when
the American's voice drew his attention.

"… like the blonde on the way in here," he said in a blus-
tering voice.

"Which one?" the Brit asked, egging him on.

"Across the lobby. She was giving me the eye," the first
man replied.

"She was a dyke," another Western voice chimed in. "The
way she took off after the other —" He stopped, recognizing
Charlie as having been with Sophie in the lobby.

Charlie pushed back his chair and bolted to the elevators, pressing the button frantically and calculating
whether it would be faster to take the stairs when the
doors finally opened and a startled couple stepped aside
to let him on.

"Sorry," he muttered, pressing the button for the fourth
floor repeatedly until the doors slid shut again. "Come on,
come on," he said, his pulse racing as the car seemed to
crawl upward. After what seemed like an eternity, the doors
opened onto a deserted fourth-floor landing. He turned
right and raced down the hallway and was almost at the door

to their room when he heard a muffled crash from inside. He grabbed the door handle, finding the door slightly ajar.

He swung it wide and saw Sophie on her back on the floor, the blonde from the photo straddling her hips with her hands clenched around Sophie's neck. The coffee table and chairs were knocked over and a lamp lay broken on the floor. He rushed at the blonde, shoving her onto her side. Sophie rolled over, gasping for air, her face scarlet, but Charlie was too focused on the other woman, who had gained her feet and was already coming at him. She had the heavy base of a lamp in one hand and was swinging it toward his head like a battle-axe. He ducked just in time, felt a whoosh of air graze his ear, and managed to send an elbow sharply upward, hitting her in the midsection and eliciting a guttural gasp.

"Knife," Sophie croaked, still gasping for air. She pointed to the floor by the corner of the room, where Charlie caught a glint of metal. He traded glances with the assailant as she lunged toward it, but he cut off her path by launching a vase at her, forcing her to stop and throw up a defensive forearm. Charlie closed the gap to the knife. The woman appeared to make a quick assessment, glancing first at Charlie, then at the now standing Sophie, and bolted for the door.

"Stop her!" Sophie gasped.

Charlie tore off out into the hallway just in time to see the blonde running off in the opposite direction from the elevators. He sprinted after her, catching the door to the stairwell before it closed and expecting to see her halfway down to the next floor.

Instead she was waiting on the landing, her hand striking him in the midsection a few inches north of where it would have landed had Charlie not hunched over in time. He swung out desperately but missed her face and grabbed her ponytail as she delivered another punch, this one shielded by his arm. He tightened his grip on her hair and yanked with all his might, causing her to shriek and jerk away in pain. Straightening up, he threw his body weight into her, slamming her into the wall, but he was unprepared for the blow she landed with her knee, straight into his crotch this time.

He folded like a lawn chair and his assailant grinned in victory, forgetting that Charlie still had a grip on her ponytail. She shoved him toward the stairs, and as he felt himself come off the first step, he got a second hand around the ponytail and pulled with everything he had, flinging the woman over him as they both tumbled down the stairs. Charlie covered his head with his arms as they bounced down the concrete steps — a dozen or more before they hit the next landing. He heard the hollow crunch of breaking bone as his hip landed heavily on the back of the woman's head at the bottom. Scrambling to his feet, he saw that she was immobile, eyes staring vacantly beyond him, her head at an impossible angle. He was standing over her when he heard the sound of the door opening above.

"Charlie? Jesus!" Sophie came running down the stairs, one hand rubbing her throat.

"I think she's dead," he muttered, collecting himself and grimacing in pain.

"I would have liked to kill the bitch myself." Sophie knelt down and checked for a pulse, then went through the woman's pockets. Other than a package of cigarettes, a disposable lighter, and some cash, there was nothing.

"She have a phone?"

Sophie stood up and shook her head, then noticed he was still a bit hunched over. "Are you okay?"

"I'll live."

"Come on. We need to get out of here now."

"Wait." Charlie stood his ground as she began to pull him down the stairs. "We need to get Steve's things."

She stared at him for a moment and then agreed. "Okay, let's hurry!"

They ran back up to the fourth floor and down the hallway to their room. Miraculously no one had been alerted by the fracas. Charlie supposed it was because the floor was sparsely populated.

"You gather our stuff, and I'll clean up," Charlie said, collecting the pieces of the broken vase and lamp off the floor as Sophie stuffed her rolling suitcase with whatever they had left out. Charlie took a pillowcase off one of the pillows and filled it with the broken lamp and vase.

"Isn't this Steve's stuff?" he asked, pointing at the floor by the bed.

"Yeah, we knocked the duffel off the chair when I was wrestling with her," Sophie said, avoiding the still-remaining pieces of shattered lamp and retrieving one of Liepa's books and the rubber Berlin bear. One of its legs had been severed by a shard of broken enamel from the lamp base. "I don't know why Steve even had this stupid thing," she said, tossing it into Charlie's open pillowcase with the rest of the debris. He was about to close it up when something metallic caught his eye. He stood there staring at the inside of the pillowcase as Sophie zipped up her suitcase.

"Come on," she said urgently, moving to the door.

"What's this?" Charlie pulled the little bear from the bag and grabbed the metallic object, the end of which was visible where the leg had separated from the torso. He gave it a tug, and out came a silver rectangle about two inches long and a half inch wide.

"It's a USB stick."

"What the hell?" Charlie said. "Give me your laptop."

"Are you crazy? Someone's going to stumble across our friend any minute." She gestured to the door.

"You're right. Let's get out of here." He headed out into the hallway and dropped the pillowcase into the garbage bag of an abandoned cleaning cart after confirming that there was no one else around. He stopped just before the elevators.

"What are you doing?" Sophie pressed the down button.

"You check out," he said. "I'll meet you in the lobby."

He rushed back toward the stairwell, pausing at an alcove near the door to the stairs containing an ice machine and next to a door to what looked like a utility closet. He glanced up and down the hall, then tried the handle. Locked. He looked for something to wrench it open with, but there was nothing. Noticing the recessed light in the ceiling above the alcove, he looked at the large ice maker and made up his mind. Grabbing one side, he slid the heavy machine forward before stepping around to the other side and doing the same. Then he covered his hand with his handkerchief, reached up, and unscrewed the light bulb overhead so that the alcove was suddenly cast in a grey gloom. Checking the hallway again, he opened the door to the stairwell and ran down to the next landing, then dragged the body back up the stairs and into the alcove. There was just enough space to get the body in behind and still push the machine back a couple of inches. In the dim light, it would be difficult to spot anything amiss. He returned to the stairs and bolted down the four flights to the lobby, just in time to see Sophie stepping away from the reception.

"We all good?"

She nodded tentatively as they headed outside and got in a cab for the airport. Once there, they were able to get seats on the last flight to Paris with a timely connection to Berlin. They had to race through security and it wasn't until they were seated on the plane that they had the opportunity to open her laptop and see the contents of the USB stick.

"It's the *MC* document," Charlie said, pointing at the file directory that appeared when Sophie plugged in the stick. "You remember the ghost title we saw on Steve's laptop? This must have been the stick he was working from."

"So we've been carrying this fucking thing around for days?" she whispered in frustration. "We're lucky I didn't toss it," she added, clicking on the document.

They both stared in silence as a large document opened onto the screen, the title underlined at the top: *Moscow Code*. It was about fifty pages in length and appeared to be part text, part notes.

"There," Charlie said, spotting Sergei Yermolov's name. "This is about United Pharma being the anchor tenant in Petr Square." They scanned the page of text and scrolled down to the next page, which was an article cut-and-pasted from a newspaper. The subject was the Customs Union agreement, effectively giving responsibility for controlling access to several of the former Soviet republics to Kazakhstan — a role that had been carried out by Russia long after the Soviet Union had crumbled.

"Go to the next page," he said as the flight attendant announced their impending departure from the gate. Sophie ignored the instruction to stow all electronics and scrolled down. The next page was a digital image that left them both staring at the screen. Under it was the text: *T. Evseeva, SVR operative.* They looked from the text back to the picture of a woman with cold blue eyes and long blond hair. The same woman whose dead body they'd left back at the Negresco Hotel.

Sophie minimized the screen, closed the file, and popped out the stick, shutting the cover of her laptop as the flight attendant walked by.

"Are you thinking what I'm thinking?" Charlie said as they buckled their seat belts.

Sophie nodded. "This plane can't get off the ground fast enough."

CHAPTER 35

It was after midnight when they touched down at Tegel Airport in Berlin. By force of habit, Charlie pulled out his BlackBerry and turned it on. He wasn't expecting any news, much less the email from Brigitte Martineau that was waiting for him. Reading it as they moved down the aisle toward the exit, he was so absorbed in the message that it took Sophie several attempts to get him to respond when they reached the gangway.

"What is it?" she repeated.

"You're not going to believe this. I've been cleared to return on the noon flight to Moscow. And your visa was renewed for another week."

"You're kidding! That's fantastic. For both of us."

"Yeah," Charlie said without much conviction.

"You don't think so?"

"I guess so. I'm just surprised it happened so quickly — my clearance, that is. As for your visa ... well, that's pretty unusual, too, now that I think about it."

"What flight are you on? I need to get a ticket."

"You're already booked on the same flight as me — Lufthansa. I assume they knew you were good for it."

They hurried outside into the cold night air — a marked

change from the south of France — and hopped in a cab. Twenty minutes later they were in a suite back at the Berlin Marriott. As soon as they were through the door, they had the laptop out on the desk. They read together for half an hour, jumping back and forth through the text.

"So Steve knew that UPI was going to sign on at Petr Square long before it was common knowledge." Charlie pointed to a portion of text. "And look at the initials — *SY.* There's no question Sergei was his source. It must have been Yermolov who let it slip that Steve was asking questions. Whoever he told, it got them both killed."

"Look at this," Sophie said, pointing to the bottom of the screen. "These are notes of a conversation with a Piotr Zhibek."

"Zhibek?" Charlie reached for Liepa's book on international crime and flipped to the section on drug smuggling. "It's a reference to a *person*, not a place," he said, indicating the scribble in the margin that they had assumed was a reference to a city in central Asia.

"It looks like this Zhibek guy's a reporter."

"You keep reading. I need to start mapping this out." Charlie grabbed the hotel notepad from the desk and drew a circle in the middle of the page around the initials *SL.*

"Too small," Sohie said, looking at the little pad. "Here." She rummaged in her purse and pulled out a lipstick. "Use that," she said, pointing to the enormous mirror over the dresser. Charlie drew his circle in the middle, then drew a line to a second one, with a *B* inside.

"That's Bayzhanov?" Sophie said.

Charlie nodded. "I think we know for sure Steve was looking into him." He drew another circle and connected it to Liepa's. "This is Sergei Yermolov." Charlie scribbled the initials in the circle.

"Here, there's a whole other section of notes on him," Sophie said, then went quiet as she scanned the text. "He told Steve a lot of senior execs were getting kickbacks from Bayzhanov's company to move United Pharma into Petr Square, even before the permit was granted."

"That would explain his fancy clothes and nice apartment, considering he was mid-level, at best."

"You remember what Steve's Russian girlfriend said about him — how he liked to throw money around."

Charlie nodded. "And if *he* was flush with Bayzhanov's cash, imagine what the top guys were getting. That would also explain why UPI signed on as anchor tenant at all."

"You mean because of the permit problems."

Charlie frowned. "There's that, but I was thinking of the rents Bayzhanov was charging for Petr Square. They were way above market, from what Rob Brooker told me. He was interested in the building as a possibility for the new embassy for a while, until he found out the rent they were asking."

Charlie tapped his finger on the circle surrounding Yermolov's name for a moment, then drew an X across it. "So who killed him, and why?"

"Bayzhanov?" Sophie suggested, standing up to join him at the mirror.

"But why? And besides, he was killed well after Steve died."

Sophie shrugged and took the lipstick from him, drawing a line from the circle representing Bayzhanov to a new one, with the initials *AS*.

"Alexander Surin."

She nodded. "We know he's got to be in Bayzhanov's pocket, since it took him all of five minutes as chair of the planning committee to green-light BayCo's project. Then there's the fact that they both own shares in the same Cypriot company." She drew another circle for Krasnikov and connected it by a dotted line to Surin's. "And I'm assuming Surin's the prime suspect for Krasnikov's fender bender in Nice."

"He's former KGB," Charlie said, remembering the information provided by the secretive journalist she'd met at the Conservatory. "Which means he's probably still got connections to the FSB or SVR, and maybe to the Evseeva woman." He took the lipstick back and drew a circle to represent Evseeva, then drew an X through it. A chill descended over the room as they considered the implications. Charlie was the first to voice their thoughts. "Someone is going to be expecting a report from Evseeva. Someone we have to assume knew we were there and sent her to kill us."

Sophie turned to stare at him. "You can't go back to Moscow, Charlie."

"What am I supposed to tell Martineau? Besides, I don't think the SVR respects borders. If they want to kill me, they can send someone to find me anywhere they want. You remember the guy they poisoned in London? He was one of theirs."

Charlie sat down heavily on the bed. Sophie continued to stare at the mirror for a while, then joined him at the end of the bed.

"What are we going to do?"

He turned to face her, then looked down at the floor. "I have no idea."

Charlie and Sophie walked north along Ebertstrasse, the vast expanse of the Tiergarten to their left as they made their way toward the Brandenburg Gate. After an early breakfast at the hotel, they had decided to get some fresh air. The sun was shining but the air was cold, and their feet crunched on the icy ground as they passed in front of the imposing facade of the U.S. Embassy. Charlie had been up early, poring over Steve Liepa's mysterious document — part rough draft of a partially finished book, part collage of notes and source material. And while there was no shortage of information, there was no outline that Charlie could find, or anything else to tell them where Liepa had been headed before his life had been snuffed out. They had dissected the document in the hotel room and over breakfast. Even as they strolled along Ebertstrasse, they were still discussing it, particularly Liepa's notes of his interview with Zhibek, the Kazakh journalist.

"It's got to be the trip Steve took to Astana," he said. A police car raced by, sirens wailing, disturbing the relative calm of that Sunday morning.

"The one Tania Ivanova said Steve was so excited about," Sophie said, sidestepping a patch of black ice, though not enough to avoid a slip. She grabbed Charlie's arm and righted herself, then left her arm entangled in his as they continued on toward the open space beyond the U.S. Embassy building that was centred by the massive classical gate featuring a general at the helm of a chariot.

"But you remember she said he seemed down when he got back ... disappointed or something?"

"Yeah." Sophie pulled a strand of windswept hair from her face. "She did say something like that. What did the notes say?"

Charlie shrugged. "It's just a bunch of questions and answers about the Customs Union thing."

"What was his obsession with *that*?"

Charlie shook his head. "I can't figure it out. It was a decision by Russia to essentially give Kazakhstan responsibility for all eastern border crossings."

"So the Kazakhs are responsible for checking passports and stuff for anyone coming in from China?"

"Yeah, and anywhere else bordering Kazakhstan," he said, recalling the map of central Asia that he had examined when he'd first seen the notes. "Which would include Tajikistan and Afghanistan, but so what?"

"That's pretty impressive," Sophie said. They'd reached the base of the Brandenburg Gate, and they looked up at the towering statue.

"Apparently, Napoleon took it with him on one of his campaigns," Charlie said. This tidbit was one of the few things he had retained from a long-ago history course.

"I guess he had to give it back." Sophie pulled her collar up in response to another gust of wind. "So this was the dividing line between East and West Berlin, right?" In the silence that followed, Sophie looked at Charlie, who seemed not to have heard her question or to even know that she had spoken at all. "Charlie?"

"Wait a sec," he finally said, visualizing the map of central Asia with Kazakhstan at its centre. "I think I get it. Once they're in the CIS, they're into Russia."

Sophie frowned. "What's the CIS?"

"It stands for the Commonwealth of Independent States, and it's like a eurozone for former Soviet Republics," Charlie explained. "They share some authorities and co-operate on some things, including border security."

"You mean, once you have your passport checked at the border in Kazakhstan, you don't have to check it again to cross into Russia?" Sophie grabbed his arm and started pulling toward the Adlon Hotel, on the far side of the open Platz. "Come on, let's get a coffee and warm up."

"I still don't get why Steve would be so interested in the whole Customs Union thing," she said after they had taken a table at the Adlon's lobby bar. "Or why he would bother going to Astana to talk to a reporter about it."

"Me, neither," Charlie said. A server arrived and took their order for coffee. "And Steve's notes," he continued, "are in shorthand, or maybe they're meant to be cryptic. Either way, it's difficult to see what exactly they were talking about. It looks like Zhibek mentioned an interview he did with a prisoner named Kuatbekov, but I can't make much sense of Steve's shorthand. Can you?"

He opened the slim laptop he'd been carrying and pulled up the document, turning it toward Sophie, who looked at the screen and shook her head after a few seconds.

"It doesn't look like any kind of shorthand I've ever seen before," she said. "And look at the bottom of the page — the notation to follow up with *PZ*, and he's got a bunch of question marks next to the initials."

Charlie nodded, moving the cursor over to the map and pausing for a second before entering Zhibek's name into the main search box. It returned a full page of hits, some in English and several in Russian or Kazakh. He skimmed through the search results while Sophie slipped off her coat and blew into her hands. He was immersed in the third entry as she looked on.

"Find anything interesting?"

Charlie pointed to the screen. "This is an obituary for a Piotr Zhibek."

"Maybe that's a common name in Kazakhstan."

"It says he was a reporter and ... look at the date."

"August fifteenth," she said. "He died two days after Steve left Astana."

Charlie stared at the screen. "It's got to be connected to Bayzhanov somehow. Astana's his hometown."

"But how?"

They paused as the server delivered a pot of coffee and a small plate of biscuits.

"I don't know," he said after the server had left. He was about to try another search when the shrill ring of his BlackBerry disturbed the calm of their table. He plucked it from his pocket and saw Brigitte Martineau's name on the caller display.

"Hi Brigitte."

"You in Berlin?"

"You bet."

"I just wanted to give you a quick debrief. I had a call from the head of Protocol at the MFA yesterday. The Moscow police have abandoned their inquiry into Yermolov's death."

"Abandoned?"

"They've ruled his death accidental and have given assurances that they won't be requiring you to provide a statement or answer questions."

Charlie was reluctant to go into how ridiculous that sounded over a cellphone connected to Moscow, given how he had found Yermolov. "That's kind of ... surprising, but good, I guess."

"I have been promised a diplomatic note to confirm all this in writing when I get into the office. I'll have my assistant send you a confirmation of receipt before you board the flight in Frankfurt. If you don't have it, don't get on the plane, understood?"

"Got it."

"And the Durant woman's visa is waiting at the Berlin embassy."

"I'll get it on the way to the airport," he said, checking his watch.

"I'll send a driver out to Domodedovo for you. We can have a chat when you get here."

"All right. I'll see you later today."

He disconnected and put the phone down. "Your visa's at the embassy here and we're good to go, but we have to get to Frankfurt."

Sophie nodded, sipping her coffee. "I guess we should head back to the hotel."

He looked at her for a moment. "Are you sure you should go back?"

"What are you talking about?"

"I mean, maybe it's not such a good idea. You could stay here and we could stay in touch by —"

"Are you kidding?" Sophie had assumed a combative pose, her spine arched and her eyes narrowed. "I wasn't there for Steve when he was still alive, and there's no way I'm going to let him down now, not when we're finally getting close."

"I'm just saying —"

"I know what you're saying, and I appreciate your concern, but this isn't negotiable."

Charlie held up his hands and picked up his phone from the tabletop. "Then I'll book us two seats to Frankfurt."

CHAPTER 36

Charlie sat on the sofa in Martineau's office while the ambassador gave her assistant some instructions. The flight to Frankfurt and on to Moscow after a brief layover had been uneventful. Charlie had received Martineau's email — confirming receipt of a diplomatic note from the Russian MFA that effectively freed Charlie from any connection to the investigation into Sergei Yermolov's death — while he and Sophie were waiting in the lounge in Frankfurt. Though he still had some lingering doubt about whether the Russians would honour the arrangement, it was as clear an indication as he could expect that they would. The drive in from the airport had taken twice as long as usual, due to a multiple car pile-up on the highway, and it was already dark by the time they hit the Garden Ring. He had insisted on dropping Sophie off at her hotel, and they had agreed to circle up once his debrief was over.

He fidgeted on the sofa as he heard Martineau wrapping up outside the open door, and he wondered if he looked as nervous as he felt. He was not looking forward to the meeting. As if on cue, she walked into the office and shut the door behind her, then took a seat opposite him.

"Glad to have you back," she began with a thin smile.

"It's good to be back," he lied.

"I imagine it's been a stressful time for you. I know I've been worried sick about this whole business."

Charlie nodded. "I'm really sorry for causing you all this trouble. I really didn't ..."

Martineau held up a hand to silence him. "I'm more interested in getting to the bottom of this whole thing, starting with your visit to Yermolov's apartment. Why on earth were you there in the first place?"

Charlie took a deep breath. "I thought he might be able to shed some light on why Liepa was the only one the police detained on that night."

Martineau frowned. "And you did this because?"

"I had met with him at his office, but he seemed reluctant to talk. I thought he would be more forthcoming at home."

"You realize it goes well beyond your role as a consular officer. I mean, you're a lawyer, so I don't have to tell you the consequences of acting outside your scope of work — the risks to yourself, not to mention the Department."

Charlie nodded. "I know all that, but I felt like I needed to try."

"Look, Charlie, I know you're committed, and you're just trying to get to the bottom of the Liepa case — and I'm sure there's a lot more to it than that whitewash the prison dared to call an official report, but this is Moscow, and there are real dangers here."

"He was a Canadian citizen, Brigitte. He deserves to have someone asking questions on his behalf, doesn't he?"

"On his behalf or his sister's?"

Charlie didn't respond. He didn't want to lie to Martineau, but he knew he was on shaky ground. He wasn't exactly objective when it came to Sophie.

"I'm going to be honest with you, Charlie. One of the reasons I lobbied to get you here is that I like the way you operate. I don't want another drone who follows the rules and punches out at four. And I'm happy to cover your back if you happen to bend a few rules along the way. But I don't want my next call from the Russians to be a request to identify your body at the morgue. Do we understand each other?"

Charlie sighed. "You know as well as I do that Liepa didn't commit suicide. That prison report was a joke — you said so yourself."

"So what do you think happened?" Martineau asked, causing Charlie to stop and look at her. He knew he should just say nothing or say he was going to toe the line. But he saw something in her eyes that made him want to level with her. What did he have to lose at this stage?

"I think he was working on some sort of exposé — investigative journalism. He was a novelist wannabe, and we found a bunch of true crime and investigative-reporting books with the stuff he kept in Berlin."

"An exposé on someone here in Moscow?"

"I think it had something to do with Dmitri Bayzhanov."

"And who's that?"

"He's the guy behind BayCo, the developer of Petr Square."

"Petr Square? The big one that just got its permit?"

Charlie nodded. "Yes, it's worth millions, but I think there's more to it than that."

Martineau paused. "Did Yermolov work for BayCo?"

"No," Charlie said, about to mention the fact that he worked for United Pharma, but something about Martineau's question struck him. He held his tongue.

"So what did you intend to find out from him?" Martineau asked, moving on.

Charlie didn't respond for a moment, just shrugged. "I don't really know. He was the only person I knew of who was with Steve Liepa the night he was arrested. I guess I was hoping he might give me a lead — anything — to go on."

Martineau proceeded to outline her discussions with the Russian MFA and her superiors back in Ottawa, whose initial reaction had been to get Charlie on the next plane to Canada.

"How this plays out is up to you, Charlie," she said as they neared the end of their meeting. "But I don't have to tell you, you're on a short leash. A very short one."

"I'll try to keep a low profile."

"I'm serious, Charlie. I don't want you sticking your neck out. Do you hear me?"

"You bet."

"And, Charlie," she added, stopping him as he reached the door, "that goes for the Durant woman, as well. I don't want her to turn into another consular case either, okay?"

"Understood."

He left her office, then bolted down the stairs and outside across the courtyard to the other building and the consular section. Once there, he flicked on the light, fell into the chair behind his desk, and clicked his computer to life. He tapped his fingers on his desktop as he waited for his web browser to open. He was supposed to meet Sophie in fifteen minutes and it would take him at least twenty to walk to her hotel. He entered *United Pharma* into the search window and waited for the company's web page to load, then clicked through the main page until he was on the list of the company's directors. As he printed the page he scanned the list onscreen, but didn't recognize any names.

Next, he found the link he had saved on his desktop to the list of individuals and companies whose shareholdings in Panamanian and Cypriot companies had been disclosed as part of the online tax-haven leak, which had first hit the news a couple of weeks earlier. One by one, he searched through the list for the names of the United Pharma directors, but halfway through, none of them had appeared on the other list. He sighed and was about to close the browser when it occurred to him to reach into his top drawer and pull out the list of names that Bill Halston, the trade officer, had come back with after they had searched Kvartal's shareholders. He glanced at the United Pharma CEO's name and went down through the Kvartal list, finding it halfway down. His heart skipped a beat as he recognized the CFO's name, as well. He tore through the rest of the names, growing more and more excited with each new hit. By the time he was done, he had confirmed that twelve of the directors of UPI were also shareholders in Kvartal. He typed a mark next to each name and printed the list, grabbing both sheets of paper off the printer and flicking off the light as he headed out the door.

"So how did it go with Martineau?" Sophie said as she greeted Charlie in the lobby of her hotel. She pecked him on the cheek and added, "You look like shit, by the way."

"Thanks. Actually, it was better than I thought."

"They're not shipping you to Antarctica?"

"Lucky for me, we don't have a mission there, or I have a feeling I might have been first on the list. Let's just say I'm on a very short leash."

"You want to get a drink?" She pointed toward the lobby bar.

"Sure."

They took a table near the door and ordered a couple of drinks, then Charlie pulled out the printouts he had made back at his office.

"What's this?"

"Martineau asked me whether Yermolov worked for BayCo, and it got me thinking about what Steve's notes said about the kickbacks the senior execs were getting, so I did a little research."

"Wouldn't kickbacks be in cash?" Sophie looked from the lists to Charlie. "I mean, it would be pretty risky to have a paper trail."

"That's true, unless the kickbacks were in offshore stock. Here." He pointed to the first printout. "This is the list of United Pharma's directors. When I compare it to this other list, twelve of the twenty names show up."

"And the second list is?"

"The list of shareholders in Kvartal."

"That's the Cypriot company that Alexander Surin also has shares in?"

Charlie nodded. "And Bayzhanov. And don't forget we wouldn't have known about any of this if it weren't for that big tax leak."

Sophie rubbed a finger over her top lip. "That's true. Even now, all we know is that they're all shareholders in the same company — Bayzhanov, the UPI directors, and Alexander Surin — one big happy family."

"But we have no idea what the shares are worth or how Kvartal gets its capital."

Sophie released a breath. "I have a feeling it's got plenty of capital."

"Me, too," Charlie said, frowning. "But I don't know how to find out for sure."

"I might know," Sophie said as her eyes turned to the revolving door at the main entrance of the hotel. Charlie followed her gaze and watched as Natalia Povetkina crossed the lobby toward the bar.

"Jesus, Sophie, we don't even know if she's reporting back to Bayzhanov. You could have told me …" Charlie trailed off as Povetkina arrived at the table and Sophie stood to greet her. Charlie did the same and then Povetkina settled in her seat.

"Can I get you a drink?" Charlie asked, to which Povetkina gave a dismissive wave.

"No, thank you. I have another appointment across town. I don't have much time."

"I was surprised to hear back from you so soon," Sophie said as Povetkina zipped open a sleek leather portfolio and slid out a glossy four-by-six photo of a woman they both quickly recognized as the blonde from the hotel in Nice.

"Tatiana Evseeva," Charlie said.

"She's SVR, right?" Sophie asked.

Povetkina shook her head. "Not anymore. She's been free-lancing for the past several years. She's worked for a couple of different private security firms based in Moscow."

"I don't suppose you know who hired her to try and kill us, do you?" Sophie said.

Povetkina returned a grim smile. "These are not the types of question I can ask, you will understand. But I did find out something else about her past." Sophie and Charlie glanced at each other. "You mentioned Alexander Surin was of interest to you," Povetkina continued. "Surin was Evseeva's *rezident* in Almaty," Povetkina said. Seeing Sophie's puzzled expression, she explained, "Her handler."

"Almaty? What was she doing there — or Surin, for that matter?"

Povetkina shrugged. "I don't know, but whatever their assignment, it seems that it was a success."

"What do you mean?" Charlie was on the edge of his seat now.

"They were both there for approximately three years. By the time they left, they had both been promoted several times. Surin ended up as a colonel before he left the SVR. He was a very successful — how do you say? — bureaucrat, and Evseeva was by all accounts also very successful. Her services were widely sought, and she had considerable assets, including a large apartment on the Arbat. She owned property in the south of France, also."

"How did you find all this out in the couple of hours since we spoke?" Sophie said, amazed.

"I have many contacts in the FSB and SVR. They are eager to share information, for a fee."

Charlie pulled out his list of Kvartal shareholders on the off chance that Evseeva was on it, but it wasn't. He looked at Povetkina. "You said Surin was a successful bureaucrat. Do you mean his recent appointment to the Moscow planning committee?"

Povetkina laughed. "That is a job he was given for a single purpose, which we all know."

"You mean to give Petr Square the green light?" Sophie said.

Povetkina nodded.

"So what were some of his other positions since leaving the FSB or the SVR or whatever?" Charlie persisted.

Povetkina shrugged. "He held several high positions, including deputy chair of GasCom — a highly coveted position. And also the chief of the Anti-Drugs Committee."

"Which does what, exactly?" Sophie asked.

"It directs resources to confront illegal importation and distribution of drugs in the Russian Federation."

"So he was, like, the drugs czar? Sorry for the expression," Charlie said, eliciting a flat grin from Povetkina.

"Yes, this was also a very powerful position."

Charlie looked at Sophie for a moment, then back to Povetkina. "And you say he was appointed to these positions because of his work in Almaty."

Povetkina shook her head. "The work was no doubt helpful, but you are not appointed to these positions without very powerful sponsors."

"You mean … the Kremlin?"

Povetkina said nothing, and Charlie wondered whether he had crossed the line. Sort of like mentioning Castro's name in Havana, where everyone referred to him by stroking their imaginary beards.

"I will try to find out more for tomorrow, but I must go now," Povetkina said, pushing the photo of Evseeva across to Sophie. "Please keep it."

"Thank you, Natalia. Stay in touch," Sophie said. She and Charlie watched her go, then Sophie folded the photo in half and tucked it into her purse.

"I'm not sure I want to keep it," she said. "It gives me the creeps." She studied Charlie, who seemed absorbed in thought. "Well, what did you make of all that?"

"It just gets more and more intriguing," he said, pulling out a file folder with a half-inch stack of paper in it. "I printed Steve's notes." He waved the server over for their bill. "I think we need to go over them again. Come on."

CHAPTER 37

They sat around the coffee table in Sophie's hotel room, the remnants of a room-service meal sitting on a tray in the corner. Charlie had re-created the diagram they had started on the mirror of the hotel room in Berlin on a sheet of legal-size paper, and he was adding circles to connect Alexander Surin and Tatiana Evseeva. Sophie took a sip of her beer as she watched him draw in the circle for Evseeva.

"Don't you think Kazakhstan's a strange place to make a career for yourself if you're a Russian?"

"What do you mean?" Charlie looked up.

"It's a bit out of way, isn't it? I would have thought if you really wanted to get ahead in the KGB, or FSB, or whatever, you'd want to do it in Moscow."

Charlie frowned as he considered the question, then reached for his BlackBerry and thumbed through the Departmental contact list until he found Doug Cullen's name.

"What are you doing now?" Sophie asked as he hit the button to dial Cullen's number.

"Just calling my counterpart in Astana — the guy I had lunch with last week. He's probably gone for the day but —" He stopped when Cullen came on the line.

"Doug? Charlie Hillier."

"Charlie, what's up?"

"Working late?"

"Damn report for Ottawa on regional security," Cullen replied. "You don't know how good you have it in Moscow. When you're in a backwater like this, you end up being a jack of all trades. Anyway, what can I do for you?"

"I wanted to ask you about a journalist who died about a month ago. He might have something to do with that case we were talking about last week."

"Oh, yeah? What's the name?"

"Piotr Zhibek."

"Doesn't ring a bell," Cullen said distractedly. "How's he connected with your guy?"

"I'm pretty sure they met while he was in Astana, but I'm not sure why."

"I can ask one of the locally engaged guys and see if he's heard of him, but I'm in a bit of a time crunch right now."

"I understand," Charlie said, trying not to sound disappointed. "If anyone's heard of him, let me know. I'll let you get back to your report."

"I'll ask around. Talk to you soon."

Charlie tossed the phone onto the bed. "It was a long shot, anyway." He turned his attention back to the chart, started drawing a dotted line between Bayzhanov and a blank circle, then tossed the pencil down on the table. "We're still missing something. Whatever it is, it connects Bayzhanov and Surin and their time in Almaty somehow."

Sophie nodded, then got up and began to pace. "And whatever it was, we have to assume that Steve uncovered it and that it was important enough for him to be killed. Krasnikov, too."

Charlie frowned. "Maybe."

"You don't agree?"

"With the first part, yes," he said. "But I'm not sure Krasnikov was killed for any other reason than to make way for someone who would green-light the Petr Square development." He turned to the laptop and opened the browser. "There's got to be something in English about this Piotr Zhibek somewhere online." He began typing in the search box and waited for a list of results, groaning when he saw that they were all indecipherable. He clicked through the next page with much the same result.

"What about Natalia's theory about Surin's sponsor — that someone in power was pulling the strings to advance his career?" Sophie said. "What if he's somehow connected to Bayzhanov, as well? That would make sense, wouldn't it?" She turned away from the window to see Charlie still staring at the screen.

"Charlie?"

He gestured at the screen. "There's an article here on Zhibek by a group called Journalists Without Borders."

"It's in English?" She approached the coffee table and looked over his shoulder to read the article's title: "There Are No Coincidences."

"It says they believe Zhibek was killed because of questions he was asking about a drug informant. A guy who was preparing to name names before he was killed in prison."

"Does it say when *that* guy was killed?" Sophie asked, as she scanned for a date. It wasn't until Charlie scrolled down a page that they both spotted the date — August 14.

"Wait a second." Charlie flipped through the printout of Liepa's notes. "That's the day before Zhibek was killed."

They both sat staring at the screen in silence for a moment, then Sophie spoke.

"So Steve shows up and interviews Zhibek — about what we're not really sure, other than a reference to the Customs

Union thing — and within two days after he leaves Astana, the reporter we think he met with dies in his sleep, and the prisoner he was possibly talking to is murdered in jail. Not to mention what happens to Steve not long after he returns to Moscow." She paused. "We've got to be close. What do his notes say again?"

Charlie flipped to the notes corresponding to the dates Liepa was in Astana and scanned them again. "There's shit-all here," he said in frustration, passing the document to Sophie. He got to his feet and then sat again, this time at the end of the bed, which made his courier bag fall and its contents spill onto the floor.

"I wish I knew what the hell was in his head — what all this gobbledygook shorthand is supposed to mean," Sophie complained. "The only thing I can understand is the part at the end, where it says 'Follow up PZ,' which isn't much help, since we know he wouldn't have had the chance to do much follow-up with Piotr Zhibek — the guy was dead within forty-eight hours of Steve leaving town."

Charlie had picked up his bag and was holding the copy of the *Moscow News* that he'd been given on the plane. "What did his notes say about PZ again?"

"You just read through them." Frustration had crept into Sophie's voice.

"Read it to me," he said, his voice oddly flat as he continued to stare at the front page of the newspaper.

"Read what to you — 'Follow up PZ'?"

"Not 'Follow up *with* PZ.'"

Sophie looked at him as though he had lost it — until he showed her the article on the bottom of the front page of the newspaper. There was a picture of a man in a sharp suit that accentuated the muscular frame that lay beneath. His face wore a boyish smile, but his eyes were pure steel with, overall, the hardened look of a former soldier, capped off by a blond brush cut. The headline beneath read, "Zhukov to Run for Mayor of Moscow."

"Who's that?"

"You've never heard of Mr. Clean?"

"Mr. Clean?"

"He's an ex-KGB man with close ties to the Kremlin. He's been all but given the mayor's chair."

"I thought the election wasn't until February."

"Hard to believe, reading this." Charlie gestured to the article.

"I still don't understand what this has to do with —"

"Listen to this," Charlie said, taking the newspaper back and reading aloud from the article: "'Zhukov's career is the stuff of legend, starting with his two tours of duty at the head of a commando unit in Chechnya and a key undercover role in breaking a sleeper cell of terrorists who were planning to bomb the Bolshoi. His appointment as the head of the anti-narcotics directorate for central Asia followed several years at the head of Moscow's anti-terrorism division of the FSB. It was only recently, when his undercover work was acknowledged by an unknown Kremlin source, that it was revealed that Zhukov dismantled the biggest heroin-distribution network in central Asia during a three-year undercover operation in Kazakhstan a decade ago.'"

He stopped reading and met Sophie's gaze. She still looked puzzled.

"Don't you see? Zhukov must have been in Kazakhstan with Surin. He's a superstar now, with all the right con-nections — he's inner circle. The type of guy who can have whomever he wants appointed as chair of some rinky-dink planning committee."

"Let me see that," Sophie said, grabbing the paper and picking up where Charlie had left off. She scanned it for a moment, then read the last part aloud. "'Pavel Zukov will be Moscow's next mayor.' Pavel Zukov," she repeated. "*PZ*. Steve's note after his conversation with the journalist was to follow up *on* Zukov, not follow up *with* Zhibek."

"And if he was in charge of the anti-narcotics directorate for central Asia, he —" Charlie bolted to the computer and typed in a new search, tapping his finger on the keyboard as he waited for the results. He found what he was looking for in the third result.

"Here it is — Zhukov was instrumental in negotiating the devolution agreement with Kazakhstan for the Customs Union."

"That again? But what does —"

"He brought down the drug lords all right, then he and Surin must have cornered the market, maybe with help from Bayzhanov."

"Cornered the market?"

"That's what's funding the Cyprus companies," he said. "Drugs. The kickbacks for signing on to the lease at Petr Square are a joke — chump change — compared to the prof-its on heroin brought in from Afghanistan. They must be bringing it in with Bayzhanov's construction shipments — he brings most of his materials through his old contacts in Almaty."

"You mean every third or fourth crate is filled with heroin instead of nails," Sophie said with a nod.

"And Zukov's got someone on his payroll checking the shipments, or not checking them is more like it, with his old network in place to make sure his monopoly stays in place. That's got to be it." Charlie nodded his head slowly. "Somehow Zukov or his people must have found out about Steve's conver-sation with Zhibek. The stakes are enormous, enough to ki —"

"Enough to kill him without a second thought. A guy with that kind of power could make a call to the prison and it's done." Angry colour rose in Sophie's cheeks. "The bastard. He's not going to get away with it."

Charlie was shaking his head now, the elation at having finally solved the mystery gone. "No, we have to get out of here. Like you said, a guy like that wields unimaginable power in a place like this. It's not safe anywhere."

They both froze at the sound of the room phone ringing. Sophie looked at Charlie before answering, waiting for his subtle nod before she picked up the receiver.

"Hello?"

Charlie watched her reaction as she listened to the caller, but he saw no sign of apprehension, and after a couple of acknowledgements, the call was over.

"That was Natalia. She says she has some new information on Surin and wants to meet now. She says it's urgent."

"She's coming here?"

"She wants to meet at Pushkin Square. She's in a rush.... What?"

"You don't think it's odd?"

"No, not really."

"We've never met anywhere but here. How did she sound?"

"She sounded normal, I guess." Sophie shrugged. "Come to think of it, she did sound kind of frazzled, and she's usually so cool and collected."

"We need to get out of here, *now*." Charlie was already on his feet and taking her by the arm. "The embassy's the only safe place."

"But what if she does have information we need?"

"Then we'll get it from her by phone, or she can come meet us at the embassy. Come on."

Realizing that he wasn't taking no for answer, she stuffed the few things she had taken out of her suitcase back in and they were heading down the hallway in a matter of seconds.

Charlie stopped in front of the elevators, his finger hesitating over the call button. "Let's take the stairs."

"You think they're in the hotel?"

"I just know that too many people seem to be aware of our movements." He swung the fire door open, grabbed her suitcase, and they raced down the stairs. When they reached the ground floor, he opened the door and stepped out into the hallway, which was to the right of the main lobby. As they approached the end of the hallway, Charlie held up his hand for Sophie to stop.

"What is it?" she whispered.

"The guy by the pillar over there." She followed his gaze to a heavy-set man in a leather jacket standing side-on to them, the curled cord of an earpiece visible under his collar, his jacket bulky enough to conceal a rocket launcher.

"This way," Charlie said quietly, redirecting them to the stairs to the parking garage. They went down a flight of concrete stairs and emerged from the stairwell at a door marked P1. "We'll go out through the side entrance," he said, pushing the door open. "And get a hotel car —"

His words were halted by a gloved hand that cut off his air supply. He struggled in vain against the bulky arms that held him and pushed him toward a white van, its side door open. He watched helplessly as another man plucked Sophie off her feet and tossed her into the van ahead of him. When the door slid shut, the van lurched forward, and Charlie and Sophie found themselves slung together on a bench seat, facing the muzzles of a pair of handguns pointed at their chests.

CHAPTER 38

As the van climbed the ramp out of the parking lot and turned right, Charlie's eyes adjusted to the dim light in the van. He found himself seated across from a bear of a man in a rear-facing seat who made the two musclemen who had bundled him and Sophie into the van so easily look frail in comparison. Charlie watched as the other man turned to the driver and growled something, the sound of his deep, gravelly voice instantly recognizable. Its effect was almost instantaneous, so that by the time their captor had turned back to face them, Charlie had made a new connection.

"Dima the Great," he said, causing Sophie to look on in puzzlement and the big man to smile.

"Impressive, Mr. Hillier." Again, there was no mistaking the distinctive voice.

"We meet again." Charlie turned to Sophie. "Meet Vladimir Oligansky."

"I warned you last time that you were in danger. You should have listened."

Charlie looked at the faces of the two bodyguards and the blond-haired driver, none of whom looked like the man he had seen in the hotel lobby.

"Someone was waiting for me in the lobby. It wasn't your men?"

Oligansky's face remained inscrutable, but Charlie could tell the wheels were in motion behind those dark eyes. He was calculating his next move, trying to decide how much Charlie knew. As Charlie sat there in the van, headed for who knew where, it came to him suddenly, and he let out a little laugh.

"Is something funny, Mr. Hillier?" Oligansky said. "Maybe you can tell us all."

Charlie turned to look at Sophie. She appeared calm, but he knew how much it was costing her.

"I'm just thinking how simply this all boils down in the end," he said, turning back to Oligansky, who didn't respond. "We've been trying to figure out how Surin and Bayzhanov were connected, and what Steve Liepa might have discovered in Astana that set this whole chain of events in motion. It all comes down to turf, doesn't it."

Oligansky moved his enormous head to the side ever so slightly, as if to indicate growing interest.

"You talk a great deal for someone whose future is … uncertain," he finally said.

"I don't think I have to worry about that. I know what you want, and I think I can help you. We can help each other."

"Please tell me," Oligansky said with a wave of his enormous hand. His two bodyguards remained motionless, their guns still trained on Charlie and Sophie.

"Krasnikov was your man, wasn't he?"

Oligansky said nothing, though Charlie thought he saw a glint in his eye, in the reflection of a headlight beam that cut through the van's interior as they turned west.

"It makes perfect sense," Charlie continued. "You're the top dog in the Moscow construction market. That's no secret, so it stands to reason that you would have your people in key positions, holding the levers, so to speak. I'm sure you were none too happy when you found out he'd been sent off a cliff in Nice, much less that his replacement was Alexander Surin." Oligansky remained impassive. "The next thing you know, Petr Square's a go, which is the death knell for you. All that construction on your turf. It must have been a bit of an insult, really. That's why you sent me his obituary, right? Because you were hoping we could expose his killers without you having to lift a finger."

Oligansky remained stone-faced, but again he moved his weight slightly to one side in his seat, as if total immobility were no longer possible. Charlie went on. "And although you didn't know what he had uncovered, you knew Steve Liepa was on to something. How did you find out, anyway?" Charlie paused, then waved a hand. "Forget I asked. I'm sure you have contacts in the police, the prisons, wherever. As for our progress" — he gestured at Sophie — "maybe Natalia was keeping you up to speed. No matter. The point is we found what Liepa was working on — all the information you need to secure your turf for a very long time." Charlie leaned forward. "But we have a small request first."

Oligansky looked at him in silence for a moment, then grinned and opened his massive palm. "And that is?"

"You take us to the Canadian Embassy now, and you let us walk through the gates and we go our separate ways. Sophie goes back to Canada — there's nothing for her here anymore — and I go, too, back to Canada or wherever, and you don't interfere."

"Why would I allow that?" Now Oligansky leaned forward, making his bulk seem even more imposing.

"Like I said. Information. Very useful and valuable information for you."

Oligansky chuckled and then grunted an order to one of his heavyweights, who began searching through Charlie's bag, pulling out the printout of Liepa's research and handing it to his boss.

"It seems I already have it." Oligansky flipped through the document.

Charlie smiled. "Good luck figuring it out. Steve had a kind of shorthand that was a little ... unorthodox. But you're a businessman, right? You want to protect your interests — the last thing you want is two more dead Canadians on your hands, and this time there will be lots of questions, and those questions will eventually lead to you. You're not the kind of guy who wants to draw unnecessary heat, am I right?"

Oligansky looked at Charlie for a moment, then waved the papers in front of him. "So tell me what's in here."

"I'd be happy to, but only if we have a deal. Do we?"

Oligansky smiled, looked at his hands for a moment, then turned around and barked an order at the driver. It was largely unintelligible, except for the address — Starokonyushenny. The Canadian Embassy.

"Start talking, Mr. Hillier. If by the time we arrive at your embassy I am satisfied that you have something to offer, I will let you go. If not," he said, his dark eyes glowing in the dim interior of the van, "I have other plans for you."

Charlie nodded, estimating he had about three minutes to make his case, otherwise he and Sophie were goners.

"Petr Square is not Bayzhanov's end game," he began. "It's just a front. Bayzhanov's going to use it to set up a distribution system for Afghan heroin, using the network set up by Surin and his old friend, Pavel Zhukov. You know they're connected, right?"

Oligansky gave a barely perceptible nod.

"Bayzhanov's been doling out shares in a certain company to United Pharma's executives as kickbacks for signing on to the outrageous lease at Petr Square."

Oligansky's eyebrows crept up slightly at the news.

"Bayzhanov's a shareholder in the same company, as is Surin, and if you trace it far enough, I'm sure you'll find that Zhukov is connected, too, probably through an intermediary. He's the Kremlin's golden boy, but even that won't protect him if you expose what he and Bayzhanov are cooking up."

Oligansky seemed to be considering the information.

"It gives you enough," Charlie added, "to send Bayzhanov back to Astana in a heartbeat. Maybe even enough to make trouble for Zhukov."

Oligansky laughed at the last statement and seemed about to say something, but held back. They continued to drive in silence for a minute or so, as Oligansky looked through the paperwork. Suddenly the van came to a stop and the big man turned to look out the front window. Charlie could see the yellow walls of the embassy and the bottom half of the flag hanging out front.

"It seems we have arrived," Oligansky said, turning back to face them.

"Decision time," Charlie said. "You let us go and I give you the name of the company at the heart of all this — that's the deal. You won't find it in there. We came up with it ourselves," he said, glancing at Sophie.

Oligansky paused, looked at the paper, then back at Charlie. "I could have a forensic accountant identify the company, you know."

Charlie nodded, trying to maintain an unconcerned expression as he wondered whether he had overplayed his hand. He was about to find out. "Maybe, but you have to ask yourself why you'd go to the trouble, not to mention risk being connected to the murder of a diplomat and a visiting surgeon. It's unnecessary and it's just not good business."

Oligansky thumbed the corner of the paper as Charlie and Sophie held their breaths. Finally he spoke. "And the name of the company?"

"Not until we're at the gate," Charlie said with a shake of his head, prompting a chortle from Oligansky.

"You amuse me, Mr. Hillier," Oligansky said, then gave a nod to the man nearest the side door to open it. They all stepped out onto the sidewalk, twenty feet from the embassy's security gate. If the diplomatic guard outside noticed that two of the men held guns, he didn't show it and seemed content to stay in the relative safety of his little hut.

"All right, Mr. Hillier. Give me the name and you can go, but I don't have to tell you what will happen if you break your silence, yes?"

"We get it, believe me," Charlie said. "It's a Cypriot company named Kvartal."

"Kvartal?" The big man shrugged and Charlie wondered whether this was the moment that he would give the nod to his men to fill them with bullets before casually hopping back in the van and driving off. Instead, he extended his hand and Charlie reciprocated, albeit reluctantly. Oligansky enveloped his hand in a bone-crushing grip.

"I hope you enjoyed your time in Moscow, Mr. Hillier. Never come back." He turned and got back in the van, followed by the two bodyguards, who slid the door shut. As the van moved off, Charlie stood there for a moment as if frozen in place.

"I can't believe that just happened," Sophie said, jarring him back to reality. He took her by the hand and hurried to the front gates before Oligansky changed his mind.

EPILOGUE

Charlie sipped his cappuccino and read the paper in the corner of the Mayfair coffee shop that had become his favourite in the past few days. And an eventful few days it had been. Once he and Sophie had walked through the gates of the embassy in Moscow, they hadn't come back out, except for the escorted ride to the airport and the hastily arranged flight to London the next morning. He had been through a quick debriefing in Moscow, but the Department had decided to go a little deeper as soon as he got to London. He had lost count of the number of hours he had spent meeting a long list of people at the Canadian High Commission to explain what he had uncovered in Moscow and the south of France. He took it as a good sign that they had let him take a room in a nearby hotel after the second day. Whether someone was watching his movements, even now, he wasn't sure, but he did feel pretty sure he was out of the woods, at least when it came to his employers. The French police also seemed prepared to accept his version of the events leading to the death of Tatiana Evseeva, corroborated as it must have been by Sophie Durant. Which left only the Russians to worry about, until this morning ...

He had been in a debriefing when word had come from Moscow that things were happening. First, Alexander Surin's body had turned up in a Dumpster outside his favourite restaurant, along with those of a couple of executives from UPI. The official story was a mugging that had gotten out of hand. It was followed shortly after, however, by word that Dmitri Bayzhanov had been arrested while trying to board a flight to Kiev, which left no doubt in Charlie's mind what was happening — Dima the Great was putting his information to good use. Charlie didn't think much of Bayzhanov's chances of ever seeing the outside of a prison again, if he survived at all.

Pavel Zhukov was the real question, though. How would Oligansky walk the delicate tightrope between using what he had and not angering Zhukov's powerful friends in the Kremlin? Charlie had a feeling if anyone knew how to play it, Oligansky would.

He looked out the window at a woman walking by with a yellow Selfridges bag, her auburn hair tied back in a ponytail. He glanced instinctively at his BlackBerry to see if Sophie had sent him any word from Toronto, but his inbox was empty. She had flown back with her brother's ashes twenty-four hours ago, after giving her version of events to Charlie's debriefers, no doubt saving him a lot of explaining. She had insisted on staying in touch, and he knew she must be busy making arrangements for Steve's funeral, but he didn't hold out much hope. After all, she was bound to forever associate him with her brother's death, not to mention having barely avoided the sort of long drive with Russian mobsters from which no one ever returns. Why was it that every woman he cared for ended up in the same predicament lately?

He had been told he might be able to return to Canada in a few days, and while he was relieved that neither the French police nor his own employers seemed to want him behind bars, he was in no particular rush to return to Ottawa. *And to what?* he asked himself as he sipped the last of his coffee and contemplated another. His posting in Moscow was obviously done, and they hadn't told him what, if anything, was on offer back at HQ. Maybe they were trying to decide about giving him some sort of discharge, though whether of the honourable variety or otherwise, he wasn't entirely sure.

His heart jumped when he saw the flashing light of his BlackBerry, but it sank again when he saw not Sophie's address, but Rob Brooker's. He clicked on the link Brooker had forwarded of an article in the day's *Moscow News* and read with increasing interest about the mayoral race set to begin in the New Year. But rather than an announcement of Zhukov's withdrawal, which Charlie half expected, it seemed that Zhukov's campaign was due to kick off in the next couple of weeks with the benefit of a new influx of campaign contributions. Charlie smiled as he clicked on the second link announcing that the Petr Square development had been sold to a consortium linked to Vladimir Oligansky, who was described in the article as a prominent Moscow-based developer.

So there it was, he thought, as he waved to the server. All's well that ends well … sort of. Oligansky maintains his turf and actually gains a prize development in exchange for supporting Zhukov's mayoral bid. Call it a market correction, or a strategic alignment, all done according to the Moscow Code. He wondered if even Steve Liepa could have foreseen the strange turn of events.

Maybe I'm safe after all, Charlie allowed himself to think as he ordered another cappuccino and scanned the coffee shop for anyone out of place.

He put the BlackBerry back down on the table and decided to leave it alone. Sophie Durant had other things on her mind right now, and so should he. Like what he was going to do when he was finally allowed to go home. The thought alarmed him at first, especially if it meant taking a desk job under the indirect control of his ex-wife. Maybe it was time to do something else. He hadn't been much help to Steve Liepa, after all.

His mind wandered to the last time he had seen his brother Brian, and Brian's offer to have him join his business occupied Charlie's mind for a brief moment. But soon his mind was back on Liepa. Hadn't he uncovered why Liepa had been killed? Hadn't at least some of Liepa's killers been punished in one way or another as a result of his efforts?

Sophie Durant was another question. He was pretty sure she would have preferred a different result, but he also knew that he had helped her find some closure. Maybe there was hope for him yet, he decided, as a fresh cappuccino arrived and the sun began to shine outside.

ACKNOWLEDGEMENTS

Thanks to everyone at Dundurn, including (but not limited to) Kirk Howard, Margaret Bryant, Michelle Melski, and especially to my editor, Allison Hirst. Thanks also to Allister Thompson for improving the manuscript, to David Jacques and Oriana Trombetti for reading and commenting on earlier drafts, and to Tara Snell for the title. Special thanks to my medical consultant, Dr. Greg Brown, for sharing his knowledge and enthusiasm.

The last word goes to my wife and first reader, Tanya. Thanks for not (always) ignoring the sign on the door!